freedom
Come All Ye

A Tale of William Wallace

By Hazel B. West

A Pay the Piper Press Book

ISBN: 1461139376

"The story of Wallace poured a Scottish prejudice in my veins which will boil there until the floodgates of life shut in eternal rest."

-Robert Burns

freedom

Come All Ye

forward

David R. Ross, in his book *On the Trail of William Wallace*, says this: "Wallace stepped from oblivion onto the pages of our history books a fully-grown man." It really is the truth. Hardly anything is known about Wallace's childhood except that he was the second son of a knight. His father was a patriot named Alan Wallace and he had two brothers who you do hear a little about in later history. Most of what we know about his life before he slew Sheriff Heselrig in Lanark to avenge his wife is contributed to the epic written by Blind Harry in the 1400s. Unfortunately, Harry's epic, *The Wallace* is not known for its accuracy. While it has a lot of good information, most of it is thought to be fiction. However, Wallace started fighting the English at a young age, if you go by Harry's account. There were many exciting things that happened to him before he steps onto the pages of historic documentation. So I decided to take some of those things and write a book about his adventures as a teenager. I tried to make it as historically accurate as possible, but without any real information to go on, I took a few liberties. Okay, a lot of liberties. But even the great authors were not always accurate when it made a good story. So this is not a history and you should not take it seriously! I am simply writing this because I think people might like to read a book about Scotland's national hero when he was younger. All the information I have found is in this book and I have added some other things to fill in the gaps.

Also, I see it fit to point out that there has been a lot of things circulating in the past couple years that William Wallace is not worthy to be Scotland's national hero anymore. This is because some people seem to think of him as a monster who killed people for no reason. Unfortunately, these are not people who have done real research and have either picked up Blind Harry (really a bit overly blood thirsty) or just watched *Braveheart* and think they know all there is to know about Wallace. So he killed men. So what? He was fighting a war. He did everything he could for his country, he died for Scotland! It was his heroics that made him Scotland's national hero, someone to look up to years after his death. Wallace was killed seven hundred years ago and he is still loved like he was by his personal companions! Someone who can last seven hundred years in the history books without being forgotten is certainly not a horrid person like some people will claim. Why must we form these ideas now? George Washington made mistakes too but do we try to disown him as the Father of America? No, we don't. Please do yourselves all a favor and read real histories. David R. Ross is a good place to start. If you want to learn more about Wallace after reading this book, please look at his sources. They are the most accurate I have found and written with love of country. Please don't form the opinion that I am telling you what to think. Everyone is entitled to their own opinion, but please make sure you have hard evidence to back it up!

As of now, please enjoy this book! I hope you find it entertaining as well as informative and remember to always look before you leap!

-Slainte, Hazel

Chapter One

There Was a Lad

William rolled over in his sleep and clutched the blankets tighter around his shoulders. He could tell that the fire had burned down because the air was cold, and a chilly draft was seeping under his covers. He was too comfortable to get up and tend to the dying flames though, so he just scrunched himself further into the blankets and drifted back off to sleep.

"William, it's time to get up." William opened his eyes a crack to see his mother standing by his bed.

"Already?" he mumbled.

"Yes, ye need to be going or you'll be late for your classes," she told him. "Breakfast is ready and hot."

She left the room and William sighed and rolled out of bed. He went to his dresser and splashed his face from the bowl of water sitting there. Once it settled again, he stared at his reflection in the bowl. Dark brown hair that fell down to his shoulders and was always a bit messy, well shaped face and strong jaw and bright blue eyes. Aye, he had his father's looks but his mother's eyes.

He quickly dressed in a new green tunic his uncle had bought him and sighed as he pulled on the leggings to go with it. He cast a longing look at his plaid, but knew it was asking for trouble wearing it in the city with the English garrisoning there now. His blood boiled at the very thought that they had come to Scotland thinking they could take it without a fight. But they had. No one had put up a fight. At least not here. He tightened his broad belt and hung his long dagger from it.

William laced on his boots and left his room to go eat breakfast. He found his mother, uncle and younger brother, John sitting at the table already, with steaming bowls of porridge in front of them. William took his seat and poured milk from a nearby pitcher onto his porridge.

"Good morning, William," his uncle said to him with a smile. "You look very fine in that new outfit."

"Thank ye," William said and shot John a glance as the younger lad giggled. "Good morning to ye too." He was silent through the rest of breakfast even though his mother and uncle talked between each other and his younger brother was forming his oatmeal into two armies. His mind was elsewhere. As soon as he had finished, he stood up to leave.

"I guess I'll be going now," he said. "I'll see ye

later."

"Here's your food, Will," his mother told him, handing him a package wrapped in a cloth. William took it and put it into his belt pouch. "Be safe."

"I will, Ma," he said and left the house.

He had lived with his uncle in Dundee for about six years now. His father, Alan Wallace and older brother, Malcolm, had gone off to fight the English when he was only ten and his mother had taken him to live with her brother in the seaside town. His uncle had insisted he go to school and learn his writing and languages. William knew that everyone hoped he would take up the priesthood like most second sons, but he never saw himself as a priest. He wanted to be the one out fighting alongside his father. Alan Wallace had taught his son to love Scotland, and William remembered all the tales his father had told him as he was a bairn sitting on his knee, of the wrongs done to their country by Edward Longshanks, the English king. They had had a king of their own, but Alexander had fallen over a cliff in a storm and broke his neck. Without an heir to carry on his name, Edward took the opportunity and claimed Scotland for himself. He put a man named John Baliol on the throne, but Baliol soon became tired of being under English rule and laws and defied Longshanks. He paid for it dearly, for Edward stripped him of his kingship and had him shipped to the Tower of London to rot. William clenched his fists with the thought of it. He hoped that some day he would get the chance to fight Longshanks' army and maybe even meet the Tyrant King who liked to call himself the "Hammer of the Scots". William snorted. "Hammer of the Scots," he muttered to himself. "He'll find we're an anvil."

He had gotten to the academy then and he stopped outside and sighed. He looked at the other lads walking around and took a step forward, going into the building.

He had never thought he learned much in his classes. Of course, now he could speak Latin and French and write in the languages as well, but his penmanship would never be what the teachers hoped and his Latin grammar left something to be desired. He rested his chin on his fist as he sat at his table and looked up at the bookshelves in the room. He fingered his quill and flicked flakes of dried ink off it by scraping it against the desktop. They were copying passages from a huge Latin tome at the moment, and William looked at it in distaste as he inked his quill and started to copy it on his parchment. He turned to the lad, Thomas, who sat next to him and shared the book.

"This is bloody boring," he whispered to him.

"Aye," Thomas replied. His penmanship was far better then William's but he had the same views as his friend.

"Why not *Beowulf?*" William wondered as he scraped his quill too hard and left a splotch on the paper he knew his teacher--tormenter, he added silently--would deem unsightly. "It's far more interesting than this."

"Aye, but it's not a Latin tome," Thomas said.

"Quiet in the back," the teacher said and looked at

the two lads dolefully.

William gave a quiet sigh and rolled his eyes comically at Thomas. "I forgot that you couldna talk. Heaven forbid!" Thomas smothered a laugh before the teacher turned his stern eyes on the lads again.

"Master Wallace, come up here," he said and William stood with a sigh and went up to the table his teacher sat at.

"Aye, sir?" he asked.

"Where were you yesterday, Master Wallace?" the teacher asked.

"Not here," William said truthfully and several of the students laughed quietly.

"Obviously," the teacher said, not amused. "Since you were not here, where were you?"

"At the burn."

"Why?"

"I was fishing."

"Did your mother and uncle know you were at the burn?" The teacher raised his eyebrow.

"No," William said defiantly, not feeling the least bit uncomfortable from the questioning. He had been in this position far too many times to care anymore. "But I dinna think they'd really care either."

"I'll see about that," the teacher said and quickly scribbled a few words out on a parchment and folded it up. "Give this to your uncle and make sure it *gets* to him this time and does not *accidentally* get into your mother's washing basket. This is a warning, but I will tell you now.

One more absence, Master Wallace, and I won't ask
questions. You will get a beating and I will personally call
on your uncle and tell him that you are doing nothing
more here then wasting his money, is that understood?"

"Aye, sir," William told him and snatched the letter
from him, marching back to his table with his head held
high.

Thomas shook his head at him. "Ye have to stop
getting on his bad side, Will. He's beaten ye before."

"It didna hurt," William said indifferently. "If I still
lived in Elderslie where I grew up as a bairn, I'd be done
with schooling and would be off fighting with my Da now.
I'm done with it here."

"Dinna do anything daft, Will," Thomas said,
keeping his head bent over his work so that the teacher
would not suspect them of anything.

"I willna," William said, going back to his work.
"The last daft thing I did was leave that wee poem on my
desk last week for the teacher to find."

Thomas clapped a hand to his mouth to smother a
laugh. "That wasnae daft, I think he deserved it. But he
was unco mad at ye to be sure!"

"Aye, he was," William said and smiled in
rememberance at the thought.

Before long, it was thankfully time to break for lunch
and William and Thomas went out to sit on the side of the
street to eat their food in the light. Two other lads came to
join them. One jostled William on the shoulder and
grinned at him.

"Ha, Will, that was braw the way ye acted. Always cool in a situation, our Will Wallace is!"

"Oh, I've had him after me too many times to bother me any more, Duncan," William told his friend but couldn't help a bit of a grin.

"Aye," said the other lad, Richard. "But if ye keep championing us here, I can only imagine what ye'll be able to do for the whole of Scotland someday against the English."

"Aye, he'd make a good champion," Thomas agreed. "I would follow ye, Will."

"I'll be sure to remember yer loyalty when the time comes," William said, half in jest.

Duncan knelt in front of William and bowed his head. "You have my fealty, brave knight," he said, and William shoved him onto his backside amid their laughter.

"Are ye going to show yer uncle that letter, William?" Richard asked.

William shrugged. "I'll do my best to lose it like all the others," he said with a small smile and the other lads grinned. "There is a fine wind today."

"Ye do ken that the teacher will find out after a while though, Will," Duncan said. "He always does."

"I'm no' afraid of him," William told them nonchalantly. "What can he really do to me? He willna beat me enough to do any damage and if he decides to kick me out, then that's no' to bad is it?"

"I suppose no'," Thomas said. "But I dinna think ye're uncle would be very happy."

William shrugged. "Nae, probably not."

They finished their lunch and by that time, the teacher had come out to tell them it was time to resume their lessons.

William stood and turned to his friends with a rueful face. "Time to go back to our dungeon."

Chapter Two

An Unfortunate Incident

William gave a sigh of relief as he shoved out of the academy with his companions and headed out to walk in the town a bit before he started for home. He smelled someone selling meat pies and his stomach growled so he bought one from the vendor. It was piping hot and tasted wonderful. William sat on the corner of the street to eat it as he watched the people walk through the town. There were the gentry of Dundee and the sea folk who came into the port with things to sell and trade, or to stay at the inns and get the latest news from the taverns. William himself often visited the taverns to listen to the talk going around. See if he could hear anything about his father. He was considering doing that very thing that afternoon, when he happened to see a group of lads about his age coming down the street a little farther away but heading in his direction. He knew who the leader of the group was immediately, for he had seen him many times before. It was young Selby, son of the man Selby who was the English governor of Dundee.

"What's he doing out today?" William wondered out loud to himself watching him with narrowed eyes.

Selby was walking up to a young lad who looked to be about twelve years old and shoved him slightly in the arm. He said something to him that William couldn't hear and then he and his fellows laughed raucously as the young lad tried to walk away from them. Selby grabbed his arm and shook him hard until the lad lost his footing and sat down hard on the cobbled street. William's blood began to boil as he witnessed the treatment of the poor young lad. Once Selby had tired of bothering the lad, he moved on down the street with his cronies. As the group passed William, Selby caused himself to brush against the young Scotsman with his shoulder. He walked a few paces then turned back and raised his nose at him.

"Oh, forgive me, did I run into you?" he asked disdainfully. "I'm surprised I didn't see you. In that fine green outfit of yours." He sneered at William and his friends sniggered.

William looked him in the eyes. "It's nothing to me. People run into others all the time in the market. I saw ye mistreating that lad over there just now. Why do ye feel ye need to exercise rudeness? Is it just because ye're really a coward and afraid to fight real battles?"

Young Selby twisted his lip disdainfully at William and crossed his arms in front of him. "So you're a bold one, are you?" He looked William over and spotted the dagger at his belt. "That's a fine dagger you carry. It's *far* too fine, like that tunic. Yes, far too fine for a lowly Scot like you. It would look better in my belt." He reached out for it, but William took a step back.

"I willna let ye have it," William said. "It is my best one. I use it for my work and to cut my meat at supper."

"How quaint," Selby said with a sneer. "But I will teach you to deny me something that I ask for." He drew his sword from his belt. "How about you fight me and we'll see who wins?"

"Fair enough," William said and drew his long dagger, falling into a crouch.

Selby's friends laughed, thinking that their companion would soon have the Scotsman begging for mercy. But they hadn't yet met with William Wallace.

As soon as Selby struck out with his sword, William leapt to the side and caught the blade on his far shorter dagger. Selby struck out at him again and had the same effect. He started to get angry then and swung around harder at the Scotsman. William blocked and dodged expertly, not letting Selby's sword touch him.

"You are far better then I thought," Selby growled as he tried to get past William's defenses. "But no Scot can win against an Englishman. I'll have you soon enough and then I'll take you to my father and he'll decide what to do with you."

"I'd love to see you try," William told him with a careless laugh and struck out, cutting Selby across the arm. The young Englishman gasped in annoyance and turned his flashing eyes to William.

"Why, you little...!" he said dangerously and drove his sword at William in hopes of stabbing him through the middle.

William leapt to one side and blocked the blow with his dagger. Because of the smaller size of his blade, though, it glanced off with the force of Selby's blow and William's dagger plunged into Selby's chest.

The Englishman dropped his sword and staggered to the ground. William just stood there with his mouth hanging open, not believing what he had just done. Selby's friends looked at him in amazement then one of them finally got his voice back and shouted at the top of his lungs for the English solders who were milling around the street.

Time to go! William shouted to himself and forced his feet to move. He left his dagger sticking into Selby and took to his heels, running off through the town with the shouting Englishmen right behind him.

William had the advantage of them though, because he knew these streets like the back of his hand and he barreled down an alley to get away from them. He knew his green tunic would attract too much attention out in the open and he wished he had not worn it.

He took another street and raced down the familiar cobbles when he saw a lady sweeping her stoop. She caught sight of him and hailed him with her hand.

"Young William! Where are ye off to so fast?"

"I'm in trouble!" he told her breathlessly, looking around for Englishmen.

"Come in, I will hide you," she told him and grabbed his arm, drawing him inside. "What happened?"

"I got into a fight with young Selby and I fear I killed him," William said. "It all happened so fast, I didna know what happened."

"Dinna fret, I will help ye, young William." The old lady looked around. "I have nowhere to hide you where they will not find you, but perhaps I can disguise ye so that they will never expect anything."

"What exactly did ye have in mind?" William asked as she bustled around.

She grabbed several things from a closet and came back over to William. "Get this on," she told him, shoving a dress over his head.

"Ye're going to make a lass out of me?" William asked indignantly as she tied a lacy scarf around his neck and clapped a bonnet over his head to conceal his messy mop of hair.

"Yes I am," the lady told him firmly. "Now sit at the spinning wheel and spin the wool."

"But I..."

"Sit!" She pushed William over to the spinning wheel and shoved him into the chair. "Do your best."

As soon as William sat down and took up the wool to spin, there was a knock on the door and it was shoved rudely in as several Englishmen marched into the house. William looked up quickly, then turned back to his spinning.

"What mean ye by bursting in here?" the lady asked indignantly. "What is it ye want?"

"We're sorry to bother you ma'am," one of the men said, stepping forward. "But we are looking for a young Scotsman. He has killed the governor's son. Perhaps you have seen him. He was wearing a green jerkin, about sixteen years of age?"

"I have been working around the house all day," the lady said.

"We have to check your house to make sure you are not hiding him," said another Englishman.

"Go ahead," the lady said cooly. "You'll find no one here but me and the girl spinning and my kitchen maid."

"We'll see about that for ourselves," said the leader of the group and they went around the house, all the while William sat spinning as well as he could, trying not to attract any attention to himself.

The Englishmen came back before too long and one nodded to the lady. "Sorry for your inconvenience, ma'am. If you see him, please make sure you tell us."

"I will," the lady said and closed the door behind them.

When they were sure it was safe, William stood up and took the bonnet off his head and laughed. He couldn't stop laughing and soon the lady started laughing along with him. William struggled out of the dress and handed the things back to her.

"Thank ye Lady Eliza," he said. "I dinna ken how I can thank ye for this."

"Dinna think anything of it, William," she told him. "But I'm going to have to ask you to stay a little bit longer. It's not going to be safe for you out in the town. There are sadly a few here who would give ye up for a few pieces of gold from Governor Selby. They are not all true like me. Stay until after dark and then you can leave when no one will be able to see you."

"But my mother and my uncle will be worried," William said. "I know how to move around town without being seen."

"I willna allow it," Lady Eliza said firmly. "Come join me for dinner. You are a young lad who can eat a lot, I trust."

William had to smile. "All right," he said, giving in. "I just dinna want to be a burden."

"Ye're no' a burden, Will," Eliza said and took his arm, drawing him into the kitchen.

They sat down at the table and the maid turned to smile at William.

"How are ye, Will?" she asked. "I havena seen ye for a while."

"I'm fine, I suppose, except for the fact that I am now a criminal," he said ruefully.

"I heard ye tell Lady Eliza," she said. "Be careful, Will. Ye know the English give no quarter to those they are after weather they're guilty or not."

"I'll be fine, Ishbel," he said. "But I dinna ken what I'll do now. I canna go back to town if I'm a wanted man."

"You have family in other places," Eliza told him softly. "You'll have no other choice then to leave this part of the country."

"I suppose ye're right," William said, suddenly hit by the enormity of it. "I guess I dinna have any other choice."

Eliza put her hand on his shoulder and gave him a smile. "Dinna worry, William. You are a strong young lad. And ye'll take anything they can throw at ye."

Ishbel set out the food and they fell to. William found that despite his misadventure, he was very hungry and he ate heartily to Lady Eliza's coaxing.

He stayed late into the night and spent most of his time pacing back and fourth anxiously. Finally, around midnight, Eliza gave in and told him he could probably go.

"Thank ye very much," William told her, taking her hand in his. "I dinna ken how I can thank ye for all this. If ye hadna helped me, I would have been thrown into the tolbooth or worse."

"It was nothing, William, as I told ye," Eliza said and led him to her back door. "Go out this way just to be safe. I hope to see ye again, William, though I dinna think there's much hope of it."

William turned to her as she opened the door for him. "One day, ma'am, I will be back and hopefully, I will bring the news that Scotland is free."

"Ah, freedom," Eliza said with a sad look in her

eyes. "I will be waiting that day right readily, William Wallace," she told him.

William nodded and slipped out the door into the dark town. He had only been out in Dundee at night a few times on his personal adventures but he knew his way around just as well in the dark as he did in the light. He slipped silently through the deserted streets, hearing the loud talking and singing from the taverns where the sailors were enjoying their nights on shore. He was always on the lookout for English soldiers. He had always been wary of them for they were oppressing his country, but now he was avoiding them for his life. He was really overwhelmed with feelings right now. He had no idea what to think. He had never wanted to cause trouble like that. But now that he had, he began to feel as if he had taken the next step and it almost made him feel like he had accomplished something. He took a deep breath. Since he was already an outlaw, what could it hurt to go the whole way and start a campaign against the English? William smiled with that thought. His misfortune earlier that day might have turned to a bit of an advantage. He was soon out of the town and made his way to his uncle's house on the Dee river. He stopped and took a deep breath. He was not looking forward to telling his family about what had happened.

Chapter Three

When Fate Calls

William opened the door to his uncle's house cautiously and slipped inside. He looked around to see if anyone was there and gave a sigh of relief. Maybe they weren't worried about him after all. He went into the kitchen and almost cried out in surprise as his mother materialized out of the darkness.

"Oh, William, I was so worried something had happened to you!" she cried, grabbing him up in her arms and looking him over to make sure he was all there. "Where have ye been?"

"Mother, I'm all right," William assured her and gently took her arms from around him. "I have to talk to you though, where's uncle?"

"I'm right here," said his uncle, coming into the

kitchen as well with a candle to light the room a bit. "William you have a lot of explaining to do. We were worried sick about you."

"I can take care of myself," William muttered as he sat down at the table to his mother's insisting.

"Would ye like something to eat, Will? You must be starving," she said.

"I already ate, thank ye," William told her and she sat down next to him.

"All right, William, tell us what happened," his uncle said with a stern look.

William took a deep sigh and started his story. "Well, after my lessons, I went to walk around the town a little bit and I met up with young Selby. He was mistreating a young lad and then he came up to me and insulted me on my finery and tried to take my dagger. I told him he couldn't have it and he drew his sword. I was forced to fight him or die, so I drew my dagger and we dueled." His mother gasped at this and grabbed his hand.

"William, did he hurt ye?" she asked.

"No, mother," he said. "I...I won, I'm afraid. Ye see, he thrust a blow at me and when I went to parry it, my dagger glanced off his blade and I stabbed him."

William's uncle turned his eyes skyward and he sighed deeply. William's mother looked at him in shock.

"You *killed* him?" she asked in disbelief.

"I never meant to," William told her firmly. "It just happened."

"You can't stay here anymore," his uncle said,

standing immediately. "You must leave this instant. The English will be here first thing in the morning looking for you. You and your mother must leave."

"What about ye?" William asked. "They willna spare ye!"

"I have friends in high places," his uncle told him insistently. "But you, dear lad, would be hung without question."

"Where will we go?" William asked.

"We'll go to my brother Richard's house in Dunipace," William's mother told him. He could tell her face was pale even in the candlelight. "Oh, William, I wish yer father was here."

"Even he couldn't do anything, Margaret," William's uncle said sadly. "But you must leave now. I will try to send your things on later. Dress as pilgrims, no one will notice you then."

"Come, William," his mother urged and they went to pack some clothes and things they would need on the journey.

William rolled all the things he would need in his plaid and tied it with two cords so he could carry it over his shoulder. Then he dressed in the drab robes his uncle had given him to wear. He took up his old dirk that his father had given him before he left and hid it under his robes in case they ran into trouble. He sighed as he took up his pack. He hated the idea of fleeing like a criminal but he also knew that it would be folly to stay and fight. He was only one, and though there might be some in Dundee who would fight with him, they would still not have a chance against the English forces, being untrained and undisciplined.

He went out of his room and found his mother and uncle waiting for him. His uncle took his hand and clasped it.

"Be safe, William. I hope to see ye again some day," he said.

"Good bye, Uncle," William said and embraced him warmly. "I hope to see ye again too."

"William!" John shouted as he ran out of his room and threw his arms around his older brother.

"Be good Johnny," William said, hugging him back. "Take care of Ma."

"Come, Will," his mother said. "We need to be gone. There's only a few hours more before sunrise."

"I want to come too!" John said, clutching his mother's hand tightly.

"No, Johnny, you need to stay here. I will be back for you soon and then we'll go back home to Elderslie." She kissed him on the forehead. "Now we must go."

So they set off in the dark night, the moon not even making any light for their escape. William couldn't help the excitement rushing through him. It was not that he was glad to be fleeing for his life, but he had to admit that he had never done anything this exciting before.

They came to a river and they drank their fill and filled their canteens to the brim. It was only a couple more hours until dawn now and they were now a good few miles from Dundee. When the sun finally came up, they laid down among some bushes and took a bit of rest. They were soon off again within a couple hours, eating a hurried breakfast as they went.

Later that day, they took a ferry over the Tay and made their way to Dunfermline Abbey. They spent the night there then the next morning, they continued on their way to Dunipace.

Chapter Four

I Tell Thee True

It had been a long time since William had been in Dunipace or had seen his uncle Richard Crawford. They had always gotten on well, for they shared many of the same views of freedom and he reminded William very much of his father. His mother told him that she would probably only stay there with him for a couple days because she wanted to go back to their home in Elderslie and see if she could hear any news of her husband and oldest son.

"Can I no' go wi' ye?" William asked her after she had told him her plans.

"Nae, William, I think it best ye stay here for a while. You're uncle will be glad to have you, ye know that. When everything calms down a bit, you can come to Elderslie as well. Hopefully by then yer father will be home and we can live as a family again."

William turned to look at her. "Mother, I dinna think we will be able to live as a family again until Edward Longshanks takes his men away from our country and forgets about us."

"Ah, Will, you are too much like yer father," his mother said sadly. "What would I do if I lost ye?"

William stopped walking and reached out to take her hand. "Ye willna, mother. Dinna worry. I willna do anything that shouldna be done."

She sighed and they continued walking, going up to the house where Richard Crawford lived.

William's uncle was very happy to see his sister and nephew and beckoned them in to the supper table where his gillies, the Scottish servants, were setting out the food.

"Please come in. I was not expecting anyone, but this is a very nice surprise," he said with a grin as he clasped William's hand and tussled his hair.

"I'm afraid we're no' just here socially, Uncle," the young Scotsman said sadly.

His uncle's hooded eyes clouded as he saw the worry in his young nephew's face. "Well, perhaps ye should tell it me then?" he inquired.

William took up his tale with a sigh and his uncle listened intently as they ate. When the lad had finished his tale, Richard ran a hand through his graying hair tiredly.

"Ah, William, I was hoping ye wouldn't get into trouble like that, but then I guess it was too much to hope for. I ken ye didn't mean it, but now you'll be made an outlaw for sure and they'll have Englishmen out looking for your head."

"I can take care of myself, Uncle," William insisted. "The only thing I worry about is that they will hurt you and my other family members to find me."

"And ye know they won't get anything out of us!" his uncle said surely. "We'd never give ye up, Will, I hope ye know that."

"That's why I worry for ye," he said quietly.

Richard reached across the table and took William's hands in his, smiling at him. "Everything will turn out all right in the end. You may as well make the best in any situation, I say. You have grown very much since the last time I saw ye, why ye're almost taller then me now! How old are ye? Sixteen?"

"Aye," William smiled back at him. "That's right. And it has been far too long since the last time I visited. I have been stuck in school for the past several years!"

"Ah, and have ye learned anything?" his uncle asked with a twinkle in his eye.

"I have learned a lot," William said slowly. "Though I dare say I learned more from what I *didna* do than from what I did."

His uncle laughed heartily and stood up. "Come sit where it's comfortable. Then we can talk more."

William's mother bade them good night, tired from the journey, and William and Richard went to sit by the fire as the sun set, looking into the flames as they spoke together.

"So how have you been, William?" his uncle asked.

"Over all, Uncle, I have been well. I have some friends at school. I suppose I'll have to send them some letters so they know what happened to me."

"Yes, you'll have plenty of time. Young John Graham still comes here to visit me some times. I'm sure he would like to see ye again too."

"Aye, I forgot about Johnny!" William said happily. "I'll have to go visit him tomorrow."

"What's on yer mind, William?" his uncle said after a few seconds. "You're oddly solemn."

William gave a small mirthless smile as he looked into the fire, watching the flames lick the logs. "I can't help but see that the Scots dinna like the English oppression. I've been thinking a lot about it these last few days. I think that if we get enough to rise, then England would have no other choice then to listen to us. If they had a chosen leader to gather men quietly a little at a time then they could rise in different places in quick attacks. Then we could attack swiftly and disappear even faster. I think it would work that way."

"Ah, Will," Richard looked to his nephew fondly. "I fear I see no way of it right now. There are far too many English here, and the Scots, I regret to say, don't care either way if we are attached to England or not. Nor do we have a leader to gather the men you talk about."

"But if we try," William told him earnestly. "Many things will be possible. I may be young, but I can see right now that nothing will ever be done unless someone makes a stand. I would take the command myself if I could."

"You are far too young, William," Richard said gently.

"Who else would?" William asked. "I am not saying I am going to take it right now, but perhaps some day I can at least help with the fight. I'm not saying I would make a good leader, but if I was put into that position, I would certainly try my best at it. You, Uncle, taught me as well as did my father, that it is right and noble for a nation to protect itself, preserve it's freedom and never bow to a foreign people. You had me learn at a young age that 'The day that makes a man a slave, takes away half his worth.' I never want to be a slave, Uncle. I think that if Scotland would stand up as I wish, then she could free her bonds that I think, sadly, she put there herself. If we had fought back then, we might not be in this position, but Baliol was too weak a ruler and the nobles were at each other's throats and because of it, Scotland is oppressed." He paused, turning to his uncle and looking him in the eyes. "But Scotland is not content with England's oppression. They would fight if given half the chance. I believe there are others who feel the same as I do and would rise to fight for her right like our ancestors in days of old. Now may not be the time; but until the time comes, I shall do all I can to assist or get others to sympathize and we will be ready when the time of action comes our way."

"Ah, William," Richard said and leaned forward in his chair, reaching out to clasp William's shoulders. "I tell thee true, Will, freedom is the best of things. Don't ever let yourself be a slave."

William grinned bravely at his uncle. "I willna, Uncle. Ye have my word on that!"

"Good!" Richard said and smiled at the young Scotsman. "Now you should be off to bed. You've had a long journey and tomorrow, you can go around the grounds. Maybe take my horse if ye wish to ride through the woods."

"Thank ye, Uncle. Good night," William stood up and went to his room where the gillies had stoked up the fire to a roaring warmness. William took off the dusty traveling habit he had worn on the journey there and climbed into his bed, pulling the thick blankets over him. He closed his eyes and despite the excitement of the last few days, he fell asleep quickly, dreaming of a land no longer oppressed by England.

Chapter Five

A New Reason

The next morning, William woke early and got out of bed. He washed his face in the water basin and quickly toweled it dry. After he had done that, he took his roll of plaid and untied it, taking all his things out of it before he spread it out on the floor and knelt to pleat it. He lay down on the pleated part and folded it over him, belting it around his waist. He stood up and gathered the extra tartan and bundled it over his chest so that it hung down behind him, pinning it with his large round broach on his left shoulder. He hung his dirk from his belt and pulled his boots on, then went out of his room, following the smell of fresh bannocks cooking on the griddle.

"Good morning, Will," Richard said as his nephew came into the kitchen. "Have a seat and get some food into ye."

William sat gladly and filled a plate with piping hot bannocks and eggs. He ate his fill while his uncle watched him approvingly.

"It seems you haven't lost yer appetite," he said with a grin.

William grinned back. "Nae, I'm afraid no'," he said.

When he was done, he stood up and pulled a handkerchief out of a pocket he had made in his plaid, tying several bannocks up in it and putting the package back into his belt pouch. "Is it all right if I go for a ride now, Uncle?" he asked. "I'll be back by this afternoon. Will ye tell my mother where I am?"

"I will do that, Will. Have a good time." Richard waved him off.

William left the house and went out to the barn where one of the gillies directed him to a horse and William took over to saddle it for himself.

"Thank ye," he said, and the gillie nodded as William tightened the girth and then mounted up, giving the horse a friendly pat on the neck before he urged it into motion and rode out of the barn, cantering it across the field to the woods that surrounded the property.

It felt wonderful to be out again with that feeling of freedom he had not felt in a long time. It was hard to believe he was living in an oppressed country when he felt like this.

His horse seemed to feel his exhilaration and ran swiftly between the trees. William held tight with his knees and leaned forward over the saddle, moving with his

mount. When they came across a burn, William slowed the
horse and stopped it on the bank of the river. William
dismounted and led his horse forward to drink. He knelt
on the bank and took a drink himself, the water cold and
sweet. Everything seemed exceptionally good that day.

He was about to mount up again when he heard
something crack in the woods behind him as if someone
had mis-stepped. He turned slowly, his hand going to the
dirk at his belt. He felt a presence and knew it was no
rabbit that he had heard. He slowly moved in the direction,
keeping his feet as silent as if he was lighter than air.

He ducked down behind a bush and looked out to
where he had heard the sound. He saw someone's boot
sticking out from behind another bush. William snuck
forward silently, moving his dirk up to hold between his
teeth. He crept closer to the hidden figure as if he was
stalking a deer and when he was within an arm's length,
he leapt forward, whipping the dirk from his mouth and
grabbed his stalker quickly, holding his arms behind his
back and pressing the dagger to his throat.

"State yer name and reason for being here, or ye
die!" William hissed to the startled captive.

"Peace, man, peace!" his stalker pleaded. "I mean ye
nae harm!"

William spun his captive around so that he could see
his face. He found a lad his age staring back at him, his
green eyes half covered by the shaggy dirty blond hair that
fell on his face. He was grinning.

"John Graham?!" William asked in surprise, looking

in disbelief at his old friend.

"Aye, who'd ye think it was, Edward Longshanks?" John laughed as William grinned and they embraced as they both laughed.

"Why'd ye sneak up on me then?" William asked.

"I didn't think ye'd take it that hard," John said with another laugh. "Ye've gotten more desperate since the last time I saw ye. I heard what happened."

"How did ye find out about that so fast?" William asked, slightly surprised.

John grinned. "I talk to the gillies on yer uncle's property. I go up there every once in a while to visit him. He misses ye a lot. Ye havena been here for at least four years."

"Nae, I havena," William said. "So now, I'm here again. And probably here to stay for a while seeing as I canna go back to Dundee, nor to Elderslie."

"I'm sorry, Will," John said. "I ken ye didna mean to kill him."

"Aye," William said. "It wasna what I had wanted. I didn't want a quarrel now."

"But now that it's happened..." John said with a mischievous smile. "What are we going to do?"

William laughed at his "we". "Well, we will do whatever we have to."

"Fighting the English together, eh?" John asked.

William looked at him. "Do ye mean it, John? Do ye really think it a good idea to start now?"

John shrugged. "Will, what else are we going to do?"

he asked. "We can find some other lads and start a rebel army and train in the art of weaponry so when the time comes..."

"We'll train in hit and run warfare," William said, starting to get excited as he stood up. "And when we get enough lads, we'll start using our knowledge on the English."

John laughed in excitement and stood up as well. "Aye! That's the William Wallace I ken! When do we start?"

"Soon I hope," William said and started back to his horse. "Need a ride back home?"

"If ye dinna mind," John said and leapt up behind William as he urged his horse into a trot and they started back through the woods. Once they got out of the forest, they sat on a hill overlooking Richard Crawford's house and William took the bannocks out of his belt pouch and shared them with John.

"So how have ye been?" William asked him.

"Och, I've been fine," John said. "As good as anyone can be living under English tyranny."

"Aye, I ken," William said. "But maybe we willna be oppressed too much longer."

"If we have anything to do with it!" John laughed and William shoved him on the shoulder. "So how have ye been besides getting into trouble with the English?"

"Getting into trouble at school," William said with a laugh. "But then that's only to be expected, isna it?"

They both laughed then and looked out to the land

in front of them with William's uncle's house to one side. William felt alive once again. He felt more life then he had in many years. There was a new reason to his life that he felt surging through his veins. He had a companion, and he was ready to take on the whole English army if he had to.

"I should probably be getting back," John told him and stood. "I'll see ye again tomorrow, Will. It's great to have ye back!"

"Bye, Johnny, I'll see ye tomorrow too!" William stood as well and mounted his horse again, waving to John before he trotted off down the hill to the barn again.

He left his horse with the gillie and went into the house where he found his mother sewing by the fire. She smiled up at him as he came in.

"Hello, Will, how have ye been today?" she asked.

"Good," William said and sat down opposite her. "I found John Graham in the woods. We talked for a while."

"That's nice, Will," his mother said. "I'll be leaving tomorrow for Dundee. I'll pick up John then head to Elderslie, I think."

"Are ye sure ye dinna want me to go with ye?" William asked. "Just on the journey?"

"No, Will, it's all right. Your uncle is sending a couple of his gillies with me so I won't be alone. I want you to stay here and stay low. Don't wander too far into the towns. I don't know how fast news has traveled. You could be taken by surprise."

"I'm always ready for trouble," William said and

stood. "I'm going to go find Uncle. I'll see you at dinner."

William spent the rest of the day talking with his uncle and that night at dinner they all sat down to a hot stew and fresh crusty bread. William fell to with gusto and was on his second bowl when there was a knock on the door. A gillie went to answer it and came back with a man who snatched the bonnet off his head.

"Yes?" Richard asked, looking up at the man.

"I came with a message for Lady Wallace," the man said and Richard motioned to his sister.

"Yes?" William's mother stood up and stepped over to him. "What do you need?"

"My Lady, I am sorry to report that your husband is dead," the messenger said sadly.

"Alan?!" she gasped, her hands pressing against her mouth.

"Dead?" William cried, standing up. "What happened?"

"He and your brother Malcolm were both killed on the field of battle," the messenger replied. "They died bravely, fighting to the last." He stepped forward and took William's mother's hand. "My Lady, I regret this news as much as ye, to be sure. I fought under yer husband and he was a brave man. One of the bravest I ken. And yer son, Malcolm, was just like him. I've never seen their equal. We have brought their bodies back to Elderslie for a proper burial. I will bring you back with me if ye wish."

"Thank you," she whispered then sunk into her chair, burying her face in her hands. William stood as if made of stone. He stepped forward and reached out for the messenger. "Where is the rest of your men? How many did my father have under his command?"

"Precious few," the messenger replied. "And even fewer are left after our fateful skirmish. The men werena ready. This was no clan fight, this was against the English and no one was ready for their style of fighting. It didn't work out and only a few of us were left with our lives." He put a strong hand on William's shoulder. "I'm sorry lad. But yer father was a brave man. We'll no' forget him, nor yer brother."

"Aye," William said slowly. "Thank ye." He pushed past the man and went toward the door.

"William..." his mother called him back.

"Leave him," Richard told her gently and rested his hands on her shoulders in comfort. "He'll be all right."

Once William got out of the house, he ran as fast as he could to the top of the hill he had sat on earlier with John. He looked out to the moonlit hills, breathing hard from his run, his mind full of too many thoughts.

His first was anger. A growl ripped from his throat and he grabbed the dirk from his belt and threw it into a nearby tree. He kicked the tree as well, not minding the pain that shot through his foot. He didn't even feel it. He ripped the dirk from the tree and threw it into the ground. His chest heaved and he dug his foot into the ground, picking up a rock and throwing it as hard as he could. He suddenly felt tired and he sank to the ground, pressing his knees to his chest. The sorrow was coming then. He could feel it and there was nothing he could do to stop it. He wrapped his arms around his legs and pressed his face into his knees as the tears came. He felt weak and foolish, but for some reason that didn't bother him. Not now. There was no one to see him anyway.

He didn't know how long he sat there. Eventually, he began to feel the cold of the night and he shivered in the breeze that blew around him. He raised his head and roughly wiped the tears from his face. He looked out to the hills, seeming to see farther than possible in the night as if he was looking all the way down to England. He swore right then that he would avenge his father if it was the last thing he did. He would fight England, he would win Scotland's freedom as his father had wanted. There was no other thought in his mind as he stood, taking his father's dirk from the ground and kissing the blade.

"I vow, Father," he said out loud. "That I will do the best I can to free Scotland. I will avenge you. I promise ye that."

Chapter Six

Fighting for a Cause

William somehow managed to get back to his bed as if in a stupor and fell asleep on top of the blankets. His uncle came in to see him a while later and looked in sympathy at the lad who had just lost his father and his brother to the enemy he himself hated more then anything. Richard Crawford pulled a blanket over his nephew and turned to put more wood on the fire as William let out a soft moan. He looked at the lad's troubled face and wished he could do more for him, but knew he couldn't. Grief would wear down in its own time. He walked quietly out of the room and closed the door silently as William slumbered on in troubled dreams.

**

When William woke the next morning, he lay in bed,

trying to make sense of what had happened the day before. He felt miserable, his heart feeling as if it had a big gaping hole cut into it. *Just another scar*, he thought to himself grimly. He didn't want to get up, but he knew his mother was bound to leave that morning, and he wanted to see her off. He reluctantly pulled himself out of bed, realizing he was still fully dressed and left the room. There was a dull pain in his foot from the night before, and he remembered his anger and felt heat flare through his veins again, making him involuntarily clench his fists. He ground his teeth. Aye, he would avenge his father the best he could. If he ever found the man responsible for his death...

When he got to the kitchen where voices could be heard, he saw his mother standing with his uncle while the gillies packed food and things for her and the messenger from the night before. They looked up when William came in and the young Scotsman was saddened further by the grief in his mother's eyes.

"I'll be leaving in a few minutes, William," she said softly. "Hopefully someday you can follow me when our land is safe and not dominated by the English."

"Aye, Mother," William replied. "I hope for that day soon, but I do not think it will be short in coming. Not when we have nae one to stand up and fight."

"William..." His mother started then stopped with a sigh. She took his hands in hers. "I don't want to loose you too. Do what you think is right but do not do anything foolish."

"I willna, Mother," William told her and squeezed

her hands comfortingly. "Please believe me."

"I do, William, I do," she said.

The messenger came up to William and took him to one side looking him seriously in the eye. "Master William, I didn't want to tell ye last night, but I have word that ye have been officially outlawed. I went to yer uncle's in Dundee first, thinking ye and yer mother were there and he told me the news. Now people have a right to be searching for you. In fact, it's more than likely. Ye have a price on yer head, William. I dare say ye shouldna stay here long. I heard easily enough where ye were heading, others with less friendly intentions might find out as well."

"What do ye suggest?" William asked.

"I suggest getting out of here. There's too many earls around here who might not mind turning ye in. Do ye have any where else ye can go?"

"I have an uncle in Ayr. I suppose I could go there," William said.

"Ayr! That's a huge English garrison town, do ye think it's wise?"

William gave a slight smile. "Aye, that was exactly what I was thinking. They wouldn't look for me there in the heart of their garrisons. Besides, my uncle, Ronald Crawford, is the sheriff of Ayr, so that should count for something."

The other man smiled slightly. "I guess ye have one there, William. Ye are a smart lad, I canna see ye getting captured too easily. Just do what ye think is wise. I think ye can trust yer own judgement. But dinna tell yer mother about yer outlawry. She would worry far too much. There's no sense in giving her more grief then she is already suffering from."

William nodded. "Aye, I understand."

They ate a quick breakfast, then William's mother took her leave and William was left to discuss his plans with his uncle.

"So I'm to loose my nephew so soon?" he said with a small smile.

"I'm afraid so, Uncle, but I will be back to visit ye from time to time. I may need an escape sometime."

"Ah, young William," Richard said with a sigh. "You have far too much sense of duty for one so young. I wonder sometimes if you are older then you appear."

William had to laugh. "I dinna think everyone would agree with that, Uncle."

"Well, do what ye wish," Richard said. "Will ye be leaving today?"

"I'll stay one more night," William told him, standing up from the table. "I want tae talk to John about it first. He has relatives down there if I remember correctly. He may want to come with me."

"Good idea," Richard said. "The journey's long and it's always nice to have a traveling partner."

"Aye," William said. "Well, I'm off. I'll see ye later."

He left the house and grabbed a horse from the stable, saddling it himself and riding it down the glen to the house of his friend John Graham.

When he got there, he met John coming up the path

on his own horse. William reigned it in as John hailed him with a laugh.

"I was just coming to see ye," he said. "How are ye?"

"Why dinna we go up in the woods to talk more privately?" William said and set his heels to his horse's sides, urging it into a canter as he led John back up the hill to the woods.

When they got up to the tree line, they sat down in the spot they had the day before, letting their horses loose to graze as they pleased.

"I saw a messenger go up to yer uncle's last night," John said. "What news?"

"Nothing good," William said bitterly. "My father and Malcolm are dead. Killed by the English."

"Och, William, I'm sorry," John said sincerely. "It always seems that when one bad thing happens, everything goes wrong."

"Aye," William said. "On top of that, I'm an outlaw with a price on my head. Though I figured as much. It doesna bother me, but it does make it a bit annoying when ye have to go around town."

"Aye, it does that," John said. "So I imagine ye'll be leaving again soon?"

"It seems I have little choice," William said. "I was going to go to my uncle's house in Ayr. I was thinking that the closer I get to the English, the harder it will be for them to find me."

John grinned. "Aye, daring Will Wallace, that's who I've always known. It's a good idea."

"Would ye like to come with me?" William asked. "Ye have relatives down there as well, dinna ye? Then we could work on recruiting lads. I'm sure there's someplace over there where we could train and hide out."

John looked thoughtful. "Aye, I bet ye're right. I like the idea. I'd like to go with ye. I'll ask my Da to make sure. I haven't been down there in a long time. Ye know, Kerlie lives down there too, I bet he'd like to help us. He probably knows some lads who'd like to get in on it too."

"Aye, I bet ye're right!" William said, getting excited again. "I was planning on leaving tomorrow morning. How's that?"

"Fine," John said. "I'll meet at yer uncle's for breakfast, then we can be on our way!"

John left to go back home to make his plans and William stood on the hilltop, patting his horse on the neck. "Aye, boy, we'll be free soon enough, dinna ye worry," he said softly. The horse nudged the side of his face with his nose as if in agreement.

Chapter Seven

Onward Once Again

William didn't sleep that night. He was too restless with his thoughts of the next day. When dawn finally came, he rolled out of bed and dressed quickly in his plaid, pulling his boots on even as he made his way out the door. He found his uncle sitting by the fire, drinking a cup of mulled ale.

"Ye're up early, William," he said. "Ready for your journey?"

"Aye," William said, sitting opposite him. "More than ready."

Before long, a knock came at the door and William got up to open it himself, finding John standing there with an excited look on his face.

"Good morning, Will," he said.

"Good morning, John, come in." William stepped aside to let his friend into the house and they made their way to the kitchen where the gillies were setting out breakfast. Richard looked up at the lads and smiled.

"Hello, John," he said. "How are ye this morning? Ready for the trip I hope. William has been up half the night."

John laughed. "Aye, so have I. But first, I would like to eat some of those wonderful smelling bannocks."

The two lads fell to with gusto and between them, all the food was soon gone. Richard looked to the lads fondly. "I must remember to have a lot of food packed for ye two."

John laughed. "I packed my bow so we can hunt on the way, but we will need some supplements."

"Meaning bannocks," William said with a grin and Richard laughed.

"All right then lads, go do what ye need to get ready, the food will be packed soon and then ye can be off."

The lads finished their breakfast then took the haversacks the gillies had packed for them and took their leave. William embraced his uncle warmly before he went out the door.

"Bye, Uncle Richard," he said. "I'll be back to visit ye soon hopefully and I will send letters whenever I can."

Richard clasped his nephew in his arms. "I will send you some too, Will. Be careful and stay out of trouble. I don't want to have to get a letter from my brother saying that ye have gotten yerself hurt or worse. And ye and John stick together on the road. It can be dangerous traveling alone in times like this."

"Dinna worry, we'll be inseparable," William said with a bit of a laugh. "We'll be fine, ye ken ye can trust us."

Richard let him go and clapped him on the shoulder. "I ken, William. Well, I won't keep you much longer then."

"Aye, we should go," William said. He turned to John. "Well, shall we?"

"Aye," John said and held his hand up to Richard. "Bye, Mr. Crawford."

"Good bye, John. Bye, William." He waved to them as they went out the door and smiled slightly.

William and John went to the stable and got their horses ready. William put his haversack over his saddle and mounted up as John positioned his things on the back of his saddle as well.

"We're off," William said.

"Tally ho and all that, eh?" John joked with a fake English accent.

William laughed and urged his horse forward, out of the barn. He and John cantered their horses neck and neck off his uncle's land and to the southwest, in the direction of Ayr on the western coast of Scotland.

The first night out, they stopped in a glen and made a small peat fire where they warmed their bannocks.

William wiped crumbs off his lap and looked up at the darkening sky, seeing the moon as it rose. "I always liked sleeping out in the heather. I never minded it."

John smiled. "Aye, me too. We'll probably have to get used to it seeing as we might be living in the woods before too long."

"Aye," William looked off into the distance, thinking of the days to come.

"What's on yer mind, Will?" John asked softly after a few seconds of silence.

William shook himself slightly. "Naething of importance, Johnny. I was just thinking of my father. I wish we still had him to lead our band. He knew many people he could get to follow. I dinna ken half of the men he did. I only wish he hadna died sae early in this cursed war."

"Do ye no' understand, Will, that ye're just like him?" John asked his friend with eyes glowing with pride. "I would give everything I had to serve under yer father. I wish mine was half the patriot he was. But, Will, I dinna think serving under his son would be much different. I would give everything to serve under *ye.*"

William smiled and turned to his friend, putting a hand on his shoulder. "Och, John, all I need is yer friendship. We're equals in this. I dinna want to be a leader. I'm just tired of no one doing anything. When a leader is found, well, then I would be more than happy to follow him."

"Yer father would be proud of ye, Will," John told him seriously.

"I ken it." William looked down, the heaviness in his

heart feeling like a lead weight. "Thank ye, John. I hope he would be."

"We'll I canna imagine him no' being proud of a son who followed in his footsteps," John said, then yawned. "Well, we should probably get some sleep. Should we take watches?"

William hesitated. "We probably should, but I'm too tired. I havena slept well for the last two nights."

"Never mind then, it will be fine for one night," John said and unbelted his plaid so he could roll it around himself and lay down in the heather. "Good night."

"Good night, John," William said, doing the same.

Soon they were sleeping peacefully by the glowing embers, dreaming of the adventures they would have in the coming days.

***

The next morning, they woke early, and were off again after a quick breakfast. They saddled their horses and mounted up. William wrapped his plaid around his shoulders in the cool morning air and urged his horse into a canter, taking the lead as they continued on their way to Ayr. John sighed contentedly in the crisp fresh breeze that blew around them.

"Och, I do love a good ride early in the morning," he said with a grin.

"So do I," William replied. "I was denied it going to school. But living out in the country now, we should be able to go on rides whenever we want to."

"Aye, at least we are starting our campaign with a

bit of personal freedom."

"Aye, I suppose ye could say that," William said and stood up in his stirrups so he could see the land ahead. "I wonder how far it is to the sea. My uncle lives outside the town a bit in a big house. We can even go down to the beach and ride or go for a swim sometimes."

"It would be a good place to practice," John said. "We could practice shooting out on the water."

"We could," William said thoughtfully. "But it might attract unwanted attention. I dinna want to do anything that will have the English on our tails."

"Aye, ye're probably right," John agreed. "But there are the woods where we should be able to go and practice without any trouble."

William nodded. "Aye. I bet they're afraid to go in the woods. The English have odd superstitions about forests. They think ghosts live there." He grinned and chuckled. "But it's really only the desperate men who canna live in proper society."

John laughed too. "Aye, just like in those tales the bards sing about Robin Hood. Ye'll be Robin Hood and we'll be yer merry men!"

William grinned at this. "Rob the rich to give to the poor. That's my kind of man!"

"Aye, mine too," John turned around in his saddle to look at his pack settled behind him. "I was going to see if maybe I could shoot a couple birds today for our supper."

"Sounds good," William said. "Tell ye what, if ye can shoot them, I'll cook them."

"Hmm, I dinna know," John said, pretending to contemplate the matter. "I dinna ken if I can trust ye with the cooking. I dinna want to have to shoot the birds and no' be able to enjoy them."

"Ye dinna trust my cooking abilities?" William asked him, pretending to be hurt.

"In other words, nae," John said and ducked a swipe from William that made his horse shy away.

"All right," William said. "If I make a passable stew, ye get first watch tonight. And if I make a terrible stew, I have to stay up all night. Deal?"

John grinned and reached over to clasp William's hand. "Deal!"

As it was, John shot two good-sized birds and William made a more than passable stew that even John had to admit was edible. William smugly lay down in his plaid as John sat at watch first and huddled by the fire. The young Scotsman closed his eyes and curled up for warmth as he drifted off to sleep.

***

The rest of their journey was uneventful and soon enough, William and John were sitting their horses on a rise looking out to the town of Ayr in the distance. William turned to his companion with a smile.

"Aye, we made it, did we no'?" he said cheerfully. "Now let's go and see if our unsuspecting relatives will welcome us with open arms."

John played along with him, bowing low in his saddle. "After ye," he said.

William urged his horse into a trot and they set off to the town by the seaside. This was just one more step on their journey and he felt again that same excitement he had felt before. They could do this. He knew it. He looked over to John and could see the same anticipation reflecting on his face. William leaned forward in his saddle and urged his horse on faster. Aye, there was nothing that could stop them now.

Chapter Eight

A New Scene

Ronald Crawford was, to put it blandly, surprised to see his nephew ride up to his stable as he was saddling his horse for an afternoon ride. He watched the young lad in curiosity as he dismounted and the stable lad came forward to take the reigns from him.

"Hello, Uncle," William said with a small smile, taking his bags from his saddle.

"Well...hello, William," Ronald Crawford said with slight hesitation. "I...well, what are ye doing here?"

"It's a rather long story, Uncle," William said a bit sheepishly, giving him a cautious grin.

"I'm quite sure it is," Ronald said a bit sternly.

William motioned to John who was loading his

baggage over his shoulders. "This is John Graham, I imagine ye ken him as well."

"Um, yes," Ronald said, shaking his head, still surprised at the events. He turned to the stable boy. "Never mind, Davie, I don't think I will be going for a ride this afternoon. Take care of these horses. Make sure they are fed and watered well."

"Aye, sir," Davie said and took the three horses to the stable.

"Now," Ronald said, turning to the two lads with his hands clasped in front of him. "I think we had best go in for a talk, shall we?"

William and John followed him into the house where Ronald made sure they had something to drink and sat them in front of the fire in his common room. He didn't sit himself but went over to a table and got a folded piece of paper from it, picking it up and tapping it against his other hand as he paced in front of them.

"Let me explain to ye what happened, Uncle," William said, slightly confused by his odd action.

"Before you explain why you are here, perhaps you would like to explain *this* to me as well." Ronald unfolded the paper with a flourish and held it in front of William's face. The young Scotsman took it to look at more closely, his face changing to a surprised look.

John, unable to control his curiosity, snatched the paper away from William and looked at it himself. "Och, two hundred pounds, William. Ye're worth far more than that!"

"D'ye think so?" William asked curiously, taking the notice back from his friend.

"This is not a joking matter," Ronald said in distress. "Please tell me why my nephew is wanted by the crown dead or alive? I may be the sheriff of Ayr, as good as that does me anymore with the English occupation, but that does not make it any easier to see my nephew in trouble with a death sentence awaiting him if he is caught."

William looked down a bit sheepishly, handing the paper back to his uncle. "I never meant anything to happen, Uncle Ronald. I swear to ye, I didna." He then related his tale about Selby and how he had heard from the messenger how his father and brother had been killed by the English and how he himself had been outlawed by the crown. Ronald shook his head through the whole narrative and when William had finished, he went to the fireplace and leaned his forehead against the mantle.

"William, this isna going to end well. You know that as well as I. Why did you come here of all places? The town is crawling with the English, lad! Did ye not know that?"

"Yes, I did, Uncle," William said. "Dinna worry, I took all into consideration. I figured that the closer I was to the English then the better chance I'd have of them not seeing me."

"A dangerous gamble to be sure," Ronald said, running a hand through his trim brown hair. "Ah, William, I don't know what to say to you. What will you do here?"

"Uncle Ronald," William stood up, he matched his

uncle for height perfectly. "I am going to do just what my father would. I am going to raise all the young lads in the vicinity. I am going to train them in the art of weapons and war and together, when the time comes, we will join the rebellion and fight as free men for the right of Scotland. And we willna stop until Scotland has her liberty and we have our own king on the throne and not some usurping English tyrant."

Ronald closed his eyes with a sigh. "William..."

William grabbed his shoulders. "Nae, Uncle, dinna try to talk me out of it. I ken what I need to do. I ken how to do it. I ken what will happen if I'm caught. I ken what will happen if I am not careful enough. I have taken everything into consideration and I ken the risks. I will take them. I am willing to give my life for Scotland as my father did, as my forefathers did many generations ago. This is what I need to do, Uncle. *Ye* ken that."

Ronald sighed deeply and finally looked his nephew in the eyes. He took hold of his arms and squeezed them tightly. "How old ye are, William," he said rather fondly. "You are just like yer father. Do what you will. I will not stop you. But know this right now. If I am caught with you under my roof, we will both be killed and most likely the rest of the family as well. I do not want my nephew to be killed under my protection, so do not do anything foolish."

"I am under no one's protection but my own," William said firmly. "But I promise not to do anything foolish. I understand my situation and I would never do anything deliberately to hurt my family."

"You're a good lad, Will," Ronald said, finally smiling and clapping his nephew on the shoulder. "Now, why don't we get you two settled? I'll put you in the guest rooms."

"I'm afraid I willna be staying, Mr. Crawford," John said, standing up. "I have my own kin to present myself to uninvited. I really had best be going, in fact. I'll see ye again in the morning, Will."

"Bye, John," William told his friend. "We can start scouting first thing in the morning. See ye then."

John waved as he left the room and William followed his uncle up the stairs and to one of the guest rooms in the big house. He unpacked his meager belongings and his uncle left him alone to rest for a few hours before supper. William lay on the bed, taking a bit of a nap, tired after his journey. When he woke later the sun was starting to go down and he got off the bed and washed up a bit, getting the dirt of travel off himself before he went down to eat.

"Did you have a good rest, William?" Ronald asked as he came in and sat down at the place that had been set for him at the long table in the dining hall.

"Aye, I did," William replied, reaching out to fill his plate from the trays of food on the table. "I'll probably be here off and on in the days to come, Uncle. We're going to try to set up a place in the woods when we get more lads. That's where we're going to train. That way no one will see us."

"Good idea," Ronald said. "The English very rarely

go into the woods. They are so deep and dark they think they hold all kinds of evil spirits."

William smiled slightly. "Aye, I thought as much. We will try not to give them any reason to do us harm."

Ronald smiled at his nephew. "I'm sure that the spirits or the Fair Folk or who really lives in those woods willna have a problem with yer wanting to set Scotland free. I dinna think half the town would either if they didna fear the English wrath so."

"Who is in charge of the English here, Uncle?" William asked curiously.

"Henry Percy," Ronald said grimly. "And a more infernal man I have never met in my life. He's not even the worse though. His right hand man, Jack Moore, is even worse than him. He's cold-hearted and enjoys being evil. He's Percy's hound dog. He follows his word and does anything to please him, no matter how vile, and takes pleasure in it all."

William took this information silently, putting it to thought. "How many English do ye think would be in the town?"

"Well nigh two hundred," Ronald told him, then held a finger warningly up at his nephew. "But don't you get any ideas, Will. You will never be able to fight them all. They have training of the English army. They would demolish any small band ye might put together."

"Dinna worry, Uncle, I told ye I wouldna do anything daft. I just want to know what we're up against, that's all."

Ronald looked back down at his food. "I'm just warning ye, Will. I don't want your ideas to turn into mass slaughter."

William sighed slightly. He was getting tired of people worrying about him and what he was doing. He pushed back his chair and looked down at his uncle. "Uncle Ronald, I am no' a lad anymore. I'm sixteen, old enough to be trustworthy, old enough to know what I can and canna do. I have gotten into trouble many times, but I have always managed to get out of it. Now, dinna think that makes me think I can get out of anything. But I know that somehow there will always be a way. And if I have strong comrades I can trust by my side, then I believe anything is possible."

"I didn't want to imply that you are too young William," Ronald said. "You have grown so much since the last time I saw you. I promise that from now on, I will do my best to trust your judgement. But please, William, do not make enemies. I know that you understand how that will go."

"I understand, Uncle," William said. He pulled away from the table. "I think I will go up to bed. I am still tired from my trip. I'll see ye in the morning."

"Good night then," Ronald told him and sat there as he watched his nephew walk off. He shook his head slightly. He only hoped he was doing what was best for the lad. Ronald thought for a moment if it would not be better to send him back to his mother. He shook his head at the thought. No, William was right, he was most likely better off here. Ronald took a deep drink of his tankard. He would have to learn to trust the lad.

Chapter Nine

Four Generals do not Make an

Army

The next morning, William woke refreshed, fully revived from his journey. He dressed quickly, then went down and ate a hurried breakfast. He didn't see his uncle, but figured he might be about his work in the town. After he had finished, he went outside and looked around at the landscape, seeing the woods in the distance. He decided to go visit John and see if they might look around a bit so he headed off in the direction of his companion's family's house, enjoying the day.

He didn't have to go far as it turned out. He soon caught sight of John walking toward him with two other lads in tow. He haled William and shouted out with a grin.

"Look who I found! Two willing recruits!"

William jogged over to them and grinned back. John pulled one of the lads forward. He had sandy curly hair that fell into his face and bright blue eyes. "Ye remember Kerlie, dinna ye?" John asked William.

"Of course!" William said and clasped Kerlie's hand. "How have ye been?"

"Och, all right," Kerlie said with a grin and pulled the other lad forward. "This is Stephen Ireland. He comes from, guess where, Ireland!"

Stephen grinned broadly at William and pumped his hand vigorously. He had jet-black hair that looked like it was never out of its natural disarray even though he tried to braid several parts to keep it out of his face. His eyes were just as black and sparkled merrily.

"Sure, and John has done nothing but talk about ye and yer plan all morning, so I decided to come and see for myself who this brave Scotsman was anyway."

"So ye'll join, Ireland?" William asked, giving a slight smile. "And ye dinna mind sticking around with a bunch of Scotsmen?"

"As long as ye aren't English," Stephen grinned back. He bowed low. "I'm at yer service."

"So how'd ye get over here?" William asked him curiously.

"I've tried to get it out of him," Kerlie said, jabbing Stephen in the ribs. "But he willna tell me."

"Sure, and I have my own reasons for fighting the

English," Stephen said, still grinning, but William detected a bitter catch to his voice.

"Well, are we going to go and scope out our domain?" John asked, motioning to the distant woods.

"Aye, if ye all like," William said. "Let's go have a look."

The four young lads marched off to the forest, talking and joking happily. When they got to the woods, they went into them without another thought. There was an immediate change in the feeling as they stepped through the trees. The sun didn't penetrate through the thick treetops. The four lads stood there for a few minutes, looking around at the scenery. John pretended to shiver.

"All right, I have to say, it is kind of scary," he said with a bit of a laugh.

William laughed and slapped him on the back. "Och, we'll get used to it, dinna worry. After a few months here, we willna think anything of it."

"Well, don't blame me then if we get kidnapped by fairies and wake up two hundred years from now, thinking we were only gone for a few hours," Stephen said with a twinkle in his eye. His face was so strait when he said it though, that William couldn't tell if he meant it or if he was only joking. He decided he wouldn't ask.

"So what will we be doing, Will?" Kerlie asked him. "John refused to tell us anything. He said ye should be the one to explain, so tell us!"

William chuckled and led them to a big tree with protruding roots and they all had a seat on it as William told them his plan.

"We're going to start a resistance. We're going to recruit all the lads we can and train them in the art of war. We're going to do it in secret so the English willna find out. I trust ye to keep it that way. We'll train and hide in here for as long as we need. We willna strike until the time is right. We will need a lot more men than we can muster to actually do any damage against the English. But if we can find some lads our age who will be willing to fight for their country, then we canna leave them to fight it on their own. That's what our goal is. Now, John, ye're my second in command. And Stephen and Kerlie, ye're my captains. Ye're also to be in charge of recruiting since ye know the lads around here."

Stephen and Kerlie saluted him solemnly. "Aye, General Wallace, we're with ye!"

William grinned. "Good, now we'll start immediately. First we need to find a place where we can make our camp. It will need to be deep enough in the woods so that no one will stumble in on it by accident. Then we'll need to start making weapons to practice with. Eventually we will need to find some real ones. I dinna ken how, but we will deal with that later. Right now, we need to move our army out!"

"Four generals dinna make an army," John said simply. "We'll have to find some more lads."

"Aye, ye're right," William said. "We will have to remedy that."

"I already know of several who would be willing,"

Kerlie offered. "I will talk to them first chance I get."

"We should come up with a way to recruit people without causing commotion," William said. "If people catch on that most of the lads are missing at once, they may get suspicious."

"What did ye have in mind, Will?" John asked.

"Perhaps, we'll have to work in shifts. Never too many of us here at once. And on no condition are we all to leave the forest at the same time. If an English patrol were to pass at that time, it would start some questions flowing that we dinna want to answer. It won't matter with just us, but when we start to get more people, then we have to be a bit more careful."

"Aye, ye're right, Will," Kerlie said. "I can get out whenever I want. No one will care and Stephen doesna have anyone anyway, so no one will worry about him."

"I told my uncle our plan," William said, "I also told him that I'd be in and out all the time. It's safer that way anyway, for both him and me. How about ye John?"

"I dinna think my relatives will care one way or another if I'm gone a lot or not," John said with a bit of a mischievous smile. "So I guess it's all all right, eh?"

"Aye," said all the lads together. William grinned.

"Well, should we start scouting around for a place?"

They tramped through the woods, Stephen cleverly blazing a trail so they could find their way out again and looked for the perfect place to make their camp. William looked at everything with scrutiny, not finding exactly what he wanted.

"See anything yet, Will?" John asked, sounding a bit tired.

William shook his head and they continued on. That was when they heard the sound of a burn running through the woods. Stephen held up his hand for a halt.

"Sure, let's all go have a drink," he suggested and everyone readily agreed, following the sound of the water.

They knelt on the bank when they found it. The water was cold and refreshing and they all gulped it gratefully. William looked up across the river and saw that there was a large clearing over there. He turned to John and pointed to it.

"See that, John? Let's cross the river and have a wee look, shall we?"

They all took off their shoes and waded across the shallow river, only up to their knees at its deepest, and soon they were standing in a clearing where sun shone through more than the rest of the place. William looked around with a small smile on his face. It would be big enough to hold practice fights in and archery and it was hemmed in by thick oaks so that whatever they left there would be hidden from the view of anyone just passing by.

"It's perfect," he said to the others as he turned to them with a grin. "Look, we'll have plenty of room to fight, and we can even have fires here at night and in the winter because there's not too many trees. What say ye?"

"Aye!" the three lads told him immediately. William turned back to the burn.

"We best be getting back now. Tomorrow, we can

come here and decide on the layout of our camp. We'll meet here first thing in the morning. Ye'll all follow Stephen's trail and we shouldna get lost."

"I hope not anyway," Stephen said with a roguish grin.

"We better not!" Kerlie said in a mock dangerous voice and Stephen pretended to shrink back from him.

"All right, lads, let's get back for some noontime food," William said and started leading the way out of the woods. "And tomorrow, we'll start seriously thinking of our plan."

***

The next morning, the four lads met in the clearing as planned and William immediately took charge, casting his eyes over the space they had and devising in his mind what he would do with it.

"I think we should set up archery targets over there," he said pointing to the left side of the clearing. "Then on the far side we can set up a roped-in place where we can hold sword and other weapon training. We'll have to make bows and arrows, John ye're good at that, I'll put ye in charge of the archery."

"Will, I use the short sword," Stephen offered. "And daggers."

"Good, that will come in handy," William said, "How about ye, Kerlie?"

"I can use a sword," he said.

"Ye and me will be the sword masters," William grinned. "Anything else, like spears and axes and things like that we can probably figure out between us. Or maybe we'll find find someone who knows how. All right then, lads. Let's get started."

They spent the rest of the day, setting up their camp. William had brought a rope along that his uncle had given him the night before and he and Kerlie worked at roping it around several trees to form a sort of square. John and Stephen looked around to find small trees they could fell to make bows. They were able to find several spry yew saplings that were strong and good bow material. They also collected some small branches for arrows.

"Next time I shoot some birds, I'll have to save the feathers," John said as he started stripping the bark from one of the saplings with his dagger. "Then we can use them for fletches." William came over to see what he had found. "Those will work out fine I think," he said. "We'll have to find something we can use for targets."

"How about some tatty bogles," Kerlie suggested. "Like the ones the farmers put in their crops to scare the birds off."

"That would work great," William said enthusiastically. "They would be more like shooting a real target in battle. I'll leave ye to collect the things we need for that."

When the sun began to get lower in the sky, the lads started on their way home. William felt good that they were able to accomplish so much that day. He smiled at his companions as they exited the woods and gave them each a pat on the back.

"Good work, lads. Tomorrow we'll take a day off and meet back here the next day. See what ye can collect for our camp. See ye then, lads."

They took their leave of each other and headed back to their respective homes. William's uncle greeted him as he came in the door.

"Ah, Will, how was your day in the woods?" he asked as William sat by the fire, putting his feet up on the hearth to warm them.

"Good, Uncle," he said. "I think we found a nice place. As soon as we get more moved in, I'll start spending the night there. I'll come back every once in a while to tell ye how things are though, of course."

Ronald smiled slightly at his nephew. "Be in no hurry, William. I only wish you could stay here without trouble. You're lucky no one can describe you. I asked around today in curiosity. No one seemed to know what you look like. But please don't go into the town unless you have to. And if you do, make sure you take precautions. And don't wear your kilt. It might cause trouble."

"Aye, Uncle, I ken," William said.

"What will you do tomorrow? Back out to the woods?"

"I actually thought I might do a little fishing, Uncle," William said. "That way we can have some tomorrow for supper. We worked hard today, so I gave the lads a day off."

"That sounds good," Ronald said, smiling slightly. "Now how about some dinner right now, eh?"

Chapter Ten

Another Unfortunate Incident

The next morning, William gathered a pole and a net after breakfast and headed out to a burn that ran a little ways from his uncle's property. It was in the other direction of the woods and William walked there slowly, enjoying the fact that the sun was shining that day. When he found the river, he saw it was a leisurely spot and once he had cast his line, he lay back in the soft grass on the bank and rested his hands behind his head, closing his eyes. Before the first hour was up he had caught five fish of good size and there were still many fish biting his line. He sat with his feet in the water, singing a boating song he had once learned from a sailor as he caught more fish. He had done it enough in Dundee when he skipped school and went to the river so he was an expert at the art. He wanted to make sure there would be enough fish for the gillies to join in the meal as well.

His net was full by the time he broke for lunch, taking the food he had packed into his belt pouch that morning. He had just finished it when he heard the sound of approaching hoof beats and looked around to find the source of them. He saw what he supposed to be five English soldiers riding his way. He kept himself at ease, not betraying his tense feeling inside as the leader of them approached him and held his hand up to halt his followers.

"Good day, gentlemen," William said, giving them a civil smile. "What service can I do ye?"

Their leader dismounted. He was a formidable man. Tall, broad-shouldered, though lithe and had greasy, strait black hair that framed his face. On his left cheek was a pink scar that seemed to suit his disposition. He wore metal bracers and gauntlets on each arm and greaves on his legs. His armor clanked as he got off the horse and walked over to William.

"What service can you do me?" he repeated, his voice a deep raspy growl. A small sinister smile flickered over his thin lips. "You can give me your fish, my lad."

William stood up to face the man, picking up his net as he did. "I will give you half of them, sir. I have more than I really need. That should be more than enough to feed you and your men."

"I'll take them all," the Englishman said adamantly. "I am not thinking of just feeding these men. I serve Earl

Percy and I will not bring him paltry amounts."

"I'm sorry, sir, but I also have someone expecting fish. I canna give them all to ye."

"You are uncommon bold, young whelp," the man said, sneering so that the scar on his cheek crinkled, giving him an even more sinister look. "You talk to me as if I was no one. I am Sir Jack Moore, Earl Henry Percy's most trusted man; General of his English battalion. It is my job to make sure he is not disappointed. Perhaps I should teach you a lesson in subordinence." He drew his sword and hovered it menacingly in front of William's face as the other men dismounted and drew their weapons following their commander.

William didn't think twice, he reached behind him and grabbed his fishing pole. Jack Moore struck out at him just as he brought it up, William caught the blow expertly. Moore was so surprised by his action that William was able to bring his foot up and kick the Englishman in the stomach, causing him to fall backwards into his men. One of the other soldiers rushed forward, but William sidestepped and cracked the pole across his head. The man slumped to the ground in a heap and William grabbed his sword as another man came up to him but he was no match for William with the sword in his hand. When that man fell as well, Jack Moore pushed his way through.

"Out of my way! The whelp's mine!" he snarled as he rushed at William, his sword upraised.

William met him fearlessly and caught the blows the furious Englishman aimed at him. He found that fighting hand to hand was not as hard as he thought it might be. William struck out and in one deft blow, knocked the sword from Moore's hand, cutting him across the brow in the same movement. Moore staggered back, clapping a hand to his head as William picked his sword up and brandished both the weapons at the remaining three men.

"Be gone!" he cried. "And next time ye think of picking on helpless folk, stop and think if they are actually helpless."

Moore raced to mount his horse. "You, whelp, the next time we meet will be a different story! The next time we meet I'll be ready and I'll flay you alive before I let you die!"

With that he was gone with the other two men who had missed William's sword blade. The Scotsman picked up the third fallen sword and gathered the three weapons and his pole under one arm. He took up the net and set off at a trot for his uncle's house. He had a horrible yet exhilarated feeling in his heart. He had actually fought and won his first real skirmish. But he knew the consequences of it. He knew them only too well.

***

Henry Percy looked at his disheveled general with disdain. "So let me get this straight, my dear friend. You found this lad fishing and asked him for his fish and when he wouldn't give them to you, he killed two of your men, and wounded you, then *you* ran off?"

"My lord, it didn't happen exactly like that," Moore said, pressing a rag to his forehead to stop the bleeding.

"You see, I asked for the fish, then when he refused, I threatened him with my sword. Before I knew what was happening, he grabbed his fishing pole and parried my blow. Then he kicked me in the gut and I was knocked on my back. When I fought him again, he disarmed me and I was forced to retreat or die."

"How many were you fighting again?" Percy asked, looking like a cat playing with a mouse.

"One, sir," Moore said in his growly voice.

"I see," Percy said slowly. "So, General Moore, you mean to tell me that you and your four men were defeated by a mere scrawny lad?"

"This was no mere lad, m'lord," Moore said from between clenched teeth. "I have reason to believe this lad was young William Wallace."

"*Here*, Jack?" Percy scoffed. "You're a fool. And William Wallace would have to be an even bigger one to come here."

"Is there another lad capable of this, I ask?" Moore exclaimed, taking the rag from his head and inspecting the blood on it. "His father and brother were a nuisance, always going off on their 'king and country' nonsense like Alexander was still alive. Alan Wallace gave me this scar." He traced the pink scar on his cheek. "And other wounds besides. And now his son, his young whelp, has given me another. I will hunt him down, and when I do, I will make him pay. I'll have his blood!"

"General Moore," Percy said, turning around to look into the fire. "If this *is* William Wallace, which, you might be right, he may very well be, then I want him. *I* will decide what to do with him. You are not to kill him, do you understand?"

Moore was silent for a moment, trying to get hold of his anger still. "Yes m'lord," he said finally.

"Good," Percy said, turning back around to give a small thin smile to his General. "That's the man I can trust. Now I will be leaving for London in the next few days. Before I get back, I want William Wallace in my dungeon, do you hear?"

Moore bowed low. "Aye, m'lord," he said.

"Delightful," Percy said with another thin smile. "Now go see the physician about that wound. Then perhaps you would like to join me for ale while we discuss this new situation?"

Moore nodded. "Yes, m'lord, that would be fine."

***

William ran into his uncle's house and into the kitchen where he hoped he could get in without being noticed. As it was though, it happened to be just at the time when Ronald Crawford was talking to one of the gillies about dinner. They both looked up with surprise as William barged in, the swords under one arm and the net full of fish on his back.

"William, what happened?" his uncle asked sharply as William closed his eyes and sighed inwardly, letting the weaponry fall to the floor.

"Uncle Ronald..." he started but the older man was at his side, grabbing his arm roughly.

"What happened to ye, lad?" he asked and William noticed for the first time that he had a wound on his arm and that it was bleeding. He winced slightly as his uncle pulled up his sleeve to see it.

"Ewan, go get some linens to bind this," Ronald said to the gillie.

Once Ewan had gone from the room, Ronald grabbed William's face in his hand and looked strait into his eyes. "All right, William, tell me what happened."

William pulled away from his uncle. "A mess, that's what happened. Look, I dinna mean to get into these things!" he cried as his uncle made to comment angrily. "They just happen!"

"Then what happened this time?" Ronald asked impatiently.

William winced with the thought. "Percy's man, Jack Moore. He wanted my fish and I told him he could have half, but he wanted them all and...well, he would have killed me for them so..."

"Did ye kill him?!" Ronald asked frantically.

"I'd praise the lad if he did," Ewan said, coming back in with the linens and a bowl of water. He took William by the arm and sat him down at the table. "That Jack Moore is no' a man. He's vile."

"Do not encourage him, Ewan," Ronald said from between clenched teeth. "William, did you or did you not kill him?"

"I didna, Uncle," William said.

"More's the pity," Ewan said under his breath as he

pushed William's sleeve up and started washing the wound out. "This is no' bad, Master Will. It's just a flesh wound."

Ronald was pacing frantically, running his hand over his face. "So now what, Will? What does this come to?"

"It comes to the fact that Moore is now out for my blood," William said. "He vowed to kill me next time we meet, but that willna happen." His face was determined and Ronald shook his head in awe of the lad, so young yet so brave.

"Does he ken who ye are?" Ronald asked.

"I dinna think so," William said. "That was pure luck for me, I'm sure."

"He'll be telling Percy by now." Ronald groaned and rubbed his hands over his eyes. "It's no longer safe for ye here, Will. What will ye do now?"

"I'll hide in the woods," he said and winced as Ewan poured hot water over his wound to clean it. "They willna find me there and I willna be putting ye in danger. I really am sorry, Uncle."

Ronald saw the sincerity in William's eyes and couldn't help but feel pity for him. "Aye, well, fate is fate. Ye canna change it. We'll just take what is set for us and that's that. But please, William *try* to stay out of trouble. I do not want to have to see my nephew on the gallows, or, even worse, his head on London Bridge. Do not make me go through that."

William stood as Ewan finished bandaging his arm.

"I willna, Uncle. My lads and I will be training out in the woods and by the time they find us, *if* they ever do, then we'll be ready for them."

"I hope for your sake, that true," Ronald said sadly, and impulsively clasped William by the shoulders. "Be safe, Will. For your mother's sake if for no one else."

William nodded solemnly. "I know. I will be, Uncle. Now I have to go before they come and talk to you about it." He went upstairs to collect all his things and then came back down to take up all the weaponry and put several fish in his bag. "Eat the fish tonight. Do not let them linger. It could go bad for everyone then. Enjoy."

"Go with him, Ewan," Ronald told the gillie. "If you know where he is, you can bring him food."

"There's nae need, we can live off the land," William said quickly, hesitant of letting anyone he didn't know see the camp.

"If it's loyalty ye're worried about, Master Will, then I can assure ye that I would never give ye away for all the money in the world," Ewan assured him, seeing his look.

"Trust Ewan," Ronald told his nephew. "He is my truest man. He will never betray ye."

William smiled at his newfound friend. "Then be my guest. Though I will admit, my abode is a humble one."

Ewan smiled at him, his green eyes twinkling. "It matters not to me. We should be off, if you have everything you need."

"Aye, I do," William said and took up the three swords he had gathered from the Englishmen and wrapped them up in his cloak, tying the parcel in several places with twine. Ewan took up a pack of food and took the fish out of William's bag to store with the other things.

"I'll make ye a nice dinner before I leave, Master Will," he told the lad with a smile.

"Thank ye," William said. Then turned to go out the door. "Bye, Uncle."

"Good bye, William," Ronald said. "I hope to see you again soon."

William and Ewan went out to the barn. William saddled his horse and Ewan slung the things over the back of a garron, one of the stout Highland ponies, and mounted bareback. William took the lead and led his companion into the forest and to the spot where his camp was. By the time they got to it, it was late afternoon and the forest was almost as dark as night. William tied his horse to a low branch so it could graze and immediately knelt to start the fire.

Between him and Ewan, they soon had a good smokeless blaze going. William and his friends had been sure to collect only the driest of wood the day before so smoke would not give them away. Ewan cleaned the fish expertly and laid them out on a stone in the fire to cook them slowly. When they were done, the two Scots sat with their feet toward the fire and talked.

"So is this resistance open to anyone?" Ewan asked, the flames glinting off his bright red hair. "Or do ye have to apply?"

"It's open to any loyal soul who loves Scotland and

doesna want to see her in English hands," William told him with passion. He turned to look at the other man. "Why, Ewan? Do ye want to join?"

Ewan nodded slowly. "Aye. I have hated every second of English tyranny. I want what every true patriot wants; freedom. But I just dinna see how to get it."

William turned to look at him. "I fear the only way to gain it back, is to fight. Defy the English and warn Longshanks to his face that he canna have us. We're no' his slaves, and that's the truth of the matter."

Ewan looked with admiration at William. "Ye are old beyond yer years, William Wallace. Even I can see that. Show me the man who would not fight under ye and I'll show ye a coward."

William smiled sheepishly. "Och, Ewan, ye flatter me. But I canna take any praise until some day in the future, when, if fate allow, I will be able to raise my sword and the Saltire over free soil and declare our liberty to the winds. I only hope I live to see that day."

"Aye, dinna we all," Ewan said quietly, looking into the flames. They danced in his green eyes. "I want to fight. Just as ye, but I dinna have the skills. Would ye teach me, William?"

William grasped his new companion's hand tightly. "Ewan, I will teach ye to fly if it means I've found a supporter."

"Well, I dinna need to know *that* much," Ewan laughed. "My only problem is that I have to work for yer uncle. I canna be gone all the time."

"But ye'd be much help to us there," William assured him. "Uncle Ronald gets all the information from the town and he can relay it to ye. If anything important happens, it would be yer job to race here and tell us. Besides that, ye can join our weapon training whenever ye have time.

Ewan smiled excitedly. "I will do what I can, Will. And I will be on the lookout for more supporters. I know many a lad already who would be ready and willing to join up wi' ye."

"Thank ye, Ewan," William said sincerely. "And, by the way, ye're a very good cook!"

They both laughed then and finished their dinner.

After they were done, Ewan stood and stretched. "I best be getting back to help make dinner for yer uncle. I'll be back within the next couple days with some more provisions and hopefully a couple recruits."

"I'll be waiting for ye," William told him. "See ye then."

Ewan rode off on his garron and William looked around the glade in the firelight. He went over to the parcel of weapons he had gathered that day and opened it up, looking at the swords. The two he had gotten from the soldiers were well made though were obviously worn and had several dings in the blades. The third sword, however, was a beauty. It was long and looked like a claymore, the broadswords the Highlanders fought with. William picked it up, looking at it hard for the first time. There was a strange feeling that came over him as if he had seen the weapon before. He brought it closer to the firelight and examined the hilt. A hot wave flooded over him as he recognized the familiar crest on the crosstree. It was an arm holding a sword with the latin *Pro Liberate* beneath it. He suddenly knew where he had seen the sword before. It was his father's.

William just sat there for a moment, looking at the sword in the flickering firelight. He knew what that meant. He knew all too well. That man, Jack Moore, had killed his father.

William stood up slowly. He took the sword in both hands and swung it in a figure-eight movement as his father had taught him as he sat in on the practices he had done with his older brother, Malcolm. The sword was a bit heavy, but it was perfectly balanced so it did not feel as heavy as it might have, nor was it unwieldy. He spun left and right, defending himself from invisible foes and danced around in the firelight in dangerous steps. He had never really wielded a sword before that day, but it felt the most natural thing ever to him. William whirled the sword around his head and brought it to rest point first in the ground in front of him.

He clasped the hilt so tight that his knuckles turned white. He breathed hard after the exertion and stared into the dark woods. His jaw was hard and set.

"I will avenge ye, Da," he said to the darkness. "I vow it. And I will do it with this sword."

The cold wind whistled eerily through the trees and William shivered, coming back to reality. He lay down by the fire and wrapped his plaid around himself, putting one of his hands on the hilt of his sword. He gazed into the fire before he drifted off to sleep.

"Do not sleep easy, Jack Moore," he said quietly, menacingly, to the flames. "Do not sleep easy until I put ye in a grave."

Chapter Eleven

A Plan of Action

The next morning, William woke up to the sound of approaching voices. He sat up, quickly rubbing sleep from his eyes and took hold of his sword hilt, ready for anything.

John Graham, Kerlie and Stephen splashed through the burn as they haled the camp.

"A Graham!" John cried out as he stepped onto the bank, holding up his hand to William. The Scotsman stood up and greeted his friends.

"Good morning, lads, how would ye like some breakfast?" he asked.

The four lads sat around the fire as William stoked it up once more and put several bannocks onto the roasting stone to heat them up. John looked up at his companion with serious eyes.

"Will, we all heard what happened yesterday," he said quietly.

"Word travels fast here doesna it?" William said blandly as he handed out the bannocks. "Aye, well, things happen, I suppose. We all need to be more careful now though. If any of the English think that ye're of the same mind as I, then they willna hesitate to hunt ye down as well. We canna be seen together in public."

Stephen smiled as he ate his bannock. "Sure, and perhaps I need to teach ye all how to disappear when ye dinna want to be seen."

"Ye know all about that, do ye?" William asked, somehow not really surprised.

Stephen grinned and his eyes sparkled. "Aye, I do. Ye'd do well to learn it, William."

"Perhaps I would," William said as he stood up. "But first things first." He took the swords he had gotten the day before and showed them to the other lads. "I got these off the Englishmen yesterday," he told them. "This can start off our armory."

John stood and took one of the broadswords from the collection and swung it back and fourth, feeling the balance. "This will work fine," he said with a smile playing over his lips. "Should we start training right now?"

William shook his head. "Nae, I want us to go out and set snares for rabbits. Then we can start on our sword practice."

John took up the snares he had brought the last time he had gone to the woods and set off with William to set them out. They walked silently for a while, looking at the ancient trees that twisted and turned around their neighbors. They stopped to put a snare in a thicket and John turned to William.

"All right, Will, what's wrong?" he asked his solemn companion. "I've known ye too long not to notice when something is troubling ye."

William sighed and leaned against a huge oak tree. He drew the sword that he had been wearing across his back and held it out to his companion. "This John," he said. "Look at the crest on the cross-tree."

John took the sword and studied it a minute. "It's your family crest," he said and looked William in the eyes as he handed it back. "Tell me, what does it mean?"

William took his father's sword and held it vertically in front of him so that it appeared as nothing more then a thin line of steal to him. "It's my Da's," he said slowly.

"Where did ye get it?"

"Jack Moore," William said and swung the sword around sticking it into the ground between his feet. "He killed my father, John. It was him."

"Then the deed must be repaid," John said simply and smiled as he put his hand on William's shoulder. "But look on the bright side, Will. At least ye have a name to the man who killed him. Now proper justice can be done."

"I suppose ye're right," William said and forced himself to smile a bit. "Well, we best be getting back.

Hopefully the snares will work and within the next couple days we might have a nice rabbit stew."

"Aye," John said enthusiastically. "I canna wait to get my hands on a sword!" He grinned and William cuffed him on the back of the head. They laughed then, feeling better about the whole thing. Comrades together in the woodlands.

***

"I am quite sure that the town will be fine in your hands while I am gone." Percy pulled on his riding gloves as he spoke to Moore. "Am I correct in my trust?"

"Aye, m'lord," Moore said with a bit of a cringe. The wound William had given him still hurt a bit and his head was aching. "I will keep the town as well as you always do. And no Scottish whelp is going to cause any trouble."

Percy gave him a thin smile and patted him on the cheek none too gently. "That's just what I want to hear. And remember I want this William Wallace here when I get back so I can have the pleasure of killing him myself."

Moore ground his teeth. He was very displeased that he would not be the one to kill the young Scotsman, but it never did to get on Henry Percy's bad side. "Aye, m'lord, it will be done."

Percy took the reigns of his horse from a servant standing by. "Good. I will hopefully be back before the end of the year. Send me a letter as soon as you capture him. Good day." And he rode off without another word.

Jack Moore sneered to himself, his scar crinkling around his eye. Yes, he would do all he could to catch

William Wallace. He would not rest until he had him locked up awaiting execution. He gave a low chuckle that sounded like steel grating on stone, and turned to go off to the barracks.

He barged in the door and all the soldiers, most half-dressed and some still sleeping, were milling around getting ready for the day. They all stood to attention as Moore came in and the captain who was standing nearest the door, saluted him.

"Sir," he said smartly. "What brings you here this morning?"

Moore walked into the building further and nudged a snoring Englishman harshly with his boot. "I hope all of you are awake enough to understand me, because I'm not going to say it again," he said loudly and several men raised themselves dazedly from their pallets. He looked around, making sure that everyone had heard, then started again. "Lord Percy has told me that he wishes that Scottish whelp, who we believe to be William Wallace, caught before he gets back from London. We are going to do that. We will look in every possible place, not just here, but I will send some of you to alert surrounding towns of his possible presence. We are not going to be made fools of again. But I will tell you right now, that you are not to kill him. We are to take him alive so that Lord Percy can do to him as he sees fit, do you understand that?"

There were nods and "Aye sirs" throughout the barracks. The captain who had spoken first held his hand up for audience. Moore turned to look at him.

"General Moore, sir, what is your first plan of action?" he asked.

"Pick six good men and send two each to three neighboring towns to warn the garrisons there. You and I will take another few and we will start asking around here to see if anyone knows anything. Spare no one questioning and be as rough as you like. Sometimes these stubborn Scots need a bit of beating before they will tell you anything."

As the soldiers finished dressing, the captain turned to Moore again.

"Is he dangerous, sir?" he asked.

"Dangerous, Captain Simpson?" Moore asked. "Define dangerous. Do you mean will he give you trouble? Yes he will. Do you mean will he fight? Yes he will. Do you mean will he kill you if you gave him the chance? Yes he will. He is a desperate person, but so are we. We are *desperate* to be rid of him, so will you have any trouble, Captain Simpson?"

Simpson stuttered out his reply. "N-no, General sir."

"I didn't think so," Moore said and turned his back. "You had all best remember it as well. And please do remember to take him alive. The man who kills him will die in his stead, and I will do the honors. You all know what I am capable of, so I will not elaborate. Is that understood?"

"Yes, sir," everyone said heartily.

Moore smiled to himself as he went out of the barracks again. They would do what he needed. He knew this. He was sure of it, in fact. "Someday, William Wallace," he said to himself. "You will be the one kneeling at my feet begging for mercy. I killed your father easily enough. I can't imagine it being any harder to kill you." He went off to saddle his horse then and wait for his men to be ready.

***

"Just a bit higher," William said as he and Kerlie were practicing with the swords. They struck out at each other slowly so as not to cause each other damage. Kerlie struck out again and William blocked the blow. They were sparring in the roped-off area with John and Stephen standing on the outside, watching them.

"Come on Kerlie, show him what ye've got!" Stephen shouted.

"Who's side are ye on?" William asked the Irishman as he and Kerlie continued fighting.

Kerlie struck out at William and the Scotsman blocked the blow and back-stepped, then he rushed forward, flipping his sword around and hooking the cross-tree behind Kerlie's leg and pulled his feet from under him.

Kerlie looked up from the ground as William placed the tip of his blade on his chest. He grinned. "Aye, and that's how ye do that."

Kerlie grinned and grabbed William's hand as he reached down to help him up. "Aye, I see that!" he said ruefully, rubbing his back.

Stephen rolled up his sleeves and drew his short

sword, hopping over the ropes. "Sure, and we'll see how good Will Wallace really is." He grinned at the Scotsman and held his sword out in front of him.

"Aye, and we'll see how good *ye* are, Irishman," William said with a slight smile back at him, also taking a ready stance.

They circled each other slowly, looking for the other to make the first move. Stephen seemed to relax for a moment, so William, taking the chance, sprang forward to strike at him. However, the Irishman wasn't there and he felt a blade pressed to his side. He looked over quickly to the right to see Stephen smiling at him.

"Try again," he said as they disengaged.

This time William didn't wait to look for an opening; he ran forward at Stephen and clashed swords with him. He got in two good hits and then the next thing he knew, he was flat on his back with his sword arm above his head, Stephen's foot on his wrist and the Irishman's blade at his throat. Stephen grinned down at him, his eyes sparkling.

"Aye, and that's how it's done!" he said cheekily.

"I see," William said then laughed and got to his feet with Stephen's help. "I can tell ye right now that I am a very very fortunate person to have ye on my side, Stephen Ireland," he said.

"Aye, ye are," Stephen told him with a strait face.

"Perhaps ye can teach us some things," William said as he sheathed his sword over his back.

"I will do that," Stephen said. "But right now, I think it's time for something to eat. What about all of ye?"

"Aye!" the lads all said and they went to the fire to put together something to eat.

Chapter Twelve

The Starting of the Army

That night all the lads slept in the woods around the campfire. William woke early as he heard the birds sing in the coming sunlight. He sat up and stretched, looking around at his still sleeping companions. John was snoring gently, his head covered by his plaid. William got up, belting his plaid back on and knelt to stoke the fire. He was fanning the flame again when he heard a crack in the woods behind him. He stood and turned, reaching down to pick up his sword. He strode over to the burn and looked into the woods behind it.

"Aye to the camp," someone called and William looked closer to see Ewan coming out of the woods with three other lads. William smiled and waved a hand to them.

"Come in. I was just starting to get ready to make breakfast."

"I'll take care of that," Ewan said and he and the lads crossed the burn and sat down by the fire. William bent to wake his comrades.

"Get up, lads, we have visitors," he told them.

"Friendly or not?" Stephen asked as he sat up, his eyes still closed and a blade in his hand.

"Friendly," William said and threw more logs on the fire. Ewan pulled out a sack he had over his shoulder and started rooting through it to find something to make breakfast with.

"So who are these lads ye brought us, Ewan?" William asked.

"This is Donald, Jacob and Keith," Ewan said, pointing to the three in turn. "They are all about yer age, I believe. I've seen them around town and they have expressed their feelings to me on more then one occasion."

"We have nowhere else to go," said Keith, the oldest of them. "We thought that we might as well try to do something worth while."

William clasped his hand. "We're glad to have ye three here then," he said. "Have any of ye any training with weaponry?"

"Nae," the lads said.

"We'll remedy that then," William said with a smile. "We are working on making wooden swords to practice with and such things as that, and John is making bows."

"I am pretty good at archery," Donald told him. "I hunt for my food all the time."

"Good then," John said with a grin. "I willna have to go out and hunt by myself all the time!"

Ewan finished cooking up a pot of porridge and spooned it out into some bowls he had brought them. "Here ye go lads," he said. "Eat up."

They all ate gratefully and when they were done, John took the three new lads with him to help make arrows and William took Ewan to one side to talk to him.

"So what's the news ye have for me, Ewan?" he asked.

The Scotsman sighed, brushing stray strands of hair from his face. "Jack Moore has been asking around for the lad William Wallace. I dinna ken how, but he seemed to have guessed it was you who attacked him and now he's out looking for ye tirelessly. He's even sent men to the nearest towns looking for ye. I fear it's only a matter of time before they think to look through these woods."

William looked down slightly. "I only knew that this would happen," he said. "I counted on it. Och well. We're so deep in here and this forest is so big that I doubt they'd find us in twenty years."

Ewan looked worried. "You best stay here, Will. Jack Moore is no' a man to cross. I have seen what he does to the people who try. It's no' pleasant. Ye need to stay away from him."

"Ewan," William turned to the man with anger flashing unbidden to his eyes. "Jack Moore killed my father, I canna run from him forever. I'll find him and then we'll have a reckoning."

"He killed your father?" Ewan asked with shock clearly in his eyes. "How do ye know that?"

William drew his sword from over his shoulder. "This is the sword I took from him," he said. "It was my father's."

Ewan opened his mouth as if he was going to say something then he closed it and looked down. "Then be careful, William. Be very careful. Because I mean what I said. Jack would not kill ye. No' at first. He'd make ye suffer horribly."

"I understand," William told him. "And I wouldna give him that chance. That is why I am not going after him right now. I will wait until I feel ready. But I will tell ye now. When I get the chance, I *will* challenge him. And I will kill him."

"I have nae doubt," Ewan said slowly.

"Please, Ewan, don't tell my uncle this," William said quickly. "He...He doesna need to know this. That information is not to leave this camp, do ye understand?"

Ewan nodded. "Aye, Will. I understand." He stood up and put his bonnet on his head. "I have to get back. Next time I come, perhaps I can start learning how to fight with a sword."

"I'll teach ye certainly," William said as he walked Ewan to the burn. The redheaded Scotsman took off his brogans and crossed the water.

"Thank ye, Will," he said as he turned around. "I'll

look forward to it."

"And thank ye for bringing us some recruits," William told him.

"There's more where that came from," Ewan told him. "I just thought it best if I only take a few at a time."

"Aye, ye're right," William said. "Well, I'll see ye in the next couple days."

"Ye too," Ewan said as he put his shoes back on and walked off into the woods again.

William went back to the fire and sat down beside Kerlie and Stephen. The two looked at him seriously.

"I couldn't help but hear," Stephen said. "Did ye say that that Jack Moore person was the one who killed your father?"

William nodded. "Aye, aye he was."

"I'm sorry William," Kerlie said.

"What are ye going to do about it?" Stephen asked him.

"Eventually, I am going to have a reckoning with him," William told the Irishman. "Until then though, we are going to stay out of trouble."

"What fun is that?" Stephen said with a grin and that twinkle in his black eyes.

"What fun indeed," William said blandly.

John called over to them. "Are ye just going to sit there and talk, or are ye going to come over here and help us make these arrows?"

William turned to his companions and raised his eyebrows. "I suppose we best go. I dinna want to get into trouble with my trusty co-commander."

They all laughed and sat down to strip bark from the thin branches they had collected for making arrows. The rest of that day, they worked on the arrows and bows. John sat braiding twine for the strings, rubbing beeswax into the fibers to soften them up a bit. "Hand me that bow I made yesterday," he told Kerlie and the other lad handed him the bow.

John took it and stood, putting his foot against one end of the bow and bending it as he strung it. He took it up and flexed it as far as it would go until it bent in a deep arch. He smiled in satisfaction. "This one turned out good," he commented. "Hand me one of those arrows we have fletched."

Donald handed him an arrow and John put it to the bow. He pulled it back and closed one if his eyes, aiming at one of the targets they had set up the day before. He struck it close to the center. He lowered the bow with a smile.

"Not bad," William said. "That's a good bow."

John nodded. "Aye, it is. I'll make a lot more like it."

"Good," William said. "Now, let's see what else we can do."

The rest of that week, they worked on making their practice swords and their bows and arrows and Ewan came to their camp every other day, bringing in a couple new recruits every time. By the end of two weeks, William had gathered twenty young men who were eager to fight. Their camp was coming together nicely. They now had several tent-like structures rigged between trees so that they could sleep comfortably even when it rained. They trained every day and William saw with satisfaction that his lads were quickly becoming fine warriors. They had also gotten some weapons from the lads who came and from Ewan who brought things from William's uncle. There was a satisfaction to all the young men as they watched their plan come together and actually working the way they had hoped. William smiled to himself one day as he watched his lads spar together. He grasped the hilt of his father's sword. It wouldn't be too much longer before they could make a move. He knew it now.

***

Jack Moore sat at the desk in his room, the light from his candle flickering with a slight draft coming in under the door. He thudded a dagger into the desk then pulled it out before thudding it back in again. It made a slow steady rhythm to go with his thoughts. He watched the candlelight flicker on the blade. There was nothing he would like to do more than take that blade to William Wallace. Make him sorry for beating Henry Percy's trusty general. Moore took the dagger into his fist and slammed it into the desk with a growl. The blade buried halfway to the hilt in the wood. He yanked it out and held it in front of him, seeing his eyes reflected in it. William Wallace would rue the day he ever crossed blades with Sir Jack Moore.

Chapter Thirteen

An Excursion

One day, William woke with the urge to wander. He turned to his companions as they were eating breakfast and said, "Would ye like to go to Lanark with me today?"

John shrugged. "Aye, if ye're going. But is it wise?"

William tossed his head indifferently. "Maybe no' but that's no reason not to do something. I want to see how big the English garrison is there and see if there are any likely candidates for recruits."

"Sounds good," Stephen said, scraping the last of his porridge out of his bowl. "When do we go?"

"Right after breakfast," William said and stood. "Change into something else though. Tartan might attract too much attention."

The lads all changed into tunics and breeches and tied their boots tightly. William went over to Keith and crouched to talk to him.

"I'm going to take John, Kerlie and Stephen on a bit of a trip today. We should be back before nightfall tomorrow if all goes well. I'm leaving ye in charge."

Keith nodded with a smile and saluted. "Aye, Wallace. I'll hold the camp for ye."

William smiled at him and clapped him on the shoulder. "Good man, we'll be leaving now. Ewan should be coming here this afternoon with more supplies."

"All right, good fortune, William," Keith waved to him and William turned to go saddle his horse. They had all brought their horses so they could have them when they needed them. They had already started to make a lean-to barn for them. William tightened the girth of the saddle and mounted up, looking over his shoulder to his companions.

"No weapons besides daggers, lads," he said and Stephen sighed as he pulled his sword from his belt and put it aside before he mounted.

"Sorry, but it's for the best," William told them, feeling naked himself without his father's sword across his back. "If we're questioned, it will go better for us if we're no found to be carrying weapons."

They nodded and William clicked his tongue to his horse and started off through the woods with his comrades at his back. Once they were out of the woods they headed northeast a bit on track for Lanark. It felt good to be out again traveling cross country. William liked the feeling of the woods, but he had to admit that, growing up where he could see the hills, he liked the openness as well.

They reached Lanark around midday and they rode in past the gates without any trouble. They went to an inn and left their horses in the barn so that they could walk around the town more freely.

"Where to?" John asked as they came out of the barn and looked around."

"I'm rather hungry," Kerlie said as his stomach growled.

William laughed. "All right, first things first then. We should go see if we can find something to eat."

They went to the market where vendors and tinkers were hawking their wares and found someone selling meat pies. William bought some for him and his friends with his dwindling supply of money and they sat on the side of the street to eat them. William looked around at the busy marketplace and pointed across the street, leaning close to John.

"See that?" he asked. "There's an English soldier. After lunch, we'll have to go and see where they bide here."

So after the lads were done, they nonchalantly made their way in the direction they had seen the Englishman going. William looked around cautiously, always on the lookout for any people who might give him trouble. John, Kerlie and Stephen were right behind him, looking around as if they were enjoying the market, making small talk and laughing happily.

William joined in the conversation but still kept a close lookout for where the barracks were. He stopped the lads as they got to the outskirts of town and pointed farther ahead.

"Look," he told them. "See that? That's the castle. Does anyone know who is head of the English garrison here?"

Kerlie thought a moment. "I think it's Heselrig. He's an English sheriff who was put in charge here."

William took that into consideration and did some estimating as he looked at the castle. "John, how many do ye think could fit in there?" he asked.

"Hard to say, Will," his companion mused. "A good few."

"Lanark is a big town," Stephen offered. "Longshanks would need at least two hundred to hold it."

William nodded. "Aye, I bet ye're about right in that assumption." He bit his lip in thought for a few minutes. "How do ye think we should go about recruiting?"

"If I can offer a suggestion," Kerlie said, "I think it best if we just look around this time and maybe next time we come here, we can start asking around."

William smiled at him. "Good advice from my chief recruiter. It's getting late though. We'd best be finding a place to stay for the night. We can look around again tomorrow before we leave."

They walked back through the town to the inn and

tavern where they left their horses and went inside to get something for dinner. After they ate, they went into the room off the tavern reserved for travelers and tinkers and found some empty straw pallets on the floor where they could sleep that night. William draped his cloak over himself as he drifted off to sleep. It was unfortunately a light, troubled sleep though, and filled with dreams of Englishmen and Jack Moore and his father.

***

The next morning, the lads woke up and stretched then went to eat some breakfast before they went out into the town again. William looked around as they stood on the side of the street and then motioned to his companions.

"Look over there, there's an Englishman. Let's follow him and see what he's doing."

The four lads made their way to the other side of the street where they fell several people behind the English soldier, following him discretely. He looked around once, but didn't seem to think about the lads walking behind him. William motioned them to go down an alley and they cut through to the other street. They found that they had come out onto a street where small apartment-like houses were built.

"This is just residential," William told them as they came out on the street. "But let's go on, we may be able to see the castle and barracks better over here."

They went on down the road and saw that there were more Englishmen about. William wondered if they were hoping to keep the townsfolk in line. He didn't know how patriotic the people of Lanark were, but he figured that if they were anything like the people in Ayr, then they were just as unhappy about the English occupation as he was.

"Look," Stephen said and pointed ahead of them. There was a group of Englishmen standing around outside a tavern talking.

William motioned to his friends. "Come on, let's go see if we can hear what they're saying."

They made their way over to an alley beside the tavern and stationed themselves behind a cart that was sitting parked outside a side door. They crouched down and William looked out from behind the cart, straining to hear what they were saying.

"I canna hear anything. How about ye? Stephen?"

All four of them were straining to hear something, but all they caught was a few snatches and drunken laughter. William started to get annoyed, deciding they were probably not going to find out anything interesting.

"*What* on earth are you *doing?!*"

William and his companions spun around to see who had spoken, guilty expressions clearly on their faces. They saw a girl standing there, hands on her hips, staring at them as if they were villains. Stephen was the first one to speak. He grinned at her and bobbed his head in respect.

"Sure, and what is a pretty lass like ye doing out here?" he asked.

"I should be asking *ye* that question," she said, crossing her arms over her chest and glaring down at them. "So I will, once again. *What* are you doing?" William stood up, an angry expression on his face. "How did ye sneak up on us? There is not a lad here who cannot tell when someone is behind him."

The girl gave him an exasperated look. She pointed behind her. "I came from *there*. I walked over *here*. Are ye happy with that?"

"Well, why dinna ye just go back over *there* and leave us alone," William told her, crossing his arms over his chest as well.

"I'm not leaving, until ye tell me why ye're here," the lass said, staying put and not looking like she would move at all.

"That's none of your business," William told her with a glare.

She smiled a bit at him. "Sir, if I know anything, it is that when more than one lad is in the same place, they are up to no good. Since ye clearly have a Scotch tongue in yer head, and ye're sitting behind this cart watching Englishmen, it only adds to my assumption."

"Listen to her," William said, turning to his companions in exasperation. He turned back to the lass. "What's yer name?"

"I willna tell ye until ye prove my assumption right," she said smugly, raising her head so that she could look down her nose to him.

William laughed then. "Ye're a bold lass," he said. "I dinna think they were usually this demanding."

"Have you ever known a lass?" she asked him in

annoyance.

"Nae, nor do I wish to," William told her firmly. "Nuisances, the lot of them."

"Well, maybe I think the same of lads who will not admit they are up to no good."

William's companions watched this intercourse with interest, trying not to smile.

"Where do ye live?" William asked her.

"Why should I tell ye that?"

"So we can take you home like proper gentlemen," William told her with a sneer.

The girl stepped closer to him and poked a finger into his chest. "If you try anything, know that I will scream, and when I do, those English soldiers ye were spying on will come over and accost ye."

"Ye wouldna dare," William said dangerously.

"Wouldn't I?" the lass said, as if daring him to try something.

"Will," John said warningly. "One of the Englishmen is looking this way. I think they heard us. Settle it quick."

"All right," William said and with a quick movement, he reached out and grabbed the lass, pressing his hand over her mouth so she couldn't scream. "Ye're coming with us, weather ye like it or no'...Och! She *bit* me!"

The lass hissed at him angrily. "Aye, I did, and I'll do it again too! Are ye trying to kidnap me?"

"I might consider it," William told her.

"Well, ye canna," she told him smugly. "Because I'm coming with ye weather ye like it or not."

William let go of her in exasperation. "And why would ye want to do that?"

"Because ye're William Wallace aren't ye?"

William and all the lads looked at her in shock. The lass rolled her eyes.

"Don't worry, it's not obvious or anything," she told them. "It's woman's intuition."

"Well, fine," William said. "But ye're no' coming with us."

She glared at him again. "And why should I no' be able to fight for my country too, Master Wallace?"

They were all silent again until Stephen once more broke the silence. "*I* like her. Can we keep her?"

William rolled his eyes at the Irishman. "Stephen..."

"Everyone needs a camp lass," the Irishman told him almost apologetically.

William looked like he was about to say something, then he sighed and turned to the lass with a small smile. "Well, I suppose we *could* use someone to cook for us full time, and care for our wounds when we beat each other about during practice."

"Just because I'm a lass doesna mean I *can* cook and fix wounds!" she said with a glare.

"Well, do ye want to come or not?" William asked her.

They stood glaring at each other for a moment until John stood and grabbed William's arm. "Will, the Englishmen look like they're starting to come over here."

William hesitated a moment, then grabbed the lass

by the arm and started going down the alley again. "All right, come on lads...and lass."

Once they were out of the alley, William turned to his charge as they walked out into the crowded street. "So what's yer name?"

"Marion Braidfoot," she told him with a bit of a smile.

"Well, miss Braidfoot, do ye have family?"

She shrugged. "I live here only part time with nothing but a house of servants. My father has a manor outside of town, but as long as I send letters, no one will worry. I do want to stop by and get a few things though if it's all right. My apartment is right here."

"Make it quick," William said and sighed as she ran off. He turned to his companions and grinned sarcastically at them. "Maybe we should just leave her here."

Stephen grinned. "Ye'd regret it, Will. Lasses don't take kindly to being swindled."

"Know all about them, do ye?" William asked with a bit of a grin.

Stephen nodded his curly head, that grin beaming on his face. "Aye, ye could say that."

Marion came out again with a satchel slung over her shoulder and grinned at them. "They think I'm heading back to my father's house," she told them. "I'll send him a long letter explaining where I am." She grinned then. "Dinna worry, I willna mention ye!"

William shook his head and took the lead, heading back to the inn where they had left their horses. "Lasses," he cursed under his breath.

They got their horses out of the barn and saddled them up again. William mounted and turned to Marion. "Find a ride, miss," he said.

Stephen offered her his hand. "Allow me, miss Braidfoot," he said and took her bag and tied it to his saddle.

"Thank you..." Marion said.

"Sure, ye can call me Stephen," the Irishman said with a grin and mounted, pulling her up behind him.

"Thank you, Stephen," Marion said coyly. William rolled his eyes.

"Is everyone ready?" he asked. "I want to get back before nightfall."

They trotted through the town but when they got out of the gate to the town, they urged their horses into a canter and headed off back toward Ayr. Marion held tight to Stephen's waist and smiled over at William who was riding next to them.

"Ye willna be disappointed," she told him. "I'll be more help to ye than ye think right now."

"I'm sure ye will be," William smirked and urged his horse onward.

Chapter Fourteen

An Uninvited Caller

On the same morning William left Lanark, Ronald Crawford received a surprise visitor.

Ewan was finishing up washing the breakfast dishes when there was a knock at the door. He stood up from the stool he had been sitting on and wiped his hands on his smock. He walked to the door that was only a little way's from the kitchen and opened it to see who was calling.

"Aye?" he said then started when he saw who it was.

"I have come to talk to Ronald Crawford." Jack Moore stood in the doorway with two men flanking him. He looked down at Ewan as if he was a piece of garbage in a rotting heap. "Is he in?"

Ewan gathered himself again and nodded, bending his head slightly in respect even though that was certainly the last thing he felt toward the vile creature who stood before him. "Aye, he's in the common room. Please follow me."

Ewan led the three men to the common room where Ronald Crawford was sitting by the fire, looking over some papers. He looked up as Ewan came in with Jack Moore. He stood up with a questioning look on his face.

"What do you mean by coming here, Moore?" he asked, not trying to disguise his disgust.

Moore walked over to him nonchalantly, pulling off his riding gloves. "Oh, forgive me, Crawford, I didn't think I was unwelcome here."

"Why should you *be* welcome here?" Crawford asked. "We do not work together. I am the sheriff and Henry Percy is in charge of the English garrison here. I do not answer to him."

"Crawford, you didn't even let me explain why I'm here," Moore sat in the other chair and stretched his feet toward the fire to warm them.

"Enlighten me," Ronald told him tightly.

Moore gave him a small smile. "I was wondering if you knew anything about this William Wallace? I heard from someone that he was your nephew. Seen him lately?"

"He *is* my nephew," Crawford said, crossing his arms. "Why should that make any difference?"

"How about you answer my other question?" Moore

snapped, leaning forward. "Has he been here lately?"

Ronald sat down stiffly in the chair he had vacated when Moore had come into the room. "He came here a few days ago."

Ewan blanched but somehow stayed silent. What was Crawford doing?

Moore smiled, his scar crinkling the corner of his eye. "Ah! Is he still here perhaps?"

"No," Crawford told him. "I sent him away. I didn't want any trouble."

"Wise of you, but why didn't you report him?" Moore asked him. "He's an outlaw, you know. If you prize yourself the sheriff of Ayr, then you should at least respect the duty of your position."

"And betray his own flesh and blood?!" Ewan blurted out before he could stop himself.

Moore looked over to him, anger stamped on his face. He stood and walked slowly over to Ewan. The Scotsman stood still, not betraying the fear that clutched at his heart. All the stories he had heard about Moore and all the things he had witnessed himself ran through his mind in the few seconds it took for the man to cross the room to him.

"Dare you speak, thrall?" Moore spat at him. "Perhaps I should teach you some manners."

"Ewan's my man, Moore, I will deal out his punishment," Ronald tried to say but Moore didn't listen to him. He raised his hand, partly covered by his gauntlet, and hit Ewan across the face with the back of it.

The force of the blow knocked Ewan down. He lay on the ground, not daring to look up lest it excite Moore to anger.

"Moore," Ronald said, anger clearly in his voice. "I can deal with my own gillies."

"You should teach them more manners in the first place then," Moore growled, turning to Ronald.

Ewan raised himself on one arm, wiping blood from the corner of his mouth. He glared in hatred at Moore's back.

"To answer your question, Jack Moore," Ronald told his visitor. "I could not have answered it better then Ewan. No matter who my nephew is, I wouldn't betray him to his enemy."

Moore looked at him dangerously. "You're treading on dangerous ground, Ronald Crawford. I *will* tell Percy about this."

"He's in London," Crawford told him. "He doesn't have time to deal with things like this."

"Oh really?" Moore raised an eyebrow. "Well, it just so happens that he gave me express orders to capture William Wallace before he gets back from London. I *will* do it too. Don't think I can't."

"You'll be hard pressed to find him," Ronald said with an indifferent shrug. "Even I don't know where he is now."

Moore looked at him intently, moving so close that Ronald could smell his stale breath. "Are you sure about that?"

"Quite," Ronald said, turning around to look into the fire. "Why should he tell me or anyone?"

Moore picked up his gloves and started to pull them on again. "Well, I guess I had better be going." He turned toward the door, beckoning to the men he had come with. Before he got out of the room he turned around. "Oh...um...Crawford? If you happen to find out anything else, you *will* tell me, right?"

Ronald gave him a hard look. "If I can find the time, Moore."

"You had better," Moore said, giving him a sneer. "Because if you don't I'll have a way of finding out for myself." He looked meaningfully at Ewan and Ronald narrowed his eyes at him.

"I will be sure to tell you everything, Moore," he told him, then gave him a slight smile. "Is that a new scar you have on your head?"

Moore's hand moved unbidingly to the red-scabbed scar above his eye. He glared at Ronald, his lip twisting in disgust. "Don't say anything, Crawford. Don't test your luck."

Ronald couldn't help a bit of a smirk as Moore strode out of the room with his men at his heels.

As soon as they had left, Ronald turned to Ewan who was still sitting on the floor and helped him up.

"Are you all right?" he asked the Scotsman.

Ewan wiped more blood from his mouth and searched with his tongue to see the damage done. "Och, nothing much damaged but my pride, sir," he said.

Ronald sighed and lowered his voice. "Listen, are you well enough to ride?"

Ewan nodded. "It's just a knock. I've had worse."

"Good. Go to William's camp and warn him. But please make sure no one is following you."

Ewan nodded. "I'll wait a bit until I'm sure that they're gone, then I'll leave."

Ronald stopped him as he made to leave the room. "Ewan," he said. "You know that I don't mind you speaking your mind, but please, do not cross Jack Moore. He'll kill you."

Ewan hung his head. "I know. I'm sorry. I just couldn't help it."

Ronald put a hand to his shoulder. "Nor could I. But right now, we have to protect Will as well as we can. So we have to be careful what we say around his enemies. If we show that we have feelings for him, then it will only give them other ideas."

Ewan nodded. "I understand. I really should be going now. William needs to know what just happened."

Ronald nodded. "All right. Be careful, Ewan."

Ewan nodded back and left the room. Ronald turned to look at the fire and leaned against the mantle, resting his head on it. He let out a deep sigh and closed his eyes.

"William, what have you gotten into?" he moaned.

Chapter Fifteen

Peat Fire Flames

William and his company got back to the camp in the woods just as the sun was setting. Marion looked around, not seeming to be surprised at all by the appearance of it as if she had expected them to live in the woods like most other outlaws.

William swung down from his horse and Keith came over to take his reigns. "It's good to at least see ye back in one piece, Will," he said. "Who's that lass wi' ye?"

"An English princess to ransom?" Donald asked with a wicked grin.

"Nae, she's our camp-lass," William told his lads with a bit of a smirk. "Stephen took a liking to her. Her name's miss Marion Braidfoot."

"Hey, our Robin Hood has found a Maid Marion!" Keith crowed with a cheeky smile before William cuffed him on the back of the head.

"She needs to make herself useful," William said, turning to look at Marion as Stephen handed her off his horse. "Go see about dinner, miss."

"Ewan already made it," Donald told him. "He's been waiting for ye to return for a few hours now. He has some news for ye."

William caught how the lad's face fell as he recounted this and he had a bad feeling that his friend was going to be bearing bad news to him that night. "Where is he? I'll talk to him right away."

"I'm here, William," Ewan said, coming up. Keith took William's horse to the lean-to barn as the others gathered around to hear what the man had to say.

"What happened, Ewan?" William asked, even in the dimming light, he caught sight of the angry bruise on his jaw.

"William, yer uncle had a visitor today," Ewan began.

"A visitor?" William stared back, suddenly interested. "What kind of a visitor?"

Ewan sighed and closed his eyes. "Jack Moore."

"What?!" William shouted. He could feel the shock from his comrades at his back as well as they heard the news. "Why was he there?"

"It seems he kens that ye're Ronald Crawford's nephew," Ewan continued. "He wanted to know if yer uncle had any information about ye."

"What did he say?"

"He didna lie, nor did he give ye away," Ewan said tiredly, sweeping his hair away from his face. "He simply said that ye had been there and that he didna ken where ye were now, which is true since he doesna ken exactly where ye stay."

"That's not the problem," William said, anger clearly written on his face. "Did he threaten my uncle, Ewan?"

Ewan shrugged. "That's the way he works, William, though I can assure ye he would torture me first before he touched yer uncle. He may be evil but he's no' foolish. Yer uncle is still the sheriff of Ayr, even if Percy is in charge of the English garrisons."

"Did he do that to ye?" William asked, indicating the bruise on Ewan's face.

"I spoke when I shouldna have," the man said ruefully. "I was lucky though. Yer uncle stopped him from doing me any more harm."

"This has to stop," William said, grinding his teeth. "We have to do something about him."

Ewan put a hand on his shoulder. "What are ye going to do, William? Your lads are not ready to fight, nor do ye have enough of them to even make a dent in Moore's men. Ye must be patient. He will be brought down eventually. All bad men are. But ye have to wait for the right time otherwise it will all be for naught and ye'll be the one who ends up dead."

William looked down, trying to keep his anger at

bay. "I know, I know, Ewan. I just...Well, I just canna get over the fact that he killed my father."

"I ken, lad, I ken," Ewan said comfortingly. "But for now, why dinna ye all come over to the campfire and have something to eat? I have a nice rabbit stew cooking. Ye'll have to thank Donald and Jacob for their hunting abilities."

Marion hurried up to William as he strode over to the fire. "All right, master Wallace, ye need to tell me what is going on. Who is this man Moore? And why was he threatening yer uncle?"

"Ye dinna need to know any of that," William told her sternly. "All ye need to worry about is cooking and cleaning our camp. That's what ye're here for."

"You're so stubborn, William Wallace!" she growled at him. "Clean? What is there to clean? Nothing! Ye have that fine man Ewan to cook for ye it seems, and as for caring for yer wounds--ye don't know any less then me, I'm sure!"

"*Me* stubborn?!" William spun around to glare at her. "*Ye're* the one who's stubborn! What do ye think ye're here for? I could just take ye back to yer father and tell him I caught ye running away from home, is that what ye want?"

She glared him down, crossing her arms. "I want to *fight*, William. Teach me how to use a sword and a bow. I will hunt and do whatever any of these lads do for their keep. I may be a lass, but I'm no a peely-wally! I have just as much right to fight for my country's freedom as ye do!"

William made an exasperated sound through his

teeth and spun around, walking off into the camp.

Ewan smiled slightly at her as he handed her a bowl of stew. "William has a lot on his mind, lass. I wouldn't bother him right now."

She took the bowl from him and smiled. "Thank ye, Ewan. Would you like to join me for dinner? I'm going to sit by Stephen."

The Irishman grinned as she sat next to him and Kerlie. "Sure, don't mind Will, he's like that sometimes. I don't think he's ever met a girl before."

Marion gave him a slight smile. "Once he sees what I can do, I don't think he will protest. I know I can fight by his side."

Stephen nodded. "I bet ye can."

John and William sat a bit farther away, talking in quiet voices about the news Ewan had given him that day.

"We canna just let Moore push people around like this," William told him.

John nodded. "Aye, I'm with ye, Will. I ken how ye feel."

William nodded and looked down into his bowl, eating hungrily despite his anxiety. "It's something we will have to do. I have a deep feeling that we are the only ones who will do anything about this."

John ate a bit more of his stew and pushed his hair back from his face. "I have a feeling it's going to be like that through the whole war, William. If no one has done anything yet, I doubt anyone will. I think it's all on our heads."

William was struck by his friend's words even though he had thought the same thing many times. It always seemed more real when someone else voiced the same thing you've only thought. He turned to John and looked him in the eye. "Aye, I think ye have the right of it, Johnny," he said. "If this man thinks he can just act the tyrant and torment anyone he wants to, then someone needs to tell him that that just willna be tolerated by everyone. There are still people in this country who are not afraid of standing up to the oppressors. If that falls into the category of only the people in this camp, then so be it."

John smiled and nodded. "Aye, Will. I'm with ye. We'll gather all the lads we can here and do all we can with them. Who knows? Perhaps they can form the resistance of Scotland one of these days?"

William smiled and held out his hand. "And ye're with me all the way, right?"

John clasped his hand tightly. "Right!"

The night was nice despite the dark feelings that lay over the camp. The fires were high and the warmth and light from them gave a bit of hope to the lads sitting there. Marion still sat between Stephan and Ewan, enjoying the fact that she was not at home doing sewing and other things she was expected to do. She smiled slightly as she looked into the fire, watching the flames change in their turn. She turned to Ewan and spoke quietly to him.

"Please, Ewan. Tell me who Jack Moore is," she said.

The Scotsman turned to her with sad eyes. "Jack Moore is a horrible man, Marion. He doesna care who he hurts when he's on a mission. There's no one he would spare his wrath."

"If he's such an awful man, then why didn't someone stand against him a long time ago?" Marion asked.

"Because he's Henry Percy's man," Ewan told her. "And he answers directly to Edward Longshanks. And if ye go against Edward Longshanks, well, a lass doesna need to hear the horrors of English tyranny. Anyway, there's no' much more to it than that, but," he leaned close to her so no one could hear him. "William has a personal fight with him. Ye see, it was Jack Moore who killed his father."

Marion looked over with surprise at the young man sitting with his head close to John's, still in deep concentration. She looked back over at Ewan, her eyes wide in the firelight. "It was him? I thought I heard something, but I didn't know the whole thing."

Ewan nodded, looking into the fire. "Aye. William's sworn to have a reckoning with him before long. So ye see, lass, he *will* be gotten rid of soon enough. It's just a matter of time."

Marion looked into the fire soberly. "His uncle, who is he?"

"He's the sheriff of Ayr," Ewan told her. "I work for him. I'm head of his gillies."

"Ah," Marion said. "Good man?"

"Very," Ewan smiled. "He's a man who kens duty, though he loves William and wouldna betray him."

Marion was silent. She found that she was immediately pulled into the feelings that abounded in the camp. She had come upon something far more real then she had expected at first. There was something going on here that could change the history of Scotland. A shiver ran down her spine at the thought. She found herself looking toward the young leader of the troop again. There was something about him...She knew he could do it.

"He can win Scotland's freedom," she said to Ewan. "He can do it."

Ewan turned to her with a smile. "Let's hope he can, Marion. Let's only hope."

William sighed as he put his bowl aside and stood up, stretching out his back, which was stiff from the long ride. "I think it's best we turn in, John," he said.

The other lad nodded and stood as well. "Aye, I'm exhausted. We have to start training again tomorrow."

William nodded and left the fire to go to a nook between the roots of a tree where he had taken to sleeping of late. He unbelted his plaid and wrapped it snugly around himself, hunkering down in the moss and loam at the foot of the tree. He looked out to his camp, watching his companions all finding places to sleep. A small smile tugged at his lips as he watched Stephen making Marion a bed out of pine bows and relinquishing his own cloak to cover it. Irish.

The news he had gotten that day clouded his mind, but the exhaustion from travel made his eyelids droop and he soon dropped off. His dreams were troubled though and caught him up so that he couldn't get out of them. Dreams of danger and death. He only hoped that it was not a look into the future.

Chapter Sixteen

In Training

"William? William, get up, it's almost mid-morning."

William opened his eyes tiredly to see John standing over him, shaking him slightly by the shoulder. He sat up and rubbed a hand across his eyes. "Did I really sleep that long?"

John nodded. "Aye, we let ye, because we thought ye might need the extra sleep, but if ye want anything to eat, ye should get up now. Stephen was eyeing yer portion rather fondly."

William groaned as he stood, readjusting his plaid. "Aye, I must have been tired after the long trip. I dinna feel like I slept that long."

John gave him a smile and led him over to the

campfire where Ewan sat with Marion, stirring the stew pot that still had a bit of porridge left in it. He grinned at William as he dished the rest into a bowl for him.

"It's a dangerous thing rising late in this camp," he told him. "There's a fair chance that ye willna get breakfast."

William had to laugh as he took the bowl and started eating. "Thank ye for saving some for me then, Ewan."

The Scotsman nodded and stood. "I had best be going, I've been away from yer uncle's too long. He'll be wanting to know that everything is all right. I'll be back within the next few days."

William nodded. "All right, Ewan, see ye then."

As the Scotsman left the camp Marion looked over at William as he ate. "So what are the plans for today, General Wallace?" she asked with a slight smirk.

"*Ye* are going to be tidying up around here and thinking about what to make us for lunch," William said firmly. "*We* will be practicing our swordplay and archery and that kind of thing."

Marion folded her arms across her chest and glared at him. "Well, if that is your wish, my bold commander, then it shall be done." She stood up and went off angrily.

"By the way, the horse stalls could use a cleaning too," William called after her and she turned slightly to give him a stormy look.

John laughed. "Aye, Will, what have we gotten into?"

William shook his head and put aside his empty

bowl. "I dinna ken, Johnny. But if we do have someone to get the things done around here then I suppose she's worth it."

John turned to look at him with a sly smile. "Ye just like her yerself, Will. That's all this is about."

William shoved him hard as John laughed. "No' in the least, John Graham!" he said. "I have never had any wish to like a lassie nor *ken* one as a matter of fact, and ye had best remember that!"

"Good," John said. "Because I dare-say Stephen will steal her from under our noses."

"He can have her if he likes her so much," William said indifferently. "Now enough talk about lasses, let's get to work."

They went over to the practice place where all the other lads were warming up with their swords, sparring amongst each other. William stood on the outside of the training place and called out to them.

"All right lads, get into yer groups. Group one will report to John and Kerlie for archery, and group two will stay here for sword practice with me and Stephen."

The two groups of lads split up and half headed over to the archery targets where John and Kerlie were handing out the bows. William stepped under the rope and entered the sparring field where Stephen was already handing out the practice swords and pairing up the lads.

"All right, does everyone have a sword and a partner?" William asked and waited for the nods and "ayes" before he continued. "Okay, then. Take a ready stance and practice the moves we showed ye yesterday."

William and Stephen faced each other. They too had practice swords in their hands for they were afraid that if they got into the fighting they might cause harm to one another. "We're going to be practicing high and low strikes today," William told them. "Aim for the head and the lower legs. There are two ways to avoid a low strike. Ye can either jump over the blow, or ye can block it with yer sword. Remember, we'll probably never have heavy armor on, so we'll have the advantage of agility. And agility can do a lot more for you than extra protection."

Marion watched them as she shoveled the dirty hay that littered the floor of the horse stalls. She made angry eyes at William as he and Stephen acted out the moves they wanted the others to learn. "Show off," she muttered under her breath as she flung the horse dung away. "'The horse stalls need to be cleaned too,'" she mocked William's voice under her breath and dug the shovel into the ground. "I'll show him, I'll clean this place in record time and then I'll go and do something more productive." One of the horses she had tied outside the barn poked its head in and nudged her face lightly as if it sympathized with her. She smiled slightly and stroked the beast on the nose. "It seems we are all servants of William Wallace. But if he is the one to win Scotland's freedom, I suppose we shouldna knock him." She sighed and picked up the shovel again. She would never get done if she didn't work.

"Good job lads, I think we have that down," William told the others encouragingly as he lowered his sword for the time being. "Now we're going to learn an attack. The English, when we fight them, will be wearing armor and ye willna be able to give them too much damage with just a sword by hack and slash. The armor, though, is weak in two places. That is at the neck and under the arm. These are going to be the vulnerable places. Try to practice striking in these patterns." He and Stephen took the field and showed them several ways to hit their intended targets.

The Irishman took a dagger from his belt. "Also, if ye happen to have a dagger, it works very good to block yer enemy's sword with yer own and attack with the dagger when they're least expecting it."

"Aye, but please dinna try it with each other," William said with a laugh as Stephen grinned and put his dagger back in its sheath.

"Aye, perhaps not the best idea," he agreed. "Come on, lads, show us what ye've got!"

Marion finished up with the horses and stood back with a sigh. She went to the burn and washed her hands off, then bent to drink and wash her sweaty face. She stood up, looking around and caught sight of John and Kerlie instructing the lads in archery. She smiled to herself and started in their direction. She stood a little bit away, watching them for a few minutes, then she approached John as he waited for the others to go retrieve their arrows. He turned to her with a smile.

"Hello, miss Marion, what can I do for ye?" he asked.

"If it's all right, I would like to train with ye, John," she said, smiling back at him.

"I dinna ken if I should let ye," John said slowly. "William may no' like it."

"He's not here right now," Marion said with a bit of annoyance. "Please, John."

He shrugged indifferently. "All right. Let me get ye a bow."

Marion smiled to herself as John returned with a bow and several arrows. "Here, wear my bracer," he said, taking the hard leather guard off his arm and handing it to her. "Ye'll get welts down yer arm otherwise. Everyone does on their first go."

Marion cinched the bracer tight and took up the bow, twanging the string experimentally. She had never actually fired one, though she had always wanted to. John took it from her and held it properly.

"Ye'll take it like this," he told her, putting one hand on the wood, and the other holding the string. "Ye'll rest the arrow right above yer hand and take the end of it between yer first two fingers like this. Use only the tips of yer fingers to touch the bowstring so it will have a quicker release."

Marion took the bow from him and fixed an arrow to it, pulling the string back and feeling the tension build. John pulled her arm that was drawn back down. "Keep it straight," he told her. "Pull it straight back with yer hand at the level of yer cheek. Just sight down the shaft and shoot at the target."

Marion closed one eye, looking straight down the shaft at the target several yards in front of her. She pointed the tip dead center, and held her breath as she released the arrow with a twang.

There was a gasp from the lads who were all watching her and she looked on at the target where she saw the arrow quivering dead center.

"Have ye done this before?" Kerlie asked her, looking surprised and a bit miffed.

Marion shook her head. "Nae, I havena," she told them truthfully.

"Bet ye canna do that again," Keith scoffed with a grin.

Marion set her jaw and took up another arrow, placing it on the bow. She took her time sighting as all the lads smirked and waited to see if she could get another good hit. She sighted down the shaft like she had done before and shot. The second arrow thudded tightly next to the first one. The lads gaped in awe. John looked pleased at his newest pupal as she turned to smile at him.

"Who said that lasses canna use weapons?" she asked him.

He grinned. "All right lads, and lass, form up again and take five paces back. Let's get to work!"

***

William was just watching the lads practice, enjoying the fact that they were improving rapidly when he heard cheering close by. After it continued for about five minutes, he turned to look at what was going on. "Keep practicing lads, I'll be right back," he said to them.

Stephen jumped the ropes behind him. "What are they doing?" he asked.

"I have nae idea," William said, wondering the same thing. They tramped over to the archery targets where the noise was coming from and stood on the outskirts of the roped off area to watch the proceedings.

Marion stood amidst the line of lads, shooting with them. All the targets were sporadic except hers which had a tight cluster of arrows right in the center of it. William stood there as he saw what was happening, crossing his arms over his chest. Stephen grinned. "Sure now, the lass is good," he said to his companion.

William snorted and went off to talk to Marion. He stood behind her as she shot another arrow and the lads cheered again. "Very good, lass," he said and she turned in surprise.

"Oh, hello," she said indifferently. "Nice of ye to stop by. We were just practicing."

William stayed there, unmoved. "And what about the stables? Did ye clean them."

Marion motioned to the lean-to. "Go have a look for yerself. I even put some new hay down."

"Fair enough," William said. "But shouldna ye be making lunch for us? I can assure ye that the lads willna be happy if they find there's nothing to eat when they are done."

"It's only been a little over an hour since we fed them breakfast," Marion told him. "I think they can wait a little longer."

"Let her practice with us, Will," Keith told his companion. "She really is good."

William turned back to Marion. "So ye really shot all those?" he asked skeptically.

"Why should I pretend any different?" she asked him hotly.

"To get me to admit I was wrong."

"Do ye?"

"No." Marion smiled slightly at him, her eyes flashing mischievously. "I bet I can outshoot ye, William Wallace."

There were "oohs" from the gathered lads. By then all the sword fighters had come over as well, to see what was going on. William looked down at Marion with a cocked eyebrow.

"I wouldna say that, miss," he said.

"Do it!" Donald shouted out before John cuffed him on the back of the head.

William took the bow from Kerlie's hands and gathered some arrows which he drove into the ground at his feet. "All right, we'll have a little competition," he said amid cheers from the gathered lads. "Best out of five shots. John. Oversee it, will ye?"

The young man stepped over to the two while Stephen and Kerlie hurried to clear the targets of all the arrows that stuck in them. "All right, ye two. What ye're going to do is wait for my mark, and then ye will shoot at the same time at yer own targets. We'll repeat this until ye have each shot five. Good luck."

He stepped over to one side as the two put arrows to their bows and sighted down the shafts to the targets. John held up his hand and then lowered it. "Shoot."

The two arrows whizzed through the air and hit their respected targets. Both were dead center. There were scattered cheers and clapping from the lads. William turned to his opponent with a small smug smile. "See? I told ye it wasn't the best idea to shoot against me, lass."

Marion ignored him and took up her second arrow. John gave the signal and they shot again. This time, William's was just a bit far off the mark while Marion's landed right next to her first one. She smirked at the Scotsman but he shrugged. "Best out of five," he told her.

William sighted again and this one landed closer to the bottom then he wanted it too. He gritted his teeth. He couldn't let himself get beaten by a lass.

"Come on William!" one of the lads cried. "Ye canna get beaten by a lass!"

"Come on Marion, ye can beat him!" someone else who sounded like Donald or Jacob shouted above him.

"Round four," John said and gave the signal. "Shoot."

William who was flustered by now, didn't take as much time as he should have on the aiming and his arrow went awry and hit one of the outer circles of the target. Marion grinned at him as more shouts of encouragement to both parties rang out from the lads.

"Come on, William, ye have to at least get the last

one," she told him as they raised their bows again.

"Last round," John called. "Shoot."

They both shot for the last time and William got a better hit this time but still farther from the center then Marion.

"Aw, bad luck, Will!" Keith called out.

"Hey look!" Donald shouted as he and Jacob ran up with cheeky grins on their faces. "Maid Marion outshot Robin Hood!"

William glared at them as he passed. John clapped a hand to his shoulder as he walked away. "Dinna take it hard, Will. She was just lucky. She'll never be able to wield a sword better then ye."

"Dinna teach her that too," William growled.

"Ye did good, Will," Kerlie said, running up and throwing his arm around his friend's shoulders. "It's no' yer fault. Ye just got all flustered. If ye had been alone, ye would have been able to land all the shots as well as she did."

William stayed silent. He looked over to the group of lads circling around their newest "recruit". He didn't want to admit it to the lads or to himself for that matter, but he was impressed. That lass had pluck and she wasn't going to let anyone tell her what she could and couldn't do. There she was standing in the circle of his lads, letting them congratulate her on her victory. Stephen was dancing her around as well as they could in the tight place and she was laughing happily. A small smile tugged unbidingly at William's lips. He shook it off immediately as John spoke to him.

"Should we continue training, Will?" he asked.

William turned around to face him. "Nae, let the lads have the rest of the day off. I need to think over a few things. How about ye get me Stephen and we can sit together over lunch and talk about our next plan of action? When we get lunch, that is."

Chapter Seventeen

A Captive

After the blow to his ego, William stayed away from his lads for the rest of the day, sitting off to one side of the camp with his commanders and talking about their next move.

"If we can somehow get information about what Moore is planning," William mused. "We need someone to go into town and get it."

"What about Ewan?" Kerlie asked.

William shook his head. "Nae, that's no' a good idea. Moore is already on to him. He knows too much anyhow. I ken he wouldna tell anything, but that's why I worry about him. Moore wouldna hesitate to torture him if he thought he knew something useful."

Stephen nodded. "Aye, I see what ye mean. I could go."

"Are ye known by face in the town?" William asked him.

Stephen gave him that enigmatic grin. "Not if I don't want to be."

Kerlie nodded. "Believe him. He has ways of getting around that are beyond our ken."

William shrugged. "Well, if ye think ye can get something, then ye have my permission to try it. But wait a couple more days. We have to be careful about what we do. Moore probably thinks that I am somewhere around here and he's more than likely looking for me. If something else happens, then we'll be found out and we'll all find ourselves on the gallows."

The other lads nodded solemnly. William gave them an encouraging smile. "And there's also the fact that my uncle could be in danger. If we get into trouble again, he'll be the first one to get Moore's vengeance. I could never put him in danger when I knew it was my own fault."

"We understand, Will," John said. "I'm glad ye're taking precautions."

William gave him a grim smile. "Well, I ken that sometimes ye canna just run forward into the fray without a sword in yer hand and comrades at yer back."

John smiled at him. "Aye, well, at least we dinna have to keep ye on yer feet."

"We all work together," William said. "We're all in this. We have to look out for each other. I ken that if I am captured then I canna do that. I canna stand the thought of ye all having to worry about my welfare. This was my idea. This is my army. I have to take care of the people in it, no' the other way around."

John looked at him seriously. "Nae, Will, what ye said first is true. We all look out for *each other*. It doesna just end wi' ye."

"Brothers in arms," William said with a nod, a smile spreading over his lips. He drew his sword from across his back and stuck it into the ground in the middle of their circle. "For freedom."

All four of the lads clasped the hilt of the sword and repeated William. "For freedom."

"Thus the resistance was made," John narrated and ducked as William reached out to cuff him on the head. They all grinned at each other. There was nothing that could stop them now.

***

There was nothing else they could do that night than eat dinner which Marion and Keith had whipped up between them and then go to bed. The next morning, William got up early and went to one of the campfires and spoke to the lads. "There's a sad lack of meat here," he said and there was a few chuckles from the lads. "So, Keith and Stephen, please see to that. Go hunting and try to get something by tonight."

They saluted him. "Aye, General Wallace!" they said together.

They finished the thin oatmeal that Marion had

cooked up for them that morning and Stephen and Keith went off on their hunting excursion. William, John and Kerlie went off with the lads to start their training again. Marion was left cleaning dishes in the burn. As she scrubbed, she looked around and watched John teaching the lads archery. She saw the stack of unused bows sitting behind him and smiled to herself. She would go hunting for herself. If it was meat that William wanted, she would get it for him.

She stood up as she finished washing, going over to the stack of bows and selected one, taking up a quiver full of arrows as well. She slung the bow over her shoulder and hung the quiver around her waist and went over to cross the burn and walked off into the woods, smiling to herself.

William sparred with Kerlie who was helping him that day since Stephen wasn't there. He didn't notice Marion leaving the camp. "I think what we're going to do today, lads, is go over the moves ye've been learning for the past few weeks. Try to put them into spontaneous attack and parry sequences. Find a partner and practice together."

Marion crept off into the woods quietly, William's instructions fading away into the dense woodlands. The peaceful surroundings made her feel happy. Some sunlight was shining through the trees and playing over the loamy ground as she padded lightly, trying to be as quiet as possible, not wanting to scare any game away. She unslung the bow from her back and set it against the ground, bending it so she could string it. She took an arrow from the quiver and set it against the string, sneaking around the trees and crouching low behind some ground growth. There was a snap of a twig to her right and she immediately looked in the direction, wondering what had caused it.

She saw Keith creeping through the bushes ahead of her. He was crouched low to the ground, his bow bent and his eyes on something in front of him. Marion turned a bit more to see what he was looking at and caught sight of a fat rabbit eating some plants, unaware of the danger. She watched as Keith stopped to sight down his shaft. He pulled back the string and let fly.

The arrow thudded a bit to the left of the rabbit and it started and bolted off into the woods. But Marion had already gotten her arrow off and it hit the rabbit before it disappeared into the bushes again. Keith looked around in surprise and grinned when he saw Marion.

"Woah! That was an amazing shot! I thought I had lost that one."

They both stepped out of hiding to see the hit and Keith bent to retrieve the arrow. He wiped it on the dead leaves and handed it back to Marion.

"Here, maybe it's a lucky arrow," he told her as she put it back into her quiver.

"Thank ye," she said and gave a satisfied smile. Her first catch!

"Come on," Keith told her. "I saw some deer tracks over this way. I would really love nothing more than a good venison stew!"

"Sounds wonderful," Marion said with a grin. "We'll have to get Ewan out here to cook it though. I wouldn't know how to make it taste good."

Keith laughed. "In my opinion, Marion, as long as ye do the hunting as good as this, I couldn't care less weather ye can cook or not."

Marion grinned. "Well, I have to earn my keep someway."

Keith suddenly shot out a hand to stop her.

"What is it?" she asked.

"Shh," Keith told her, immediately dropping behind some bushes. "Look!"

Marion looked ahead and saw a deer standing in a glade. Keith turned to her and pointed to it. "Can ye shoot it?" he asked.

"I think so," Marion told him and raised her bow slowly, putting an arrow to it. She sighted down the shaft as she drew the string back, then held her breath and let go with a twang.

It was a perfect hit. Right through the neck. Keith looked on in shock, his mouth hanging open.

"That was amazing!" she cried. "I thought we would have to chase it down, but nae!"

Marion couldn't help a smile at her success. A rabbit and a deer and all in her first hunting trip. Now William would have to admit that she was worth more then a camp dishwasher.

"Let's see if we can get this back to camp," Keith told her as they went to admire Marion's shot. Keith looked around and found a long branch which he brought over to the deer and set about tying it's feet to the branch so they could carry it with more ease. "This should work," he said. "Can ye manage to carry a side?"

Marion nodded and they each took up one end of the stick, carrying their supper off to the camp.

***

Ewan came into the camp with fresh provisions before the hunters returned and William excused himself from practice to go and meet him.

"Hi, Ewan, how are things going at my uncle's?" he asked.

"Nothing more has happened," Ewan told him, setting down a sack of oats he had brought. "I havena seen Jack Moore for several days."

"Well, that could either be good or bad," William mused, but he smiled up at his friend. "Will ye get a chance to practice with us today? We're mainly just sparring right now."

Ewan smiled back. "I think I have the time today. Then I'll make ye some dinner before I leave tonight."

"I sent Stephen and Keith out hunting," William said. "They should have something by the end of the day."

"How's Marion becoming aquatinted with the camp life?" Ewan asked, as they started out for the sparring field.

William snorted. "Quite fine. She thinks she can shoot arrows better than the rest of us." He looked around the camp. "Dinna ken where she is right now. Probably enlisting in my swordsmen ranks."

"At least she's no' one of those lasses who needs caring for every minute," Ewan said.

William shrugged. "Never known any lasses really."

They stepped over the ropes and into the fighting ring. William got a sword for Ewan and they started training alongside the other lads.

Marion and Keith crossed the river with their baggage and Keith haled the camp.

"Look what we brought for ye, everyone!" he shouted and everyone looked over at them.

"Venison!" Donald and Jacob shouted as they saw what the hunters brought.

William looked over and frowned as he saw Marion with Keith. "I'll be back," he told the others and left the fighters. Kerlie and Ewan followed him as he crossed the camp to meet with the hunters. Marion looked up at him with a smile as he came to greet them.

"Ye wanted meat, William?" Marion asked him.

William looked at her indifferently. "Aye, I did. And I suppose ye're responsible for this, are ye?"

Keith stepped in, grinning. "Aye! She shot the deer in one go! Just like that, if ye please!"

Ewan seemed thoroughly impressed. "Good job, Marion," he told her. "Ye should be proud. I'll be able to make a good supper with that."

"Thank ye, Ewan," Marion said, brushing past William to smile at the redheaded man. "I trust ye'll make us all a fine dinner tonight!"

He bowed gallantly to her. "I will certainly do my

best," he told her.

"Stephen will be surprised when he comes back," Kerlie said with a grin. "What if he brings back a deer too?"

"Then we'll just have more meat!" John said and helped Keith take the deer over to a place where Ewan could take care of it.

William watched his lads congratulating and thanking Marion profusely. That smile tried to tug at his lips again, but he brushed it off, not wanting to admit that he was *really* impressed this time and also pleasantly surprised that they were going to get venison that night and not just rabbit stew. He gave a small annoyed sigh and turned back to the training field. He looked at the surrounding woods for Stephen but shrugged. He'd come back when he was ready. He knew that he at least didn't have to worry about the young Irishman.

***

Stephen slipped silently through the woods, his bow held at his side. He hadn't found anything, but he wasn't done yet. He crept through the trees and looked around, constantly searching for anything he could shoot.

There was a sound farther to his right and he stopped and stood still, listening hard. He caught the sound of voices and immediately knew it was not an animal he had heard. He crept closer to the voices and crouched low under a hollow at the foot of a tree, looking out to a clearing where he saw three men talking together.

"So are we going to find something to eat or what?"

one asked, and Stephen could clearly hear the man's flat English accent. He listened harder.

"We were supposed to be looking for the Scottish lad," said another man. He looked to be in charge. "We shouldn't make him mad. You haven't known him as long as I have."

"But we have to eat," said the third man. "General Moore couldn't be too mad if we landed him a deer."

"No, we need to stay on our mission," the second man said, starting to sound tired. "Look, just search for a little bit longer then you can hunt, all right?"

"All right, then we'll split up so we can cover more ground," the third man said.

"Fine, meet back here in a half hour." The two men left their commander and slipped off into the woods, soon disappearing between the trees. The commander stood still in the clearing, looking around as if he were a bit worried to be alone in the woods. Stephen smiled to himself and slipped from his hiding place, moving to the side of the tree sheltered from the Englishman's view and scaled it, climbing up into a branch some ten feet off the ground. He hid himself in some branches and looked down at the Englishman below him.

The man looked around as if he had heard something. Stephen rustled the branches around him a bit and grinned as the man jumped slightly. He drew a sword from his belt and turned around in a circle, looking at the surrounding woodlands with fear. He backed up against the tree and held the sword out in front of him. Stephen took up several acorns from one of the branches and threw them a bit away from the tree. The Englishman jumped slightly and spun around, now backing away from the tree.

"Who's there?" he asked, his voice shaking. "Who is it?"

Stephen smothered a laugh and watched as the man moved farther away from the tree, his back to Stephen. The Irishman edged forward on the branch he was perched on and dropped down lightly on the ground behind the Englishman.

"Looking for someone?"

The Englishman turned around with a shout and started when he saw Stephen. He brandished the sword in front of him. "Wh-who are you?" he asked.

"No one in particular," Stephen told him with a grin.

The man backed up, slowly. He was shaking so hard that the sword wavered in front of him. "Are-are you a spirit?"

Stephen shook his head, still grinning. "No, try again."

"A-a...fairy?" he stuttered.

Stephen grinned even harder. "Maybe," he said.

The man gulped visibly. "Don't enchant me. Please!"

"Why should I do that?"

"That's what fairies do," the man said, still clutching his sword.

"Maybe I'm not a fairy," Stephen said, still grinning and seeming relaxed on the outside, though inside he was as tense as a coiled spring.

The Englishman seemed to be trying to gather himself again and he reached out with his other hand to grasp the hilt of his sword. He stopped backing away and planted his feet wide in the loam. "I'm not afraid to fight you," he said but his voice still wavered, giving away his fear.

"If I am a fairy, ye know you can't kill me with a normal blade," Stephan said matter-of-factly. "And ye also know it's bad luck to kill one of the Fair Folk."

The man gulped again and brandished his sword. "You aren't though, are you? You're fooling me."

"Perhaps," Stephen said, spreading his arms to show that he was unarmed. "But perhaps not."

The man seemed to think this over a minute, then it seemed he had worked out a struggle in his mind and he charged forward at Stephen with a cry.

The Irishman side-stepped as the man was just ready to skewer him and whipped a dagger from his belt, pressing it to the Englishman's throat. The man stopped in mid-stride.

"Drop the sword if ye wish to live," Stephen told him.

The man dropped the blade instantly. "All right, all right, please, don't kill me!"

Stephen grinned as he spun the man around and tied his hands tightly. "Don't worry, I'm not going to kill ye. We need information and ye're going to be the one to give it."

The man nodded. "All right, fine."

Stephen took a bag he had brought for his game and put it over the man's head. "Can't have ye seeing anything ye're not supposed to." he said and pressed the dagger point into the man's back.

"Let's go," he said and grinned at his triumph. He might not have gotten anything to eat, but he had surely gotten something William would be pleased to have!

Chapter Eighteen

Information and Celebration

William was very surprised to see Stephen coming into the camp from the back with his captive. He couldn't help a grin spreading over his face as he ran to meet his comrade.

"Well, now, what's this Stephen? Couldn't find a deer so ye had to resort to an Englishman?"

The man Stephen had in his grasp quivered and moaned in the bag that covered his head. Stephen grinned and saluted to William. "I found him all alone in the woods and thought he looked lost so I decided to bring him back here. He may have information we need."

William grinned back and called over to John and Kerlie. "All right lads. How would ye like to help interrogate a prisoner?"

They gathered around the man as Stephen and William worked at tying him to a tree so he couldn't escape. The young Scotsman pulled the bag from the man's head and looked him over. His face betrayed his fright and his eyes looked this way and that as if trying to find a place he could escape. He was young, probably only twenty-five or so, William thought, and he was clean-shaven. William opened his mouth to speak but the man blurted out first.

"Please!" he cried. "Please do not let that devilish leprechaun do anything to me!"

William turned with amusement to Stephen who stood right behind him. "What have ye been telling him, man?"

Stephen grinned, winking at William so that the Englishman couldn't see him. "All kinds of horrors, General Wallace. I don't think he'll be too much trouble for ye!"

William smothered a grin and turned back to his captive who could barely keep his footing for fear. "I'll give ye a deal, my friend," he said in a commanding voice. "If ye tell me what I need to know, then I'll keep Mad Stephen Ireland away from ye. How does that sound?"

The man gulped. "Wh-what do you need to know?"

"First of all, who do ye serve?" William asked. "Are ye one of Jack Moore's men?"

The man nodded. "Aye."

The four lads exchanged looks and William turned back to the man. "Good. Now, tell me, what has he been up to lately?"

"L-looking for the rebel Wallace," the man stuttered.

"I am the rebel Wallace," William told him sternly. "And he willna find me. Ye can tell him that when ye see him again. *If* ye get the chance that is."

The man bit his lip, but seemed unwilling to say anything else. William looked him in the eyes. "And tell me. What does Jack Moore wish to do with the 'rebel Wallace' if he happens to be successful in finding him?"

The man shook his head. "Things you wouldn't want to hear. But Earl Percy wishes you to stand trial. The General won't kill you until m'lord Percy gets back from London."

William turned to his companions with a smile. "Do ye hear that, lads? I'm to have a trial. That's far more than I expected from a bunch of Sassenachs!" He turned back to the man. "What's yer name?"

"Ca-Captain Henry Simpson," he said slowly.

"Ah, so ye're a captain?" William said with a raised eyebrow. "I have to admit that I am surprised. I took ye for a common soldier. I would think that a captain in His Most English Majesty's army would be far more brave and valiant." His companions chuckled at this as Simpson's face turned red. William looked him in the eyes again. "Well, *Captain* Simpson, will ye tell me what ye're commander's next move is?"

The man shook his head. "No, I won't tell you."

"Ye won't?" William asked.

"No," the man said again, as if trying to gain back some of his lost dignity.

"Are ye sure about that?"

Simpson started to shake his head, then he nodded. "Aye. Commander Moore would kill me if he knew I had told you anything."

"There are many things that are worse then death," William said seriously. "Are ye still quite sure ye dinna want to tell me?"

Simpson nodded resolutely.

William shrugged indifferently. "All right, then. Stephen?"

The Irishman grinned at Simpson and pulled a knife from his belt and a swatch of leather he sharpened it on, taking his time as he inspected the blade and checked its sharpness. Simpson looked as if he was trying to compose himself, but was failing miserably. Sweat beaded on his brow. Stephen slowly put the leather back into his belt pouch and stepped forward with the dagger. Simpson closed his eyes, already wincing, then he suddenly seemed to loose his nerve completely.

"All right! All right! I'll tell you!" he cried and Stephen sheathed his dagger again.

William smiled at his captive. "Good choice. So. The plans?"

Simpson swallowed hard. "He-Moore, he's having us search every inch of this accursed forest. I tried to tell him it wasn't a good idea, but he wouldn't listen. Now we're stuck looking through all of it."

"It was a good idea, because as ye can see, we are here," William told him, spreading his arms and bowing mockingly. "But he'll be hard pressed to find out where *exactly* we are. This is a huge forest. We willna be found if we dinna want to be."

"He's determined to find you before Percy gets back," Simpson told him a bit proudly. "And when Jack Moore sets his mind to something, it gets done."

William nodded. "Aye? At least he's a man of action. More befitting what I want to see in an adversary. Unlike peely-wally men who get to be captains only because of their position in life." Before Simpson could retort, William turned around to his comrades. "What do ye say, lads? Should we let him go or should we eat him for supper." Simpson groaned in terror.

The look William gave the others made them keep their faces strait. "Well, we did just get that deer today," John mused, pretending to mull it over. "He looks kinda skinny anyway. I bet he's tough."

"And surely ye want to have him bring a message back to Moore for ye," Kerlie said. "He canna do that if we pick his bones clean."

William pretended to think it over for a few minutes then he nodded. "Aye, ye're right, lads. We'll let him go. I'll write a note for him to bring back to Moore and then we can send him on his way first thing tomorrow morning."

"What shall we do with him tonight?" John asked.

"Leave him there. He'll be fine. I dinna think he's going anywhere." William beckoned to his lads. "But I think a wee bit of a celebration is in order. How about a wee ceili tonight?"

Stephen grinned. "Sure, and that sounds fine. And what was this I heard about a deer?"

They laughed happily as they went over to the cooking fire where Ewan had started to cook the stew. He looked up at them with a bit of a grin.

"Congratulations, William, yer first prisoner of war!" he said with a wink.

"It's Stephen who should be thanked," William told him, sitting down on one of the logs. "I dinna ken what ye told him, but whatever it was it sure helped! Ye deserve an extra portion tonight!"

"What will ye do with the man, William?" Marion asked him from where she sat chopping vegetables to put in the stew. "Ye willna kill him will ye?"

William shook his head in annoyance. "Nae, lass, why should I kill him? I'm no' a cold blooded Englishman!"

"Excuse me then for insulting ye," Marion said hotly as she threw the vegetables into the big stew pot. "Dinna forget who ye have to thank for dinner tonight," she added.

Stephen grinned. "Sure, do ye mean to tell me that *ye* shot the deer, Marion?"

William sighed and stood up to go and write the letter. He wasn't going to let the lass ruin his small victory. He wondered suddenly why he felt it a victory. They had only managed to find out that they were in greater danger. Perhaps it was all in the fact that they had successfully captured, interrogated and struck fear into an Englishman without doing him any bodily harm. He grinned to himself again. A bloodless victory. Always the best.

He took a satchel, now serving as a pillow for his bedroll, and pulled out some parchment and a quill and ink. He started penning a letter to Moore and then folded it up and tied it with a bit of twine. He tucked it into his belt pouch and stood again to go to the campfire. The light was beginning to dim, and John and Kerlie were building up all the fires to start lighting them. They grinned at William as he came over to them.

"Well, how are we to celebrate our victory?" Kerlie asked him. "Feasting, music, dance?"

"How else do ye celebrate a victory?" William asked him, grinning back. "Aye, we'll see who can play. I heard Ewan can play the pipes."

Ewan, who had heard him, turned and smiled sheepishly. "I'm no' really that good, but I'll give it a go, Will."

"As long as ye can skirl in tune, we willna care, Ewan," William told him in good humor. "How is that stew coming?"

"Fine," the redheaded man told him. "I think it will be done within another hour."

"Good," William said and then set about helping build the fires and got a flint and his dirk to strike the flame.

Soon the stew was done and bubbling in the pot and Ewan and Marion served it to the lads with a piece of crusty bread and a hunk of cheese each that William's uncle had told Ewan to bring them.

The lads sat on the logs around the fires and ate their stew with relish. William soaked his bread in the broth and sighed happily.

"Och, this is the best thing I've eaten in a long time. Ye work wonders in the kitchen, Ewan."

The Scotsman, who sat beside him, smiled and nodded in the direction of Marion sitting with Stephen and Keith and laughing with them. "She shot the deer, I only made the stew."

"Aye, that's right!" John said, raising his tankard in Marion's direction. "Three cheers for Marion Braidfoot!" he cried.

She ducked her head modestly as the lads cheered her to an echo. William glared down into his stew but didn't say anything.

After they had polished off any food that could be found, the lads urged Ewan to take up his pipes and they danced around the fires, shouting happily. Marion was in the center of it all. None of the lads wanted to be caught without a dance with her so they all flocked to her side. She changed hands all the time, her face flushed happily as she laughed with the lads. William and John laid their swords out on the ground and danced over them, leaping and hopping and turning around each other. After a while, they stopped to catch their breath and watched Stephen dancing with Marion in the center of a circle where the lads were clapping in time to the music. John turned to William and trotted off.

"If ye canna beat them, ye may as well join them, Will," he said with a grin and joined in the dancers, grabbing Marion himself and dancing a reel with her.

William hung back for only another second, then he too joined the group and danced with the others. Ewan played on and on tirelessly, dancing as he blew on his pipes. One of the lads took up a hand drum and beat on it for accompaniment and another took up a whistle and gave the Scotsman a breather.

Suddenly, William found Marion flung into his arms and she grabbed him, not stopping the dancing.

"Hello William," she said breathlessly as she spun around with the young Scotsman.

"Hello, Marion, enjoying the night?" he asked her, his mood too good to feel anger toward her or anyone else that night.

"Quite," she said and slowed. "Would you mind horribly if I stopped? I need to catch my breath and get something to drink."

"Not at all," William said and let go of her as they got out of the circle of lads. She panted to catch her breath and took her tankard from beside a log and drank deeply from it.

"That's better," she said and looked with gleaming eyes at the dancing lads. "Ye'd think they never saw a lass before."

William had to laugh a bit at this. "Aye, it does seem that way sometimes. Ye're certainly popular when it comes to dancing."

She turned to smile at him. Her face was flushed and pretty and her eyes caught the light from the fire. He had to admit that she was a nice looking lass. Even though he had no one to compare her to.

"I, uh..." he cleared his throat. "I never did thank ye for the dinner. It was very good."

She smiled at him with a pleased expression in her eyes. "You're welcome," she said. "Now that I have mastered the bow, will ye let me learn the art of the sword?" She reached to one side where William had stuck his father's sword into the ground and pulled it out, holding it in front of her.

"Nae, dinna stretch yer luck, lassie," William told her, his smile disappearing as he reached out to take the sword from her. "This sword is far to heavy for ye anyway."

She crossed her arms and returned his frown. "Aye, I should know never to ask too much of ye, William Wallace," she said in annoyance and lifted her face so she could look down her nose at him like she always did when she was displeased. "It's all right though. Because I know that I will always be able to shoot better then ye." She gave him a slight smile and turned to join the dancers again even as he opened his mouth to reply.

William sighed in exasperation and shook his head. He looked at his sword and then stuck it back into the ground. How was he ever going to fight a war when he had a lassie to deal with who plagued him more than the enemy himself? But, for all he knew, William could not answer his own question.

"If ye canna beat them, then ye may as well join them," he repeated what John said and smiled to himself as he joined the dancers once more.

The lads danced long into the night. There were no worries in the camp this night, it was only music and dancing and laughing. But there was an underlying feeling of impending danger. Something perhaps only William and his closets friends felt. They knew in their hearts that this might be one of the last nights that they would have a reason to celebrate. There was something coming that took hold of their senses and told them to be alert. Aye, there was something in the air. Something dark.

Chapter Nineteen

There are Many Things Worse than Death

The next morning, William and his four companions went to their captive who had spent the whole night tied to the tree. He looked as if he had lost some of his unease after he knew he was to be spared. He stayed silent as Kerlie untied him and he stepped away from the tree, rubbing his stiff limbs where the ropes had cut the circulation. William pulled the letter he had written out of his belt pouch and handed it to the man.

"Do not lose this. I want it to get to Jack Moore expressly," he said in no uncertain terms.

The man nodded, knowing Stephen was standing at

his back. "Aye, it will be done."

William nodded as he handed over the letter and Simpson tucked it safely into his tunic. William motioned to Kerlie. "Tie his hands behind his back and get that sack Stephen used yesterday. We dinna want to chance him finding his way back here."

They did what he asked but before the hood was put back over his head, Simpson spoke to William. "If I may just ask you one question?" he said and when William turned to him, he continued. "Why didn't you kill me?"

"Killing a man in cold blood is the act of a coward," William told him firmly. "There is nae honor in it. Besides, I need someone to carry my letter."

"You are very merciful for an outlaw and rebel," Simpson said with a bit of disgust in his voice.

William leaned close to him and gave him a small smile. "Actually, I wasna. If *I* had killed ye, then I can assure ye that it would have been very quick and painless. But I'm afraid I canna say the same for Jack Moore."

Simpson's face paled visibly and he swallowed hard as Stephen put the hood back over his head. "Do ye wish me to escort him out?" the Irishman asked William.

"If ye wish," William said. "Take him right to the wood fringe."

Stephen saluted and took hold of the hooded man's shoulders and started to lead him out of the back of the camp so that he wouldn't notice the river and started off through the dense trees. William turned back to his companions and nodded toward the fires. "Well, how about some breakfast? Then we can get back to work."

They walked off back to the campfires as Stephen made his way through the woods with his prisoner.

***

Stephen got his charge to the wood fringe in good time, and once they stepped out of the trees, he took the hood from his head and smiled at Simpson.

"Sure, that wasn't so bad, was it?" he asked. "Be on yer way then."

Simpson looked at him indignantly. "My arms are still tied."

Stephen nodded. "Aye, that they are. That's so ye tell the truth of what happened. I know yer type. Always making up stories. And don't forget to mention the 'divilish leprechaun' to the other lads, all right?"

Simpson glared at him but backed away at the same time and started heading off on the long walk to the town. Stephen watched his progress for a few minutes then turned and slipped off back through the woods.

When he got back to the camp, breakfast was nearly done and the lads were starting to practice again. He sat down on the log next to Marion and she smiled at him.

"Would ye like something to eat, Stephen?" she asked him and reached for a bowl to dish some oatmeal into it.

"Hey, did ye send him on his way, Stephen?" John called out as he saw him sitting there.

"Aye, I did that!" Stephen called back to him. "He was none too happy I think. We pretty much condemned the poor man to death."

John shrugged. "Well, at least it's no' on our hands!"

Marion handed Stephen the bowl of porridge. "Stephen, please tell me. How long do ye think it will be before Jack Moore finds our camp?"

Stephen shrugged as he ate. "Who can say, lassie? If he swept the whole place with all his men it still might take him several weeks to find us. And if we start to move around as well, that would confuse them." He turned to smile at her and patted her hand. "Don't worry, Marion, we won't let anything happen to ye."

"It's not myself I'm worried about," Marion told him. "It's everyone here. This Moore man is awful from what I've heard. I don't want to think of what would happen if he found us. William may be guaranteed a trial, but the rest of you..." she shuddered slightly and Stephen reached over to take her hands gently in his. She looked into his black eyes.

"We do not have to be seen if we don't want to. We know these woods better than any Englishman. We live here, we work here, these are our trees. We can get around in places where no one else can. They would never find us until it was too late."

"But what if it came to a fight?" Marion asked. "We only have about twenty-five people here at the time being. What do the English have?"

"A lot more," Stephen told her with a grin. He reached up to touch the side of his head. "But we have the brains sure enough. Don't worry. We'll get through this."

Marion smiled then. She found it hard to worry with the Irishman smiling at her. "Aye, I believe we will. Thank ye, Stephen."

"Any time," he told her then leaned close and whispered. "How would ye like to learn how to use a sword?"

A smile spread over her face. "Really?"

"Aye," he said with a grin and wink. "Come on!"

They left the campfire and went over to a secluded place behind the horse stalls. William saw them go and shook his head. He had no idea what they were up to but he had other things to worry about. He turned back to his group of lads. "All right, back to practice," he told them. "Everyone get swords and partners."

***

Jack Moore was sitting at the head of the table in the house where Percy and his officers were staying in Ayr, eating his breakfast, when a servant came in and stood respectfully by his side, bowing his head as he spoke.

"General, there is a man of your regiment who wishes to see you," he said.

Moore wiped grease off his mouth with the back of his hand and belched. "Bring him in."

The servant turned and went out of the room. He came back a few minutes later with several of the guard and Captain Simpson, still tied, between them. They all looked flustered and worried. Jack stood up as he saw them and smiled thinly.

"What is this? Ah, my brave Captain Simpson. I was

wondering where you had gotten to. The two other men you went with came back last night and said they had lost you. What has happened?"

"I-I was captured," Simpson said, stuttering.

"By who?" Moore asked him, his voice was unusually calm and easy.

"He said an evil fairy captured him," said a young man who stood on Simpson's left. There was not a scorning note in his voice, but rather a fearful tremor.

"Untie him," Moore commanded.

The men cut the ropes that bound Simpson and he sighed gratefully and rubbed life back into his arms. Moore stepped close to him.

"What was that you said?" he asked him slowly, smiling so that his cheek scar crinkled. "Who captured you?"

"He dropped out of no where," Simpson began. "And spoke with an Irish tongue. He had an oddness about him. I only figured he was some kind of fairy or spirit. You know they haunt those woods."

Moore's attitude changed then. He brought up his hand and struck Simpson across the face so hard that he fell to the ground with a moan.

"You fool!" he cried. "Are you so stupid as to believe in fairies?!"

Simpson didn't say anything. Moore grabbed him by the front of his tunic and hauled him to his feet again. "There's nothing I hate worse than a coward," he growled. "At least the Scots seem to have some *backbone*. You can't let them seem the better."

Simpson reached into his tunic, pulling out the letter. "I-I was brought to William Wallace," he said.

"You were what?" Moore asked, suddenly interested. "Tell me again."

"I was taken to see William Wallace. He gave me this letter to give to you."

Moore snatched the letter from Simpson's hand and opened it. He read it out loud to himself:

"To Jack Moore, esteemed commander of His Majesty Edward Longshanks' esteemed army:

Here is your bold Captain Simpson back safe and sound. He gave us sufficient information so we decided not to eat him and rather that we would send him back to you as a messenger. There is no way to send a letter back for we took the utmost precautions in transporting him, but keep what I have to say in mind.

First of all, I would like you to know that we are not on any condition going to surrender to you, and do not even consider thinking that I will be in your hands by the time Henry Percy makes his way back from London. You'll be hard pressed to find your way to our camp. Only those who know where it is can find it.

Also, my uncle, Ronald Crawford has no part in this. Do not bother him again with even the smallest problems or you will answer for it one way or another.

And lastly, do not despair, my dear friend. We will *meet again someday. I know that you killed my father. We will have a*

reckoning, Jack Moore. We both know this. Do not sleep easy.
        Your Most Honored Enemy, William Wallace"

Jack smiled to himself, crumpling the letter in his hands and letting it fall to the floor. "That insolent little wretch. I'll show him when I find him again." He turned back to Simpson and saw that the man was quivering visibly. Moore looked him up and down. "So he said he got information out of you. What did you tell him?"

        "N-nothing, sir," Simpson said.

        "Nothing?" Moore repeated simply. "Nothing, you say? And yet he let you go without a mark. You must have readily given the information. Perhaps you will be just as willing to tell me?"

        "He-he asked for p-plans," Simpson said. "I just t-told him that you would look everywhere you could for him. There was nothing much else to tell."

        Moore nodded and seemed to think a bit and turned back to Simpson. "No, perhaps not. There isn't much more to tell, is there?"

        Simpson didn't answer. Was afraid to. His legs were shaking so much that he sunk to his knees, trying to keep the rest of himself from shaking as hard.

        Moore knelt on one knee so that he could look into the other man's eyes. He put a hand under Simpson's chin and raised his face. "Tell me, Captain. Do you fear death?"

        Simpson nodded slightly. Moore patted his cheek with a small smile.

        "That's good then," he said. "Because I'm not going

to kill you."

Simpson looked up at his commander with a glint of hope in his eyes. "Y-you're not, sir?"

Moore shook his head. "No," he said kindly. "Why should I kill you?" Simpson started to get a bad feeling in his stomach as he looked into Moore's eyes. The commander leaned closer to him. "But you'll be demoted. I can't have a captain in my army made a laughing stalk. And to make sure it doesn't happen again, I'm going to make an... *example* out of you." Simpson broke out in a cold sweat as Jack stood up and motioned to the other men who gathered around. "String him up by his thumbs," he said. "And call all the other men here to watch his punishment." He turned to Simpson again, who had renewed his trembling as the men rigged a rope over one of the ceiling rafters. Moore slid a wickedly shaped dagger from his belt and checked its sharpness against his thumb. He grinned dangerously at his former captain. "Now. What is it you were saying about William Wallace's camp?"

***

William and his sword-fighting group finished with their practices right before the midday meal was done and dispersed to go have lunch. Marion and Stephen were taking care of it, stirring up a bit of rabbit stew from the one Marion had shot the day before. William sat next to them, watching them out of the corner of his eye.

"What have ye been doing today?" he asked them.

"Nothing much," Stephen told him with his grin.

"Just talking and making this fine stew."

William nodded, still looking at them suspiciously, but figuring that if there were two people in his camp who were impossible to get information out of, it was the Irishman and the lass.

"So is it done?" he asked.

Stephen nodded. "Aye it is. Marion, call John and his men over here would ye?"

Marion left and William turned to Stephen. "So did the brave Captain Simpson cause any problems on yer march?"

Stephen grinned. "Nae. But if he had, he wouldn't have caused them for long after I had a wee bit of a talk with him. Just like when I first found him."

William smiled. "I sure am glad I have ye Stephen. If ye hadna had a...wee talk wi' the man, then I doubt I could have gotten anything out of him at all."

Stephen winked at him. "Aye. And once again, I bet ye're glad I'm on yer side?"

William grinned at him. "Should I be, Stephen?"

The Irishman started chuckling slightly, then it turned into a laugh that made his black eyes sparkle. William joined in and Stephen slapped him on the shoulder as his laughter subsided.

"Aye, William. That ye should be. That ye should be!"

Chapter Twenty

Another Encounter

Over the next couple of weeks, William picked up the pace of their training, knowing that one wrong move now could give them all away. They still had lads coming in who Ewan sent their way and soon enough, William had two score under his command. They had also gathered a good supply of weaponry for their army. The only problem with getting more and more people, was the fact that their camp was getting a bit crowded and they had to hunt more for enough food to feed them all. Ewan came almost every day to bring provisions like oats and flour to make bannocks and such things as that. He was teaching Marion how to cook and she was becoming quite a good chef. There was never a time when something wasn't bubbling on the campfire.

William had to send people hunting every day, usually in groups for safety in case they were to meet any Englishmen in the woods again. Between that and training, there was not much time for anything else but eating and sleeping and William did very little of that.

However, whenever there was an extra moment, Stephen took Marion aside and taught her how to use a sword and a dagger. They never told anyone else, thinking it best to keep it a secret, but the Irishman was making a fine swordswoman out of his student.

One day, they were sparring while William was busy teaching the sword fighters as he did every day. Marion stood her ground well and parried Stephen's attacks. Marion took the upper hand and started throwing strikes at Stephen. The Irishman changed to defense and stepped back, light on his feet. There was not a blow he couldn't parry, but Marion's striking was not inferior. After a while, Stephen knocked her sword aside and grabbed her wrist.

"All right, that's enough of that for now," he said to her with a smile and let her go. Marion dropped the sword to her side.

"Tell me truthfully, Stephen," she said. "How am I doing?"

The Irishman nodded his head. "Ye're doing really good, lassie. I daresay ye're learning better then the lads. Quicker too."

She smiled at this and sat down on a tree root. Stephen sat on the ground cross-legged beside her. She picked at the bark of the tree and sighed.

"What will it all come to, Stephen?" she asked suddenly.

The Irishman turned to look at her with his black sparkling eyes. "What do ye mean?"

"Jack Moore and his men. What will it all come to?"

Stephen was silent. Marion had never seen him at a loss for words, but he was silent for a few minutes before he turned back to her and spoke again. "I can't tell ye, Marion," he told her as if he was unused to saying the words. "I can't tell ye. It's...far away. I can only tell that our future is dark."

Now it was Marion's turn to be silent. "There's nothing we can't do if we try, Stephen," she told him. "And...William. He's the one who will try it. He won't stop and that's the truth."

Stephen smiled up at her again. "Sure and that's why we need to keep him safe. We're here to protect him. That's our job."

Marion smiled back at him. She reached out and clasped his hand. "Aye. That's our job."

***

Keith and Kerlie were leading a hunting party of five in the woods, hoping to find enough food to make a passable dinner for the camp. They were a couple miles from the camp for they had hunted the surrounding woods to exhaustion in the past few weeks and needed new ground.

Kerlie motioned his lads to spread out and cover more ground. He crept away from them, his bow drawn, and sharpened his hearing to that of a hunter. He caught a slight sound of movement in the trees ahead of him. He knew none of his companions were in that direction and so he crouched to his knees and closed his eyes, listening harder to try and place the sound so he could shoot. Before he could shoot, an arrow shot out of the trees in front of him and sliced across his arm.

He leapt up, dropping the bow and yanking the sword from its sheath. "Attack!" he cried. "Attack! Rally to me, lads! Rally!"

The six other lads Kerlie had come with rushed to his side and formed a tight formation at his back. Just at that moment, what looked to be about ten Englishmen rushed out of the trees and fell on the Scots.

Kerlie was the first to parry a blow. He clashed his sword against that of the Englishmen who attacked him and pressed it to one side, his instincts taking over. The Englishman sneered at him and tried to press harder, trying to shove Kerlie onto his back. But the young Scotsman stood his ground firmly and parried all the blows struck at him. The Englishman growled then and stuck out a foot, kicking Kerlie's legs from under him. The Scotsman fell heavily on his back, the breath whooshing from his lungs. He coughed, trying to get the air back into his lungs as the Englishman stood over him, readying for the deathblow.

"Kerlie!" Keith shouted out to his friend as he leapt

forward and struck the Englishman down with one sure blow. The man crumpled to the ground with a gasp and stayed still. Keith helped Kerlie to his feet. "Ye all right, mate?"

Kerlie nodded and ran off to join the rest of the fight.

It was over in a few minutes. The Scots soon had all the Englishmen pinned down. There were two dead and several with wounds. The rest dropped their swords and raised their hands as the Scotsmen stood them down, swords pointed in their direction.

Kerlie walked toward them. He turned to one and addressed him. "I trust ye're from Jack Moore?" he asked.

The Englishman nodded. "Yes, we are."

"Your business here?" Kerlie asked.

"Hunting," the Englishman told him. "We have to eat."

"And can ye not do that somewhere else?" Kerlie asked him.

The Englishman glared at him. "This is better hunting ground," he said.

Kerlie raised his eyebrow. "Oh? And have ye heard about the evil forest spirit that haunts these woods?"

The Englishman looked down his nose and snorted. "You fool me. I don't believe in that."

"Don't say that!"

Kerlie looked at the Englishman standing next to the one he was interrogating. The man looked scared and his eyes roved around as if he half expected to see the "evil forest spirit" come out of the woods. Kerlie grinned at him.

"Aye, that's right, my friend," he said. "Don't say anything against the spirits and the Fair Folk. Nothing good ever comes of it."

"Do you know where it is?"

"Shut up, Randall," the first Englishman told his companion and the other one stayed silent for a while. Kerlie gave him one last smile and turned back to the Englishman he had begun interrogating.

"Ye should listen to yer friend," he told him seriously. "I trust ye know what happened to the Captain Simpson?"

This shut them all up. They shared looks with each other and seemed to pale a bit. Kerlie caught this and a smile spread over his face. "Aye? I catch fear in the air? May I ask what became of Captain Simpson?"

"General Moore made an example of him," said the Englishman named Randall, his voice quivering. "I daren't speak the details."

"Well, think of it all again," Kerlie told them in a low voice. "Think over every detail of it. Now whatever it was, I can assure ye it was not nearly as bad as what the evil forest spirit would do to ye if he caught ye."

They were all silent again. Kerlie rested his sword over his shoulder. "But I willna let the spirit hurt ye. Nae, I have a better idea. Ye're going to go back to yer commander and give him this message in the name of William Wallace, commander of the Free Scot's Army: If we find any of ye in our woods again, we willna ask questions, but will immediately decide on a plan of action and there will most likely not be any of ye to send back to yer commander. Do ye understand that?"

The Englishmen nodded. Kerlie smiled at them. "Well, go on then, show yerselves out. And bring yer dead with ye. We're no' going to bury them."

The Englishmen didn't waste any time. They shuffled out of the clearing, carrying the two dead and were soon gone. Kerlie smiled to himself at their victory. He turned to the lads and gave them a grin. "Well, I suppose we could have eaten the Englishmen, but they were probably pretty bland. It's not like that fine Italian food our ancestors feasted on during the Roman invasion."

This earned him several guffaws and he sheathed his sword. "Let's get back and tell Wallace what happened."

"Kerlie, Donald's hurt," Keith said and Kerlie turned around to see him kneeling on the ground beside the young lad. Donald was leaning against Keith's arm and clasping a hand to his shoulder.

Kerlie ran to him and knelt down as well. "Donald, are ye all right?"

"I was stabbed," he said weakly as Kerlie ripped a strip from his cloak to press to the wound.

"It's no' too bad," he assured him with a smile. "Come on, we'll get ye back to the camp and see what Marion can do for ye. Here, put yer arms around my neck." Kerlie took the younger lad into his arms and heaved him up. "Keith, ye and the others pick up those weapons. Let's go, lads."

They started off on their way back to their camp.

They all had mixed feelings. Good feelings about their triumph. But dark ones about their new danger. The Englishmen were getting closer. They all knew this.

Stephen and Marion were the first ones to see the returning hunting party. They rose from their seats and ran to meet them.

"What happened?" Marion asked as she saw Donald in Kerlie's arms.

"We were attacked," Kerlie told them grimly. "Wish ye were there," he shared a wink with Stephen, but there was no light in either of their eyes. The Irishman looked at Donald's pale face and motioned to the camp fire.

"Here, let's get him taken care of," he said. "Come on."

They walked into the camp and sat Donald down against a log. He winced and Stephen knelt beside him and opened his shirt to see the wound in his shoulder. "Sure, it's not very deep. I bet it hurts though."

Donald gave him a rueful smile and closed his eyes as Stephen wiped the blood from him. Marion knelt beside him and looked over Stephen's shoulder.

"What can I do?" she asked him.

"Boil some water to wash this out," Stephen told her. "And see if you can find something clean to bind it with."

Marion did as he asked and by then, John and his archers had come over to see what was going on. John immediately ran to them and knelt beside the young lad.

"What happened? Were ye attacked?"

Keith nodded. "Aye, we were. But, Johnny, ye

should have heard Kerlie. He was so cool and cocky and he told those Englishmen just as good as Will would have!"

"Tell me, Keith!" Jacob said, coming up. "Tell me what he said!"

"What is going on?"

They all turned to see William coming up with his sword fighters. He looked around, seeing all the different expressions on his comrade's faces. "Tell me now!" he commanded. "What-is-going-on?!"

Kerlie stood up and turned to his friend. "Will," he started and began again. "Will, we were attacked in the woods when we were hunting. There was a hunting party of Englishmen there and they surprised us."

"What became of these Englishmen?" William asked, his face tight with worry.

"Two were killed," Kerlie told him. "The rest I sent on their way back to Moore with a message."

"What kind of message?"

"The kind ye would have given them," Kerlie said a bit proudly. "Dinna worry, Will. They willna be back."

"Aye, he scared half the wits from them!" Keith added with a laugh.

"*They* may not be back," William said in a low voice. "But Moore *will*. He willna give up that easily. There's nothing we can do about it now but fight back or die. Before long he'll find our camp and then we'll have to fight it out. Did we loose anyone?"

Kerlie shook his head. "Nae, William, we were lucky. Only Donald was wounded."

William looked a bit more relieved then he had before though still seemed to fight some inner battle. "Then at least we do not have to bury one of our own. Kerlie, see to that wound."

Kerlie suddenly remembered that he had been cut by the arrow that had first started the fight. He noticed that his whole right sleeve was bloody. He sighed. "Aye, Will. I forgot about that." Marion beckoned him over and cleaned the wound out with hot scalding water. Kerlie winced at the heat.

"Sorry," she told him gently. "Stephen says that the heat is good. It cleans it. This is pretty deep."

Kerlie shrugged. "When ye're in the middle of a fight, ye dinna have time to think about pain."

They looked over to one side and saw William pacing back and fourth by himself. He looked incredibly haggard with worry and decision. Kerlie shook his head as Marion bandaged his arm. "I dinna envy him the position of leader," he said. "Especially since he thinks he's all alone with it. He doesna understand that we're all here for support."

Marion tied off the bandage. "One day he'll wake up and see what we're here for. Dinna worry Kerlie. He will. I know it."

Kerlie still looked worriedly over to his friend. "I hope he does. He'll ruin himself like this."

William turned to his men after a while. "Stephen, is Donald going to be all right?"

The Irishman nodded with satisfaction. "Aye, I think

we caught the wound in time to clean it so it won't go bad," he said and tussled Donald's hair with a grin. "Ye just rest up, laddie. Ye'll be all right soon enough. Before long ye'll be able to swing yer sword again."

The young Scotsman smiled up at him, and William turned to Marion.

"Make some porridge for supper," he told her. "I dinna want anyone going out in these woods again tonight."

She nodded and started to get to it, taking the big cauldron up to go fill it in the stream. William looked around at the forty odd lads who sat around the fires. "This has gone too far," he addressed them. "Way too far. The last Englishman, the one Stephen captured, that was nothing. This, this is a different story. One of our lads has been hurt on account of Jack Moore's men. They're no' all gawks and numpitys. Some of them have brains and aren't afraid of anything. We can take no more chances now. It's kill or be killed. We are going to spend every day from this on devoting any extra time to learning the art of fighting. We will not stop until we have every move mastered. We can, I repeat, take no chances anymore. Something has to be done about the English. What? I see no other way then to fight them. If they willna learn, we'll fight them again. I, personally, will fight them until Jack Moore is dead. Until that day, our only priority is to learn and train and fight when need be. Do ye all understand that?"

There were nods and 'ayes' from the gathered lads. William turned his back to them and took the sword from over his shoulder. He ran his thumb over the crest on the crosstree. Jack Moore would pay soon enough. He knew it.

Chapter Twenty-One

Divided We Fall

The next few days they lived up to William's expectations, fighting every minute of the day they were not eating or sleeping. William drilled them hard, not taking any excuses. He was in a bad temper. He had not slept since the fight and only ate when John, Kerlie or Stephen pressed food on him. At night he would walk the camp restlessly, or practiced silently with his sword in the sparring field while everyone but the sentries were sleeping

One night, Marion woke up to see him shadow fighting in the field and got up in hopes of persuading him to go to sleep.

"William, ye'll make yerself sick if ye dinna sleep

soon," she warned him as he turned around at her approach.

"Leave me alone, lass," he growled at her. "I am already sick. Sick in the heart. I have a duty to my country and my command. I will no' fail them!"

Marion got a bit angry with him. She didn't like to be yelled at. "Oh, do ye? I wouldna have known. Ye go on about it so many times a day, I've learned to block it out. Sleep, Wallace. Otherwise ye'll end up passing out and then ye'll be an invalid. I dinna think ye'd like that very much."

"That's no' of yer concern!" William told her sharply, turning his back on her. "*Ye* best get some sleep though. It might curb yer tongue."

I have half a mind to knock ye out myself! she shouted silently, but clamped her lips tight shut and spun on her heel, going back to lay down on her pallet. She watched William stand on the field, resting sword on the ground and clasping the hilt tight with both hands. His shoulders were tense and shook slightly. She wondered silently as she drifted off to sleep again weather he was angry or if he was weeping.

***

The next morning started far too early for all the lads. William was calling them to a muster almost before they had eaten a quick breakfast. Ewan had come to make it for them and looked up, slightly surprised when William came over to them.

"Come on lads, hurry up and eat. We have work to

do."

Ewan looked over to Marion but she shook her head. "Dinna protest," she told him. "Ye best go too."

Most of the lads appeared in the training field still munching hot bannocks. William stood at their head, calling out his orders.

"John, ye take a fourth of them and Stephen and Kerlie, the same. Let's practice our tactics again. Come on."

They all took up their wood swords and separated into their respective groups. They fought tiredly. It was a hot day, it now being midsummer and though the woods were usually cooler due to their shade, there was no wind that day to move the air around. All the lads sweated heavily but they all kept on without complaining, not wanting to excite William to anger.

They were about half an hour into their fighting, when John noticed Donald starting to lag. He stopped his division and went to the young lad.

"Are ye all right, Donald?" he asked him kindly.

"My arm is starting to hurt," he said. "Can I rest for a few minutes?"

John looked to all his lads, seeing that their faces were red and their hair plastered to their foreheads with sweat. "Let's all take a break," he told them and led them in the direction of the water bucket.

William noticed them leave the ring and turned to his division. "Keep practicing, I'll be right back."

He went over to John who sat wiping his face and neck with a wet cloth from the bucket. "What are ye doing?

It's no' time for a break yet. We just started."

"They're exhausted, William," John told him tiredly, motioning to the lads who took turns drinking from the bucket and splashing water over their flushed faces. "They need a wee rest."

"We dinna have time for a 'wee rest'!" William cried, his already flushed face getting redder. "Do ye not understand our danger, John? Donald could have died! Do ye not understand that?"

John stood up to face his friend in the eyes, his anger starting to boil as well. "Aye, I understand. I also understand that his wound will never heal properly if he is made to fight constantly! Ye're killing us all with this, Will. We dinna get to eat enough, nor sleep enough. We're up late into the night and rise way before the dawn! Ye're no' succeeding in making an army, ye're only succeeding in running us all down so that if we ever *did* have to meet the English in a battle we wouldna have enough energy to fight it and we would all end up dead. Dead just like yer father." John immediately wished he hadn't mentioned William's father, but he was mad and knew it would strike true.

"My father!" William shouted back at him. By now the rest of the camp was turned to him, but he didn't notice them. He was too busy venting his anger at John. "Ye leave my father out o' this, John Graham! He was a good man. He never would have betrayed his country and friends, and he didna! He *died* defending them! Would ye do the same?!"

"Ye know I would, William," John told him. "Ye know that. I told ye as much many times!"

"Do ye still hold by it?" William pressed, his blue eyes flashing.

"Ye're no' yerself, Will," John said starting to get worried for his friend. He reached out to touch William's arm. "Are ye fevered?"

William swatted his hand away. "Leave me alone! I'm fine. Stop worrying about me!"

John clenched his fists. "I only worry about ye because I'm yer friend, Will. We all are."

"Well, stop!" William shouted at him. "I canna take it anymore!"

John's anger snapped then. "Ye know what I canna take anymore? I canna take how ye seem to think ye're better then all of us. Ye know in yer heart that ye would be nothing without the rest of us, but ye willna admit it. So ye take total control and try to run us into the ground! This willna do, Will. We all have respect for ye. Do ye want to loose that?!"

William looked taken aback at his outburst, but he soon regained his composure. "Is that what ye think, John?" he asked slowly.

"Aye, it is," John told him firmly.

William nodded slowly. "I thought so. Well, if ye're having second thoughts, perhaps ye should leave."

"That's no' what I meant by that, William," John told him.

"I wasna suggesting it," William told him firmly. "I

was ordering it."

John took a step back as if he were slapped. His anger was replaced with astonishment. "Ye...Ye want me to leave, Will?"

William nodded. "Aye, John. I do."

The other Scotsman swallowed hard and nodded once. "As ye wish. I'll leave. Good bye, Will." He turned on his heel and strode out of the camp.

"John," Marion said, and was about to go after him but Ewan held her back.

"Nae, lass. Stay out of this."

She turned to him with tears in her eyes. "Oh, Ewan, what are we going to do about William? He's not himself."

"He'll realize what he's done soon enough," Ewan told her quietly. "It's no' the time for us to help him."

William stood where he had and stared after the place where John had disappeared. He looked at the lads who had been sitting behind John and seemed to realize for the first time that they really did look haggard and Donald's face was creased in pain which he strove to hide. He turned around at last and addressed his company.

"We'll..." he started and cleared his throat. "Um...We'll...That's enough practice for the day." And then he turned as fast as he could and strode to his sleeping place where he sat down and buried his face in his hands. *What have I done?* he wondered.

***

Jack Moore had called all his men together. He had been musing ever since his hunting party had come back with two dead and another message from the rebel Wallace. Oh yes, he had made an example out of them too. He had flogged them so hard, they wouldn't be able to wear a shirt for a week. He smiled at the memory and looked at his men as he rubbed his scruffy goatee.

"I suppose you are all wondering what we are going to do," he said to them. He enjoyed the look of worry on their faces. "Well, we're going to go to the woods and we are going to look around until we find the rebel Wallace's camp. I am going with you this time to make sure things are...done right." He looked specifically at the no longer captain, Simpson. The man looked down at his feet quickly. Moore smiled thinly and started speaking again. "We are not going to stop until we have Wallace in our clutches. Is this all understood?"

Everyone nodded and said, "Yes, General Moore."

Moore smiled to himself again and snapped his fingers at Simpson. The man came forward like a whipped dog, and in truth, he wasn't much more than that, Moore thought with an inward chuckle. He put a hand to Simpson's shoulder and enjoyed the fact that he shrunk away from him.

"Mr. Simpson," he said. "You will go mounted as I am. That way you can be right where I need you. You are to be my scout. Perhaps you could manage to show us the way to where you met up with this 'evil leprechaun' as you swear on your eyes you saw?"

"I do not know if I can find the place..." Simpson started to say when Moore dug his fingers into his shoulder, where he knew there was a wound. Simpson winced.

"What were you saying?" Moore asked him.

"I would be...glad...to show you the way, my liege," Simpson told him, his lip trembling.

"Excellent," Moore said and let him go, beckoning to the stable boy who stood close by with two horses. Moore took the reigns of one and motioned Simpson to take the other. He mounted up and turned his horse around so that he could address his men again.

"Come on then, my bold hunting hounds, let's go see if we can catch some Scotsmen." He dug his spurs into his horse's side and started off through the town. He was determined to get somewhere this time. He wouldn't stop until he had.

***

John didn't know how long he was stumbling through the forest. He wasn't aware of his surroundings. From the sunlight seeping through the trees, he knew it couldn't be too long past noon. But he wasn't thinking of that either. All he could think of was his fight with William. He kept playing it over and over again in his head and he couldn't get rid of it. He gave a hopeless cry and pressed his clenched fists to his temples, trying in vain to get it out of his head. Weather it was his distracted mind or if it was just chance timing, he would never know, but one minute he was looking down at his feet and the next, he was running strait into an English soldier. He quickly looked up and around and saw he was staring at the mounted figure of Jack Moore.

"Well, well, well," the Englishman said in his growling voice, a satisfied grin on his face. "What have we here?"

Chapter Twenty-Two

Defiant

John just stared at them for a moment in shock, not knowing what to do. Then when his mind cleared a bit he suddenly realized that he didn't even have his sword in his belt. He started backing away slowly, then turned and ran as fast as he could through the woods. Jack Moore signaled his men.

"Archers, bring him down. Aim for his legs," he commanded them.

The archers stepped to the front of the troop and began to shoot at John. The Scotsman evaded the first few by dodging around trees, but one well-aimed shot struck him in the upper leg and he fell with a muffled cry, sprawling on the ground. Moore spurred his horse into movement and rode over to where the young Scotsman had fallen, his men following him.

At the sound of hoof beats, John raised his face from the loam and looked up into Jack Moore's evil face again. He knew he was caught. There was no way he could get away from all of them with his wounded leg, but if he was going to die, he wanted to see it coming. He put on a brave face as Jack Moore made his eyes bore into his new prisoner's.

"So, I have caught you," he said. "I hope you will cooperate with me. If you do, no more harm will come to you, if you don't...well, let's just say it will be far from pleasant. Get him on his feet, we're going to set up camp for the night."

John swallowed hard as two soldiers stepped forward to haul him to his feet none to gently. He knew he was going to be tortured. He would have to be strong.

"Come on you nasty little Scot," one said with a sneer. "You're not going to get the best of us this time!"

They went a little farther into the woods to a clearing and Moore dismounted from his horse, commanding the men to set up the tents and get a campfire going. The men who held John came over to their commander and dropped their prisoner at his feet. Moore looked down at him with his cold eyes and John stared back at him unwavering.

"Are you one of Wallace's scrawny little followers?" Moore asked him.

John nodded. "Aye, I am," he said defiantly.

Moore beckoned Simpson over to him and the man stepped over cautiously, making sure he was just out of Jack's reach. "Mr. Simpson, do you know this boy?"

Simpson nodded. "Yes, my liege, he was one of the ones who interrogated me."

"Ah, very good then," Moore said with a dangerous grin. "We will be repaying a favor as well today, it seems." He reached down and grabbed a fistful of John's hair, raising him painfully to his feet. John tried not to wince as he stood face to face with their mortal enemy.

"We'll see what we can get out of you," Moore told him menacingly. "You'll beg for death before I'm done with you."

"I wouldna be so sure," John said, somehow finding defiance to put into his voice. "Us Scots arena afraid of pain like ye cringin' Sassenachs." He spat at Moore's feet.

The next thing he knew, he was lying on the ground, the whole right side of his face throbbing. He tried to raise himself, but Moore kicked him in the ribs and John fell onto his back with a gasp. He looked up and saw Moore standing over him with a face red with anger.

"There is nothing I hate more than defiance and insolence to one's betters!" he told the Scotsman dangerously. He reached down and hauled John up by the front of his shirt. "Someone bring me rope," he called to his men. Several soldiers ran to assist him and he pressed John against the trunk of a tree and had him tied to it.

"There," Jack said with a bit of satisfaction. "Now we can get to our business." He looked John in the eyes and the Scotsman didn't look away. "I trust you know that I must find the rebel Wallace as an express duty to England? You're going to help me with that. You are going to show me exactly where his camp is and when he sees that I will kill you if he does not give himself up, then, if he is as loyal as everyone seems to think Scots are, he will come along with me without any trouble at all."

"You'd never get that far," John told him firmly. "William is determined to kill ye. He *will* do it."

"Not if I was to kill you first," Moore told him with that awful sneer. "And I will. Slowly. So if you value your life and the life of all your friends, then you will tell me."

"I will not," John said and Moore hit the other side of his face so that now it was throbbing like the right side.

"Maybe I didn't make myself completely clear," Moore told him. "Do I need to repeat myself perhaps?"

John shook his head. "Nae."

"Then do you agree?"

"Never," John told him defiantly.

Moore was silent for a moment. He looked John over, spotting the broken off arrow still sticking from him. He turned to him with what he thought was a kind smile. "Oh, forgive me, I forgot you were shot. Let me take that out for you." He reached out and yanked the arrow from John's leg, making the Scotsman cry out in pain. Only the ropes that bond him kept John from falling to the ground.

"Are you still so sure you do not want to show me the camp?" Moore asked as if he were trying to get a child to do something.

John shook his head resolutely. "Do what ye will to me. I'll never tell ye," he said, his voice weak

Moore nodded slowly and took a knife from his belt. He ran his thumb along it to check its sharpness. Simpson backed away involuntarily. Moore looked at his reflection in the knife blade and asked again. "I'll give you one last chance. Will you do it?"

"NO!" John shouted and gasped as Moore sliced him down his left arm with the sharp blade.

"This blade is sharp," Moore told him as he wiped the blood from it with his thumb. "But when I kill you in front of Wallace tomorrow, I will use the dullest one I can find." He sheathed the dagger back in his belt. "I won't do any more to you now because I at least want you coherent tomorrow when we break camp and you are to lead us to your camp. But don't get too comfortable. There are some very...unpleasant things coming." And with that he turned away and spoke to his men. "Go and see what you can find in these woods to eat. We'll have a nice supper before our victory tomorrow."

John shuddered in pain and the fear he had struggled to keep inside. It was not fear only for himself but for all his comrades. He knew that Moore wouldn't spare them. And William...William wouldn't fight if he knew it would put anyone's life in danger. He'd give himself up and...

John refused to think of the only outcome this could have. He closed his eyes, half swooning, and tried to will his mind to go blank.

***

It was almost evening now. The whole camp was silent. No one dared speak nor did they have all that much to say in the first place. Marion sat with Stephen and Kerlie by the campfire roasting some fish they had caught in their little burn that day. Ewan had gone back to Crawford's house to make him dinner that night so they were cooking alone. John still hadn't come back.

William stayed in his sleeping place though he didn't sleep. Couldn't. His mind was too troubled. He was so ashamed of what he had said. He wouldn't have minded if Jack Moore had come right then and killed him where he lay. Finally, when his mind wouldn't give him any peace at all, he stood up, smelling the cooking fish and went to the campfire. He noticed that several of the lads tried their best not to stare at him, though he didn't care. He thought he must look like a monster. He certainly felt like one.

Kerlie looked up at him with a kind smile. "Want some fish, William?" he asked his friend.

William shook his head once and stayed standing. "Has...has John come back yet?" he asked them haltingly.

They shook their heads silently. He caught sight of Marion looking down quickly as she brushed a tear from her eye. He felt even worse then, knowing that his comrades regretted his decision as much as he did. He sighed, a new worry clouding his mind. All he could think of was the English patrols that seemed to be in the woods of late.

"Ye should eat, William," Stephen told him with concern on his face.

William shook his head again. "Nae, I'm going to go find John and bring him back. Ye all stay here. It's best if I go alone."

"Will..." Kerlie started to stand up but Stephen pulled him back down.

No one said anything as William positioned his sword across his back and left the camp. When he was gone though, Marion turned to Stephen, tears in her eyes.

"Shouldna someone go after him?" she asked. "John could be captured by the English and William will just get himself killed."

Stephen shook his head. "Nae, lassie. I think this is something we need to leave to him. I don't think it a good idea for any of us to interfere."

***

William walked through the woods, not really knowing where to look. He went the same way that he had seen John go earlier and tried to follow his trail through the loam and bruised undergrowth. There was no rhyme or reason to his trail and William began to wonder weather it was John's trail or if it was just one that belonged to a deer or one of his lads who had gone out hunting.

But then he found a torn piece of fabric caught on a low tree branch and he took it into his fingers and felt it's coarse texture. It was a light brown color. The same shade as John's sark.

He knew then that he was going in the right

direction and followed on a little bit faster than he had been. He found several strands of John's hair on another branch a little farther on and went even faster. Then he came to a place where there seemed to be more then just one set of tracks. He knelt to study them and instantly saw the prints of a horse. And heavy mailed boots.

His heart beat heavily in his chest and he searched frantically in the damp loam for more signs. That was when he saw the blood spattered on the dead leaves.

He sat back on his heels and looked in disbelief at the sight. How could he have been so stupid? If John was dead, he would never, never forgive himself. When he got his sense back again, he realized that there was not nearly enough blood on the ground for a fatal wound. Nor did he know for a fact that it was John's. He began to feel better but only slightly. It is never a good idea to lie to yourself.

He was just thinking of his next plan of action when he heard voices and looked around frantically for a hiding place. He immediately found a tree with a huge hollow under its roots and took no time in leaping under it and squeezing himself as small as he could.

He was just in time, for only a few seconds later, two English soldiers showed up in the place he had been standing just a few moments before. They were talking together as they searched for something that could pass as dinner.

"Maybe if we're lucky, we can shoot a deer," one said. "Or at least a few rabbits."

"Aye," said the other and William could hear him

rustling around in the undergrowth. "I wonder if we'll get a victory feast when we capture William Wallace."

"Huh," the first man snorted. "Not from Jack Moore, we won't. Maybe when Lord Percy gets back though. At least he treated us like humans."

"Shh," the other man said warningly. "You never know who's listening. If Jack Moore hears ye, he'll have ye strung up just like he did to poor Captain Simpson. He's a broken man now. He was never really brave, but at least he had some constitution."

"Aye," the first man said in agreement. "I wonder what that evil fairy threatened to do to him? I tell ye mate, I wouldn't want to meet that devilish being face to face."

"Nor I," said the other Englishman. "Though I can't imagine it would be too much worse than what Jack Moore does to those who displease him."

"Like that Scot today," said the first man with a laugh and William's heart skipped a beat. "That's different. He's a prisoner of war. They're not supposed to be treated like guests of honor. But we, as men who serve under Moore, shouldn't be tortured like that."

William didn't listen to the rest of what they said as they moved farther off into the woods. What had they done to John? He immediately regretted having asked Ewan once about some of the atrocities Jack Moore had performed. The Scotsman had been reluctant to tell them then, and now William's mind was full of the horrors he wished not to think of happening to one of his good friends.

"I have to save him," he said to himself. "Dinna worry, John, I willna let him torture ye anymore."

He stayed where he was silently as he watched the woods darken with the setting sun. The two Englishmen had come back the way they had left and seemed to have something for their troubles. William marked their progress as he watched their backs and figured their camp wasn't too far away. Now that it was dark, he could actually see the light of a campfire in the distance between the trees. It would be several more hours before he could make his move. He wanted to make sure the camp was asleep. He had no idea weather John would be guarded or not, or where he was in the camp, but he did know that he was not leaving until he had gotten him out of there. He touched the blade of his sword, still slung across his back. He had a feeling that anyone who got in his way would be taken care of quickly enough.

***

John watched the camp fall asleep. The smell of the cooking food had made his stomach growl and he realized he had eaten nothing but a bannock all day. *What does it matter?* he thought to himself. *They're going to kill me tomorrow anyway.*

Moore hadn't set a sentry over him and he was indifferent with it. The knots were tight around his arms and chest and he knew that even if he did manage to get out, he could never find the strength to get back to the camp before it was too late.

He watched as Moore retired to his tent and the rest

of the Englishmen laid down to sleep around the campfires. There were two sentries but they seemed to be sharing in a bottle of something one had pulled from under his cloak and John didn't think they would be awake for too much longer. He was right in his assumption, for it was only half an hour past when he saw them nod off and lean against the trees at their backs and soon he could even make out their snores as they slumbered deeply.

He closed his eyes himself, so tired, though not in a position comfortable enough to sleep. He listened to the crackling of the campfires, burning low for the night and the snoring of the men. Then he heard something else. It sounded like stealthy footsteps walking through the damp loam of the forest floor. He lifted his head and looked out into the surrounding trees to see if he could spot it. Perhaps it was an animal, but it seemed too big and too loud for that.

He caught sight then of a shadowy figure slinking through the trees, edging slowly around the edge of the camp, trying to stay out of the light cast by the fires. In a sudden moment of delirium, he wondered if there were in fact, fairies living in the woods as Stephen seemed to believe whenever he saw something just a bit out of the ordinary.

He nearly jumped right out of his bonds as he felt a hand on his shoulder from behind and a voice that was so familiar to him. "John? Is it ye?"

"Will?" the Scotsman asked as his friend came around the tree and he saw his face in the dim light of the fires. William seemed relieved to see him alive. He took his dirk from his belt and started cutting the ropes that bound John.

"Hush," he told him firmly though not unkindly. "We dinna want to wake anyone up. There now, that's all the ropes. Och, I'm sorry I forgot, ye're probably hurt."

John had fallen to the ground as William cut the last of the ropes away, his legs simply giving out. He had to laugh though, whether in relief or just joy at seeing that William was no longer mad at him. He grabbed his friend's forearms as William reached down to help him up and stood gingerly, the pain in his leg taking his breath away for a few moments.

William put his shoulder under John's arm and started to lead him off into the woods. "Come on, mate. We'll get ye back to camp and see to yer wounds. I'm just glad ye're all right."

"Och, Will, I'll never be able to thank ye enough for coming to save me like that."

They were silent for a moment, then William turned to his companion in the moonlight. "John, I'm sorry for what I said earlier. Ye were right. I wasna myself. I dinna ken what came over me."

John waved his hand tiredly. "We both said things we shouldna have, Will. Dinna worry. Even the best of friends get into the worst of fights."

William smiled. "Aye, I suppose ye're right. Though it's foolish to make enemies out of our brothers in arms when we have so many in other places."

"Aye, it is," John agreed. They were by now a good half-mile from the English camp and William felt that John was lagging a bit, his breath coming in labored puffs. Finally John slipped from William's grasp and lay on the forest floor, clutching his leg with a pained look on his face.

"Och, Will, I canna go anymore," he said breathlessly. "Let me rest here for a few minutes."

William knelt by his friend with concern. "Och, John, I'm sorry, I should have seen to yer wounds. Where are ye hurt?"

"I was shot in the leg," John said and motioned to the bloody wound on his thigh. Not able to see very well, William felt the wound and his hands came away sticky with blood.

"John, I'm a fool," he said angrily. "Ye'll bleed to death if this isna bound." William ripped several strips from his cloak and made a makeshift bandage out of them. When he was done with that, he turned his back to John and spoke to him.

"Here, John, get on my back, I'll carry ye," he said.

"I'm as heavy as ye, Will," John protested, though weakly.

"Ye'll never make it back otherwise," William told him, and John knew he was right. He wrapped his arms around William's shoulders and his friend stood, staggering slightly under his weight, but as soon as he grew accustomed to it, he started off again into the woods, back to their camp. William grabbed hold of John's arms to steady him and new worry filled him as he felt how hot he was.

"John, ye're warm, do ye feel fevered?" he asked seriously.

"I don't know," John murmured to him. "I don't know why I should feel warm. I'm rather cold."

William moved even quicker then. He only hoped someone would know what to do for a fever.

It was another hour before they got back to camp and everyone looked up with relief as they saw William come in with John, though they immediately became concerned when they saw his condition.

"Stephen, Marion, I need yer help," he called to them hurriedly and they immediately ran to his aid. William laid John down as gently as he could on his bed and put a hand to his forehead. "Stephen, he's burning with fever," he said quickly. John had fallen into delirium on the way back and now his eyes fluttered slightly as they laid him on the bed.

Stephen looked to Kerlie who was hovering behind him. "Get a bucket of water from the burn," he said.

Marion brought over two torches she had lit from the fire and stuck them in the ground by John's bedside so they could see more clearly. William was untying the makeshift bandage he had bound John's wound with and shook his head as he saw how deep it was in the light. He took a clean rag Stephen handed him and pressed it to the wound that was still bleeding slightly.

"I have no idea how much blood he's lost," William

told them and Stephen reached over, taking the rag himself and looking at the wound closely.

"Sure, it's deep," he said grimly. "He most likely lost a bit of blood. Looks like someone ripped an arrow out of him. Your handy work, Will?"

William shook his head, anger coming back into his features. "No, not mine. It was Jack Moore's handy work. I only wish he were here right now. I'd love to shoot *him* full of arrows and rip them out one by one."

Marion wet a rag from the bucket Kerlie had just brought back and wiped it over John's flushed and sweaty face. "Dinna worry about Jack Moore right now," she told William. "We have to worry about John."

William turned to Stephen. "Do ye know how to treat a fever?" He asked.

The Irishman sighed. "I only know how to dress a wound to prevent fever. Once it's set in, I don't know any more then ye."

"We have to do something for him!" William said frantically. He turned in desperation to Marion. "Do ye know anything?!"

"No," she said a bit harshly. She hadn't meant to snap, but she couldn't help it. "I've told ye I dinna know about healing."

William ran a hand though his hair and sighed in desperation. "We have to do something," he said again.

Stephen put a hand on his shoulder. "We'll do our best, Will," he said.

William sat down at John's head and bathed his face

and chest with the cold water wishing he could do more. All the lads in the camp had gathered around to see what had happened. Their faces were all stony and none of them spoke a word. None of them seemed to dare.

It was late into the night now, long past midnight and William and his closest companions still sat by John's bedside. His breathing had become labored now and he moaned and tossed in the throws of the fever. It was worse now. He was so warm, William could sense his heat from where he sat beside him. He kept bathing him with cold water, but doubted that it was really doing anything.

Eventually, he could take no more of it and stood to walk off to a more secluded place. He couldn't stand to see John in so much pain anymore. Especially since he knew it was all his fault. He left the light of the fires and found a dark spot in the woods where he leaned his head against a tree and kicked its trunk several times. His foot hurt from the impact, but he didn't care. "How could I be so stupid?" he asked over and over again to himself. "I've put my own comrade's life in danger. I don't deserve to be a leader. I may as well give myself up to Moore."

"Don't start thinking that, William."

He turned around with start and saw Marion standing behind him. He could barely make out her expression in the darkness, but he knew that she was not angry with him for once.

"Why are ye here?" he asked her with a grunt. He still didn't feel like being civil even if she was.

She stepped closer to him. "I just thought it might

give ye a bit of comfort to be able to talk to someone," she told him gently. "It always helps me."

William was silent for a moment, breathing hard then he sighed and leaned back against the tree. "It was my fault, John is laying there," he said softly, his voice barely above a whisper. "I should be the one dying, not him."

"John is not dying," she told him though immediately regretted it. She knew he spoke the truth and wondered why she didn't just tell it to him.

"Yes he is," William told her firmly, his voice catching. "And it's all my fault."

Marion stepped forward until she leaned against the tree trunk beside him. "It's not your fault, William," she told him gently. "It isn't."

"Yes it is!" he shouted at her and stepped away from the tree. "*I* was the one who sent him away. If I had never fought with him over a stupid wee matter, then he would be fine right now and nothing bad would have happened!"

"William..." she started, but he held up a hand to stop her, turning away.

"Dinna say it again," William told her. "It only makes me feel worse. I like it better when someone is to blame, even if it's me. It doesna seem fair that someone else should die for my mistake." His voice broke again, and this time Marion caught a slight sob in it. He fell to his knees and buried his face in his hands. "I canna loose him too," he said in a muffled voice. "I already lost my father and my blood brother, I canna loose my other brother too."

Marion felt tears unbidingly fall down her cheeks.

She knelt beside William and put her arms around his shoulders comfortingly. He rested his head against her shoulder as if all his energy had left him.

"We'll find a way," she told him. "We'll save him. Now think, William. Is there anyone ye know who can help him?"

He was silent for a moment then he sat up suddenly and looked into her eyes with the first ray of hope she had seen from him in days. He grabbed her hands in his and clutched them tightly. "Marion!" he cried. "I know exactly who to go to. I'll be back within the next couple hours! Thank ye!" He kissed her quickly on the cheek and then leapt to his feet, running off to the horse stable.

Marion stood and watched him run off. She put a hand to the spot where he had kissed her and smiled. Aye, she had no doubt that things would turn out all right now.

Chapter Twenty-Three

Brothers in Arms

William rode his horse faster than he thought he had ever ridden it before in his life. He tore out of the woods and went galloping down the glen to his uncle's house, standing very lonely looking in the moonlight. He leapt off his horse as he got there and handed the reigns to a startled stable gillie who was blundering out of the barn, rubbing his eyes.

"Water him quickly, I'll need him again soon," William told the gillie and raced off to the kitchen and burst through the door.

Ewan was sleeping on his pallet by the fire and he leapt up, dagger in hand, as William burst in.

"For pity's sake, William!" he cried. "What ails ye? Is

something wrong?"

"Ewan?" the voice came from the hallway and in another few seconds, Ronald Crawford appeared tussled and barefooted with a robe hurriedly thrown over his nightshirt. When he saw William standing there in the kitchen with his desperate look, he immediately lit a lamp so they could all see each other. "William what are ye doing here, lad? Are ye out of yer mind?"

"Uncle Ronald, John was wounded, I need to get him help right away," William said in a rush of words. "Please, tell me this. Is Lady Margaret still living here in Ayr?"

"Your old nurse?" Ronald asked. "Aye, she lives right in town. She'll be the one to help John. Ewan, go with him and show him the way."

The red-haired Scotsman grabbed his plaid he had been using as a blanket and belted it on, grabbing a cloak to conceal his features. He handed one to William as well. "Here, take this, we should take no chances of being seen."

William declined. "Dinna worry, Jack Moore and most of his men are in our woods. We have nae fear of them tonight." He and Ewan swept out of the house and went to the stable where the gillie stood with William's horse at the watering trough.

"Saddle me a horse, Rob, and quick," Ewan told the man and he hurried off to the barn to get another mount for Ewan.

The two Scotsmen were off again in a few minutes heading for the town of Ayr. Ewan took the lead and trotted his horse through the deserted streets to the house of the lady who had been William's nurse when he was just a bairn. She was the best healer for many miles and people had always come to her for advice and remedies. William trusted that she would be able to help John.

Ewan dismounted first and was soon followed by William. They tied their horses up and Ewan knocked on the door.

There was a few minutes pause then William heard footsteps on the other side of the door and it opened revealing an old woman with a heavy shawl wrapped around her shoulders.

"Yes?" she asked then smiled when she saw who it was.

"Ah, Ewan, what brings ye here tonight? Has someone taken ill? Who is this fine young lad, ye have with ye?"

William stepped forward and took her hand in his. He couldn't help but smile despite the circumstances. "Margaret, it's me, William."

"Not William Wallace!" the old woman said, taken aback. She took William's face in her hands and looked him up and down. "Oh, my dear, ye have grown so much since the last time I saw ye! Come into the kitchen where there's light." She led them in even as William explained.

"I'm afraid we didna come for a social call, Margaret," he told her. "My friend has been wounded badly and he's suffering from a high fever. Ye're the only one I know who can help him."

"How long has he been like this?" Margaret asked, immediately taking up a satchel and looking around her room for the things she would need.

"He was wounded earlier today," William told her. "An arrow wound. He's been fevered for...maybe five hours now."

She nodded and put some fresh white linen into her bag as well. "Yes, I imagine his fever worsened?"

William nodded. "Aye. We have to go now. I just hope we already arena too late."

Margaret hushed him gently. "Shh, William. Everything will be all right." She looked at him for a few moments. "Oh William, ye look so much like yer father. And I dare-say ye take after him in mind and heart as well as looks."

William nodded. "Ye speak the truth, Margaret," he told her.

"But take my advice and do not come back here in the light of day," the old lady told him as she checked through her bag one more time to make sure she had everything she needed. "That awful man Jack Moore has been asking everyone if they know anything about ye. I'm sure Ewan and yer uncle both have warned ye of the dangers though."

Ewan nodded. "Aye, we have, m'lady, but William is strong-willed. It was lucky for us this night that Moore and his men are away."

Margaret doused the candlelight and left the room. "Just do be careful, William," she told him with motherly concern. "Now are we ready to go?"

"As long as ye are, we are," William told her and they went out of the house to mount their horses again. Ewan took the old lady onto his own saddle and they started off again for William's camp in the woods.

"I wish we could bring him to my uncle's house," William said sadly. "But I think it would go badly."

Ewan nodded. "Aye, it would. Now, may I ask how John was wounded and how ye came to know that Jack Moore and most his men are hiding in the woods?"

So on their way back, William related the story sadly, his face burning with the recollection of how foolish he had been. Ewan simply smiled kindly at him and said. "Let's just make sure it doesna happen again, eh?"

William nodded, finally feeling better than he had all day. They were soon at the camp just as the sky began to turn a shade of dark blue in the coming dawn. Ewan leapt down and helped Margaret off the horse as Keith and Jacob came to take care of the horses. William led Margaret over to John immediately. Marion, Stephen and Kerlie still sat around him administering to him the best they could. They all looked up with relief as they saw the old healer with William.

Margaret took over immediately, kneeling beside John and putting her ear to his chest to hear his heartbeat. She frowned a bit as she felt his forehead and realized how hot it was, but she sat back on her heels and opened her bag, rooting through it. She turned to Marion.

"Help me with this, will ye lass?" she asked and

Marion moved over to her side.

"Yes?" she asked.

"Could ye boil me some water? I need to mix it with this," she said as she pulled a dried herb out of the bag that had been wrapped in a cloth. Marion nodded and went to the fire where she boiled some water and got a bowl to mix the herb in. Margaret smiled at her as she brought her the things she needed.

"Thank ye. What's yer name?"

"Marion," the lass said as she watched Margaret crush the plant into the bowl and pour a bit of the water over it. She reached out and gently undid the bindings of John's wound and inspected it with a critical eye.

"This will help it keep from getting infected," she told them as she smeared the paste she had made of the plant onto the wound. Once she was done with that, she took the rest to spread over the wound on his arm. Then she took the linen out of her bag and tore it into strips, making bandages to bind up his wounds with.

Once she was done with that, she took a little vial out of her bag and popped the cork of it, then she raised John's head and poured it between his lips. He coughed a bit on the liquid, though he swallowed it without too much trouble. By now, all the occupants in the camp had calmed visibly as if Margaret's presence made everyone easy. She took up a blanket that lay at the foot of the pallet John was laying on and pulled it up to his chin, tucking it around him.

"There," she said. "He should be fine now. His fever

should be broken before too long." She looked around at the exhausted and relieved faces that watched her in the dim light of the early morning. She smiled at them all kindly. "You all need rest, my dears. Go to sleep. I'll watch over him. Then Ewan and I will make you a fine breakfast when you wake up."

Everyone took her up on that, and soon they all lay down by the fires and fell into an exhausted sleep. William still sat beside John, looking down into his now calm face. Margaret looked at him and saw how tired he was.

"William you look terrible," she told him. "How long has it been since ye last slept?"

"I dinna rightly know," William said. "Several days, I think."

Margaret stood and took his arm, pulling him up beside her. "This won't do, Will! Come here, where do ye sleep?"

She took him to his bed between the roots of the tree and he sunk down on the pallet there. Margaret pushed him down even as he protested and tucked his blankets up around him as she had done when he was only a wee bairn.

"Dinna say anything, William, ye just need to rest. Go to sleep."

As if by some magic, his eyelids drooped and he slid off into a wonderful dreamless sleep, comforted by the fact that everything was all right now.

Chapter Twenty-four

Recovery

It was not a happy day in the camp of Jack Moore. Jack woke that morning to voices speaking low outside his tent. He cracked one of his eyes open and listened to them.

"Should we wake him up?" one mused.

"I daren't, you do it," protested another.

"Not me," said a third. "Let Simpson do it."

"You want to get that poor man in more trouble? No, I suppose *I'll* do it if anyone does it."

Jack slipped silently from his cot and walked over to the tent flaps where he could see the outlines of the men standing outside. He stood there a moment, letting them draw the flap back slowly and smiled when they started, seeing him standing there only a few inches in front of the first man.

"What is it you need to tell me?" he asked them.

The man in front gulped visibly, the color draining from his face. "Um..we...uh..."

"Y*eeesss*..." Moore encouraged, gesturing with his hand for him to go on.

The man gulped again and stuttered out his reply. "Well...um...General Moore...it...um...it seems that we have...*lost* our prisoner."

Moore stared at him, still with that slight smile on his face. He raised an eyebrow. "You mean he...died?"

Working up his courage, the man shook his head. "No, m'lord. He's...gone."

"Left?"

"Yes, sir."

Moore's expression didn't change. He looked around at the men who stood in front of him. He nodded his head slightly as if he understood them. "Oh, I see. He *got away*." The men looked at him warily, backing away slightly, not really sure of what to think of the situation.

"Where are the men who I put on watch last night?" Moore asked.

The men all looked to each other, then out of their group, they shoved forward two drowsy-looking men with fear plastered on their faces. Moore stepped slowly toward them.

"I set you on watch last night," he told them, his voice still calm. "I fed you, I gave you drink, I gave you reliefs and this is how you repay me?"

The men were quaking in their skin by now, and Moore kept stepping toward them in slow measured strides. He was soon only a foot from them.

"This is how you repay me," he repeated, snatching an empty flask from one's belt. "Drinking yourself to sleep when you are supposed to be watching over the camp so that our prisoner would not escape. What have you to say for yourselves?"

"We...we didn't think he would escape, him being wounded so," said the fattest of the two. "I don't know 'ow he did it unless 'e had help."

Moore nodded. "Aye. Help that wouldn't have *gotten here* if you had stayed awake."

"We're sorry, sir," said the other of the two. "It won't happen again."

"I know," Moore told them with a smile and put a hand to each of their shoulders. "I know it won't." They cringed as he squeezed them hard. He reached up and patted them on the cheeks. He turned to his men. "Take these two dogs and truss them up. I want them taught a lesson before we go."

He turned back to the two men, pulling a knotted whip from the back of his belt. He smiled evilly at them, his scar crinkling. "I do hope you like the forest, my dear lads," he told them menacingly. "For I think you'll be staying here for a good long time."

They trembled as the men came and tied them up as Moore cracked his whip.

***

It was already noon by the time William woke that day. He felt better than he had for days, once again refreshed and his mind felt clearer too. He sat up and stretched his tense muscles that he had actually let rest for the first time in days and looked around at the camp. Some of the lads were still curled up under their cloaks and plaids asleep, but others were sitting beside the fire and talking or eating. He got to his feet and went over to the place where he had left John earlier. He looked to be asleep so William sat quietly by his side and took his hand gently.

"I hope ye're feeling better, Johnny," he whispered to him.

"I am rather, thank ye, Will."

William was slightly surprised as John opened his eyes and a small tired smile touched his lips. He squeezed William's hand back lightly.

"Aye, I feel all right, though I'm rather hungry. No one thought it decent to bring me something."

William laughed at him. "All right, well, I'll go see what Margaret has for us and I think I'll join ye."

William stood and went to the campfires. Margaret looked up at him from where she was sitting, stirring a pot of something that smelled sweet and made William's stomach growl hungrily. She smiled at him. "Well, look who's finally awake," she teased.

He grinned. "Aye, well, like I said, I havena slept for several days."

She took up a bowl and dished out some porridge into it. "Here ye go, Will. Enjoy it. I managed to bring some honey along."

William's mouth watered as he took the bowl. "Wonderful," he said then suddenly remembered his invalid friend. "Och, I almost forgot, John is awake and he says he's hungry."

"Ah," said Margaret and dished out another bowl. "I thought he would come around soon. His fever broke about an hour ago." She stood up and went with William to his friend. John looked up at them with a smile. He looked pale but not as bad as he had the night before. William sat next to him and John sniffed the air appreciatively.

"Och, is that honey I smell?" he asked.

"Yes it is," Margaret told him.

"Wonderful," John said. "Help me sit up, Will."

William put an arm behind John's shoulders and raised him so that he could rest his back against a tree trunk. He winced and touched his bruised ribs gingerly. Margaret knelt beside him and gave him the bowl of porridge.

"Eat this, lad, and I'll check yer wounds and re-bandage them."

John spooned the porridge hungrily as did William while Margaret unbound John's wounds and looked them over. She smiled up at him as she tore new bandages. "They'll heal well, John, dinna ye worry. Now if ye can put that bowl down for a minute, I have to bandage yer arm again."

John reluctantly put his bowl aside as Margaret

wrapped his arm up once more then she put it back into his hands when she had finished. "There ye go, Johnny lad, eat up and get yer strength back."

"Does that mean I get second helpings?" he asked her with a cheeky grin as he handed her his empty bowl.

She smiled at him and took it. "Of course ye do, love," she told him.

William handed her his own as well. "What about me?"

"Ye too, Will, but dinna tell the others," she warned. "Though that Irish lad of yers charmed his own second helping off of me. Ye just canna say no to him."

William laughed. "Aye, that's Stephen for ye. But he can be very scary to the enemy. He threatens them and all with a smile on his face too."

John laughed and William joined along. Then the wounded lad winced and caught his breath. "Och, I forgot my ribs," he said.

"Sorry, I didna mean to make ye laugh," William told him.

"That's okay," John said. "We havena laughed for a while. We need to do it more."

William nodded in agreement. "Aye, that we do." He was silent for a moment then he said, "I for one am going to change the way we work around here. From now on, we work as hard as we can, but we still take time out to be friends and comrades and brothers in arms like we used to be. We founded our resistance on that, and I never should have let it fall apart." He grinned sheepishly. "And

I dinna think it too out of the question to have a few ceilis now and again."

John gave him a mischievous grin. "Hmm, that sounds like ye wish to dance with Marion again."

William shoved him lightly, but couldn't keep a smile from spreading over his lips. "I think ye had best stop talking, Johnny, and get some rest before ye say something really off the mark."

"But my porridge," said John as Margaret came back with their second helpings.

"Well..." William said. "After that then."

They laughed again and both felt wonderful. They knew that they would never have discord in their own camp again.

***

The next few days in the camp were slow and steady. John got better and better and he was soon able to move around a bit with the help of a crutch Kerlie had made him. By John's request, Marion had taken up the archery training. William had been slightly reluctant of it, but he agreed finally. Things were different between them since the night John had been sick. Marion still pondered the fact that he had kissed her. She wasn't sure it meant anything or not. He had been swamped in every emotion known to man and she figured it was most likely just a reaction of relief more then anything. Though she herself had a new respect for him. He was more like the lad she had first met now. She found herself watching him teaching his sword fighters one afternoon. He looked very brave swinging his sword. She couldn't imagine an Englishman in his right mind not being afraid of him.

"Marion?"

She turned and saw Keith looking at her, holding his bow pointed to the ground. "How did ye want us to shoot this target?"

"Oh, sorry," Marion said, shaking her head and turning back to her command. Her first command. She smiled as she looked at them. "We're going to swing it so we can get the feeling of shooting moving targets. Remember, the English aren't just going to stand still and let ye shoot them. This will also help you when you go hunting." Donald stood by the new target they had rigged that hung over the branch of a tree so that it could swing. He gave it a good shove and then leapt out of the way as Marion gave them the signal to fire. There was a scattering of arrows that hit it and the surrounding trees.

"Good first try," Marion told them encouragingly, giving them kind smiles. "Let's try again."

She hadn't noticed that William had come over to stand several feet behind her, watching her as she encouraged her command. He smiled slightly, admiring her easy, kind way of teaching. After the lads had shot off another round, he spoke out, "You are doing a fine job, Commander Braidfoot." Marion spun around, slightly surprised to see William standing behind her, his arms crossed over his chest. She smiled as it brought to mind the day he had first caught her doing archery, though now it was an amused smile on his face and not an annoyed expression.

"Thank you, General Wallace," she nodded to him with a curtsey, trying to keep from giggling. "I am glad to be of service to you since John is not in the best."

William nodded back at her. "Well, ye are that." His smile turned apologetic then. "I fear I will have to ask yer forgiveness though. I didna at first see ye for who ye are, but now, I for one am happy to serve with ye." He held out his hand to her and she took it and shook it as heartily as any man. She grinned.

"Thank ye, William," she told him. "But I will have to beg pardon myself, as well, for I can assure ye I know how annoying I can be at times."

William laughed at this, his blue eyes sparkling. "Aye, but I suppose that is the way of lasses is it no'?"

Marion giggled then. "I suppose it is. For, it is known that women were only put on this earth to vex men."

"Isn't that the truth," William said good-naturedly.

Marion turned serious then. "It's good to see ye back in yer normal humor again, Will," she told him truthfully. "I was worried about ye when ye weren't sleeping and eating."

William nodded. "Thank ye. I promise, I willna do that again. I understand the consequences it has now." He sighed as he looked over to John leaning against his crutch while he was talking and laughing with Stephen and Kerlie. "Aye, dinna worry. I'll try to act the commander *and* the comrade from now on." He smiled at her again and nodded. "Carry on then, Commander Braidfoot. I have some things to see to before dinner." Then he turned and left.

Marion sighed happily as she watched him leave, then she turned back to her command. "All right, let's finish up practice so we can get something to eat," she told them. "Donald, swing that target again, let's try this until we can all get good hits."

Chapter Twenty-five

Two Men from the Woods

It was several days after the incident with Jack Moore now, and William's camp was recovering from their hard experience. That morning, William sent Stephen and Marion out to hunt while he stayed and took up his training again with Kerlie. John sat against a tree beside them, braiding twine for new bowstrings. With all the new lads coming day to day, he was always busy making new bows now, and he was glad of it, for he knew he would go mad otherwise, not being able to do anything.

As they took a quick break for drinks, William crouched down beside his friend and offered him the pitcher. John drank from it and handed it back to William, wiping a hand across his mouth.

"How are ye?" William asked him.

John smiled slightly. "Well, William. I'm feeling much better. Still sore when I move, but not nearly as bad as it was before."

"Good," William said, smiling back. "Dinna worry, ye'll be fully recovered again soon and doing all the things ye used to."

John nodded. "Aye, I ken. Margaret really is a good healer. Though I dare-say it was her good food more than her care that got me back on my feet so soon."

William laughed. "Aye, I dare-say it is! She's a right good cook, even better than Ewan." He stood as the lads came back into the field. "Well, I guess it's back to work with us, then we can have some lunch."

John nodded. "Sounds good to me," he said, taking up his strings again.

William took his place again with Kerlie at the head of the contingent. "All right, lads, we all know what to do now. Show me all ye know."

They clashed away with their swords and William looked on in admiration and pride at his army. They were exactly what he had been hoping for.

***

Marion and Stephen crept through the woods on the lookout for anything that might be good for their supper. So far, they hadn't come across anything that seemed likely, so they traveled deeper into the woods. There was a noise then that sounded like someone or something approaching. Stephen signaled Marion to crouch behind some bushes and she dropped behind them as the Irishman slid off in the other direction behind the noise he had heard. Marion had her bow taught and ready for whatever might pop out of the woods.

Stephen slipped silently through the trees, keeping a sharp ear on the blundering sound. It was big, sounded almost like two beasts. It couldn't be anything but a deer and yet, deer weren't usually that loud. It almost sounded like...

Then Stephen came upon his quarry. It was none other than two men stumbling through the undergrowth. They were both wearing the outfits of English soldiers and Stephen knew they must be up to no good.

He smiled to himself and crept up close behind them, reaching out to put a hand each on their shoulders. The two men froze stiffly. Stephen leaned close to their ears and whispered, "What is your business in our woods?"

The two men were struck speechless and Stephen took the opportunity and quickly grabbed a rope from his belt and bound their hands up. Marion came out of the bushes in front of them, her bow still raised and taught.

"Who are ye?" she asked them. "What do ye want?"

"Aye," said Stephen. "Why dinna ye tell us that?"

"Who are *you*?" one of the men asked, the fattest one.

"No one to be trifled with," Stephen told him with a grin. "Besides that, you don't need to know."

"You can't talk to us like that," said the other.

"We're soldiers of the crown. You're nothing but an outlaw."

"Soldiers of the crown, ye say?" Stephen said incredulously. "If ye are, then where are yer weapons? I see none on ye, nor do ye look very well kept for being in the royal army. In fact, it looks like ye've been in these woods for days on end."

The men refused to say any more so Stephen shrugged. "Well, if you don't want to tell me any more, I'll just take ye to my leader, and he'll get it out of ye." He shoved the two men in front of him and knocked his bow, pressing the tip of the arrow into the fat one's back. "Come, Marion, take care of that other one. If he tries to get away, shoot him."

Marion stepped forward and pressed her arrow into the other man's back then she and Stephen set off for their camp with their new prisoners. The lass turned to grin at her companion.

"Do ye always come back with nothing but English captives?" she teased him.

He grinned back at her. "Sure, it seems to be a growing coincidence. We'll have to go back out and find some food after William decides what to do with these two. That is, if we don't end up just eating them. They look like they have enough meat on their bones." He prodded the fat man with his arrow again.

The man grunted and turned around to glare at the Irishman. "I know you're only bluffing."

Stephen gave him as evil a grin as he could muster,

which was actually very frightening. "Think only what ye wish to think, my friend," he said.

Marion stifled a giggle as they pressed on through the woods with their captives. The two Englishmen stumbled along, pricked by the points of the arrows as they were led in the direction of the Scots' camp. When they finally came to it, Stephen and Marion pressed their captives harder and shoved them into the camp. William and the other lads looked up at them curiously from where they were sitting eating lunch. The young Scotsman stood and grinned at his friends.

"Well, Stephen, once again, I send ye to get food and ye come back with Englishmen. Are ye bent on eating them?"

Stephen laughed good-naturedly. "Well, that's just the luck I have, Will. I didn't get anything out of these two, but I thought you might like the honors this time. Then we'll go back and do some real hunting."

William stepped up to the two men who were still bound and looked them over. John and Kerlie came up to flank him. "Stephen, I think ye can unbind their hands. They have no weapons, and as long as ye keep yer arrows pointed at them everything should be fine." He looked the men in the eye then and folded his arms across his chest. "Well, tell me then, what are ye doing here? It is a very rare thing to see two English soldiers running around the woods with no swords and looking as if they've been here for several days. Are ye lost, perhaps?"

The fat man twisted his lip contemptuously at

William. "I am not going to tell a scruffy whelp anything. You're uncommon bold for one so young."

William grinned at him. "I'm Scottish, that's why. And I would reconsider that, if I were ye. Stephen there knows some very...creative... forms of torture. I'm sure he could get the information out of ye even if I canna."

The other man took a more pleasant tone with William. "Please, we've been lost in the woods for days and we've hardly eaten anything. We're starving!"

William looked them over skeptically. "Well, ye hardly look it, but I suppose that if ye give me the information I need, then I'll make sure ye get something to eat. How does that sound?"

The two men looked at each other and then turned back to William and his companions. "Fine, what do you need to know?" the fat one asked.

"Where is Jack Moore?" William asked them sternly.

"Not 'ere," the man grunted. "He left us here to rot after he flogged the hides off of us."

"And what, might I ask, caused him to do that to ye?" William asked, sounding as if he were making light conversation.

The man glared and pointed at John. "Because we were supposed to be watching *him* but he got away. Not our fault!"

William smirked slightly. "Oh, did he? Well, Johnny, I suppose ye should apologize to these gentlemen then, for the inconvenience ye caused them."

John smirked back. "So sorry, gentlemen. Meant

nothing by it, ye ken."

The fat man's face turned red as he realized they were being mocked. "We don't bandy insults with the likes of yew!" he sneered.

William turned to him with cold eyes. "As a captive in my camp, ye shouldna be having the say at all."

The man glared back at him, but said nothing more. William turned to his companion and addressed him instead. "Okay, so Jack Moore left ye here to rot. Now where is he? Has he gone back to Ayr?"

The man nodded. "Aye. He has."

"What are his next plans?" William asked him.

The man shrugged. "I don't know."

"Are ye sure?" William asked.

"I'm only a soldier," the man pleaded. "I don't know anything. We are never told plans unless we have to enact them."

William nodded slowly. "All right. But ye most likely have an *idea* of what his next plan might be. Would ye care to elaborate?"

"No, we wouldn't!" the fat man shouted. "We've already been tortured enough, we're tired, hungry, and we just want to get out of these cursed woods!"

William nodded understandingly to them. "Aye, my friends, I understand. These woods are rather deterring for those who do not know them. That is why you should stay out of them. These are our woods. They are not meant for people who do not know them. They can be the ruin of them. Stephen knows a story about a man who stumbled in here unawares." William turned to wink at his companion.

Stephen nodded solemnly. "Aye, the story of Fin O'Flanagan. Wandered in here in the dark of night and was captured by the Fair Folk who invited him to a dance and when he walked out again, it was a hundred years later and he didn't think more then a few hours passed."

The men didn't look sure whether they should believe the Irishman or not. Finally the fat man snorted contemptuously. "We don't believe in yer fairy stories, Irishman. Yore all soft in the 'ead. Now we told ye what ye wanted, how about some food?"

William held up his hands. "Not quite yet. I still think ye know more about Jack Moore then ye're willing to tell. We need to know all we can. Ye're not getting food unless ye tell us."

"We know nothing!" the fat man said. "Not all Englishmen you catch will be willing to tell ye whatever ye want under pain of torture. We're not all fools and afraid of pain!"

"Ah, finally, a tough one!" Kerlie said with a cheeky grin. "What are ye going to do to him, William?"

William pretended to think. "Well, I dinna want to start torture right away, Kerlie. I think a few days without food will do them good though. They may very well talk."

"You said you'd feed us!" the fat man cried, obviously angry.

William shook a finger at him as if he was a naughty child. "Correction. I said I'd feed ye *if* ye gave me the information I needed. Since ye refuse, ye can sit and contemplate what ye are going to tell me, and when ye think of it, *then* I will give ye food!"

The man's face turned bright red with anger. "There's no way I'm letting a mere lad do this to me! This camp is full of nothing more than young whelps who should still be home listening to their mothers! I'm not doing *anything* you want us to!"

The other man nodded agreement and the two of them stood there with their arms crossed over their chests, not moving or speaking.

William shrugged. "All right, if that's the way ye're thinking, I canna make ye do anything ye dinna want to. But know that our 'mere lads' outnumber ye about twenty to one, and if it came to a fight, who do ye really think would win?"

The man scoffed. "Ha, fight! I'd love to see how well ye seem to think ye can fight! I'd be sure to take a few with me if it came to that! No lad can fight against a man in the army of Edward I of England."

"Is that so?" William challenged. "Well, the next time ye see old Longshanks, ye can tell him this: I, William Wallace, hold myself personally responsible for the restoration of freedom in Scotland and its Free Scots Army and when it comes to war, he will be the sorry one. Will ye tell him that?"

"Do ye think I'm daft, lad?" the fat man laughed contemptuously. "When I get out of here, I'm going to personally tell Jack Moore that there is nothing here but little boys playing a game and when he finds that out, he'll march through these woods until he finds ye, and then he'll kill ye one by one. How do ye like that?"

"Why are ye so sure, ye'll ever get out of here?" William asked him coldly. "We don't always let prisoners go, ye ken." He turned to his companions. "John, Kerlie, get their hands tied up again. Then take them to a safe place and make sure they are secure. And make sure they have nothing to eat until they tell us what we need to know." He turned and started back off to the campfires.

John and Kerlie went over to the two men and reached for their hands to bind them. A look passed between the fat man and his companion and before the two Scotsmen knew what was happening, the fat Englishman had grabbed Kerlie's sword and shoved him to the ground so hard that he hit his head and lay there dazed. The other man had grabbed John's sword at the same time and shoved him hard so that he overbalanced on his crutch and fell with a gasp. The two Englishmen ran forward with the swords raised, heading strait for William's unprotected back.

"William!" Marion screamed.

The young Scotsman whirled just in time to see the fat man's sword start to swing down at him. He instinctively raised an arm over his head. And then both the men stopped in their tracks. They staggered to the ground and lay there unmoving. William took a closer look and saw that they each had an arrow protruding from their back. He looked up and saw Marion and Stephen standing there with their bows raised. He didn't say anything for a few seconds as all the camp lads looked in awe at what had just happened. Finally, William stepped forward carefully, stepping over the bodies and then quickened his pace as he saw his companions on the ground. He crouched down by John and helped him up. "Are ye all right, mate?"

"Are *ye*?" John gasped as William took him around the waist and heaved him to his feet again. Marion handed him his crutch and he steadied himself. "William, I thought he was going to kill ye!"

"So did I," William admitted as he went to kneel by Stephen who was seeing to Kerlie. His comrade was sitting dazed but all right. He looked from William to the Irishman with confused eyes.

"What happened?" he asked.

"Nothing that came of anything," William said, relief finally washing over him. He looked to Marion again. "Thanks to some."

She blushed slightly. "I canna let them murder our leader," was all she said.

Stephen pulled Kerlie to his feet and they started over to the campfires. William motioned to the two dead Englishmen. "Keith, ye take some men and find a place to bury them farther from the camp. Marion, Stephen." He turned back to them. "If ye could, go back out and see if ye can get us something for dinner. If ye want, ye can try yer luck at fishing in the burn."

The two nodded and went off to do what he asked. William sat down between John and Kerlie, sighing heavily. He ran a hand through his tangled hair and closed his eyes. John put a hand on his shoulder.

"Everything will be all right, Will," he said. "Ye're just lucky to have such good and loyal friends." He smiled. "We all are."

William forced a small smile and sat up straighter. "I count that blessing every day, Johnny, and that's the truth. I'd be dead long ago if I didna."

"Och, I think ye'd make it," Kerlie told him with a wink. "Though ye may no' be as happy."

William laughed a bit then. "Aye, ye're probably right." He put his arms around their shoulders and slapped them on the back. "But as it is, I am terribly glad to have loyal companions like ye."

That night they sat around the fires roasting fish and talking quietly amongst themselves. None of them mentioned what had happened earlier that day, though they were all thinking it. William was oddly quiet as he ate. Marion sat beside him, and she could see that he was thinking deeply about something so she didn't try to interrupt him.

After they had finished eating, William stood and addressed the lads. He looked out at them, his face glowing in the firelight and they all sat rapt as they listened to what he had to say. "Comrades," he began. "We all know that eventually we will end up fighting. We all know that we canna stay here in hiding forever. It *will* come to battle with Jack Moore. I ken ye all know this and I also ken that ye are all ready. We have trained for long months and we have all gotten better and better. I have no doubt that we could give the English a good fight if it came to that. And it will. War is on the horizon. There's nothing we can do to stop it. We may be able to delay it, but stop it, nae. And why should we? Fighting is in our future. I have sworn to kill Jack Moore. He slew my father and he wouldna hesitate to kill me as well, or any of ye here. I promise to do my best to prevent that, but I have learned that a leader can only do so much, and though he is responsible for whatever goes on in his army, he canna stop everything that happens. But remember this, my lads, we fight for freedom, and freedom alone. There is no bigger or better prize to be had than that. My uncle told me once that freedom was the best of things. This is certainly the truth. Without freedom, ye canna enjoy anything that life gives ye. Without freedom, there is truly no reason for being. That is why we must fight to uphold that right of freedom, not only for ourselves, but for the whole of Scotland. Freedom is the reason we fight. English tyranny canna last forever. And it willna if we have anything to do with it. Will ye fight with me for that right?"

There was a deafening cheer from the gathered lads. William knew that not one objected to it. "Comrades, sons of Scotland, this is the day for our fight. It is coming. We all must be ready for it." He drew his sword from across his back and struck it into the ground between his feet. "My fellow patriots, we will go to battle with the cry of freedom on our lips and we will show the English that we are no' afraid of them! That we willna stay under their tyranny anymore! We are Freemen! Freemen and Scotsmen! And it is as Freemen and Scotsmen that we fight, and if we fall on the field it will be as Freemen and Scotsmen we fall. England canna take away that freedom any more then they can take away our right to be Scotsmen!" He raised his sword in the air. "Alba gu Brath!"

"Alba gu Brath!" the whole camp took up his cry whole-heartedly.

Marion shouted along with tears falling down her cheeks. The sight of William standing with his sword raised above his head speaking such true words to his men brought them to her eyes. *She* would fight with him, to the death if need be. Watch him stop her this time! She caught his eye as he looked over his cheering companions and he smiled at her. She smiled back and held up a hand to him. He nodded then turned back to sit down by the fire. Marion sighed in anticipation. The fight was near. She could feel it.

Chapter Twenty-Six

A Foolhardy Venture

The next few weeks they spent training hard for battle. William had his lads split into two groups and made them stage battles between themselves. It was good practice, rather fun, and all the lads seemed to enjoy it a lot. They all tried to take it seriously however, though there was usually a lot of laughing and joking amongst them as they practiced.

William was leading one "army" that day and John, who had recovered sufficiently, was leading the other. They were lined up on either side of the training field facing each other. William and John stood at the heads of their "armies" and were taunting each other before they charged.

"Is it that ye're taking yer time? Or is it that ye're just too scared to fight?" William shouted across the way.

"Oh?" John countered. "I was going to ask the same of ye! If ye're so bold then why dinna ye make the first move?"

"Och, so that's what it comes down to!" William said. "All right then, lads, let's show them what we can do, shall we?" He raised his wooden sword and started forward, his lads behind him. John also started forward and the two "armies" met in the middle, clashing their wooden swords together heartily. Stephen struck Keith a blow across the back and the lad staggered and pretended to fall.

"Hey, ye killed me, ye crazy Irishman!" he shouted as he lay on the ground, covering his head so as not to get trampled.

Stephen laughed insanely and ran off again. William and John fought one on one, leader against leader, laughing breathlessly as they tried to beat the other down. William struck him a blow to the shoulder but John kept up his guard and finally struck William a blow to the head. The Scotsman stumbled unsteadily to the ground with a grin plastered on his face. "All right, all right, ye win this time," he said.

John grinned back at him and gave him a hand up. "That was a braw fight. I say we should have some lunch though, what do ye think, Will?"

William nodded, rubbing his head ruefully. "Aye, I'm famished. Let's go see what Marion and Ewan have cooked up for us today." There were always bruises when they were done, but they all laughed heartily, as they rubbed their minor hurts, sitting down by the fires.

Ewan smiled up at William as he came to sit beside him. "How was the fight today, William?"

"Good," William replied as he excepted a bowl from him. "I think the lads will do fine in a real fight. This stew looks delicious."

They all ate heartily, hungry from their exertion that day. When they were done, Ewan stood to take his leave.

"I had best be getting back to yer uncle's house," he told William.

The young Scotsman stood as well. "I think I'll come with ye, Ewan. I want to see my uncle again."

Ewan shrugged. "All right. I dinna think it will be too dangerous. Jack Moore hasna come again since that one time."

William nodded and turned to John, Kerlie and Stephen. "Ye're in charge," he said. "I might stay the night so I'll probably be back sometime tomorrow. See ye then."

"All right, Will," John said. "Be careful."

William nodded and took a short sword from the armory and grabbed his cloak, then he and Ewan strode off through the woods on their way to Ronald Crawford's house.

William looked around at the brightness as he stepped out of the woods. It was not something he was used to now since he had been living under the tree cover for so long in the half-light. Ewan grinned at him.

"It is a lot lighter out here, isna it?" he said.

William nodded. "Aye."

They started off again and soon they were at William's uncle's house. Ronald Crawford had just come back from a ride and was helping the groom curry out the horse he had been riding. He looked up as he saw William and Ewan coming up the path to the house.

"Well, William, to what do I owe this surprise?" he asked.

William smiled at him as he waved. "No surprise, Uncle, I just thought I would come to visit ye tonight."

Ronald left his horse to the care of the gillie and led his nephew inside with a hand on his shoulder. "I'm glad to see ye again, Will, and not for only a few minutes in the middle of the night."

William grinned ruefully. "Well, that was a necessity."

"How's John?" Ronald asked as they went into the house.

"All better now," William told him happily. "Able to raise a sword again anyway."

"And that's all that matters, I suppose," Ronald said blandly with a small sigh.

"In our position, aye, Uncle," William told him seriously. "When it's life or death, it's best to choose life."

Ronald nodded slowly. "Aye, perhaps ye're right, my lad." He smiled then. "But let's not talk of such things right now. I got a letter from your mother the other day. She asked after your health. I tell you true when I say that I daren't tell her the truth of it. The only thing I told her was that you were well. I didn't say anything about your fishing incident."

William looked to him gratefully. "Thank ye, Uncle. I fear for her health sometimes. Losing my da took a lot out of her and I think she's no' in the best of health anymore."

"I fear the same thing," Ronald said as they sat in the common room. "Aye, William, ye canna let her lose ye too."

"I'll do my best in that," William told him, stretching his feet out to the fire. He settled into the chair he was sitting in, contented. "It feels odd to have a roof over my head again," he said with a slight laugh.

Ronald laughed with him. "I can imagine it is! I don't know how you can stand to live in such a dark wild place."

William shrugged. "It's in my blood, Uncle. My father was no stranger to hardships, knight that he was. He often slept out in the woods and heather when he was on the march."

Ronald nodded. "I suppose you're right." He sighed tiredly as he gazed into the fire. "William, I know what you're doing is dangerous, and I have said before that I do not approve of it, but hear me now when I say this. I am extremely proud of you. I look at you and I hear you speak and I see your father. I know that I could never attain such bravery as you do, William."

William smiled slightly at his uncle. "There are different types of bravery, Uncle. I know that you are brave. Perhaps not in the same way as that of myself and my father, but ye are brave."

Ronald Crawford smiled slightly at this and kept staring into the fire. "Perhaps, Will. Perhaps."

They were silent for the next few minutes then William spoke up again. "While I am here, Uncle, I wondered if I could write a letter to Uncle Richard and have ye send it for me. I told him I would keep him up to date on what was going on. I haven't had the time or resources to do it since I went into the woods so I forgot."

"That's fine," Ronald said, standing to go over to his desk where he pulled some paper and ink out of the open top. "You can write it right here if you wish. I am going to go talk to Ewan about fixing a room for you. That is if you are planning on staying the night?"

William nodded. "I had planned on it. I wished to go and see Margaret tomorrow as well before I went back to my camp."

Ronald looked a bit uneasy then. "Be careful going into town, William, though I know I don't have to tell you that."

William nodded. "Dinna worry, Uncle, I'll take utmost precautions. I wish everyone would stop worrying about me. Ye all ken I can take care of myself."

Ronald nodded and forced a smile. "Yes, I know. I'm sorry, Will. I just haven't realized yet how much older ye have gotten in only these past few months."

He left William to his writing and went off to find Ewan. William sat down at the desk and dipped the quill into the inkwell and started penning a letter to his uncle. It took him a while, making sure he mentioned all his friends and their adventures lightly so as not to alarm his uncle in any way. When he had finished, he folded it up and sealed it with his Uncle Ronald's seal and put it into his belt pouch to give to the messenger later.

He left the parlor and went into the kitchen where he found Ewan getting things ready to make supper. He smiled at William as the young Scotsman came in.

"Who do I give a letter to, Ewan?" William asked.

"There's a messenger who comes every other day to take the letters from yer uncle," the redheaded man said as he straitened up from the fire, pushing his hair from his damp forehead, flushed from the heat. "I'll take it for ye, if ye wish, and make sure it gets to him."

William thanked him as he handed his companion the letter and sat at the little table where Ewan had a lump of dough he was kneading. He pushed the heels of his hands into it until it formed a smooth ball that he put on a paddle and pushed into the oven. William watched him work silently, then Ewan turned around to smile at him.

"I left one of the maids to get a room ready for ye. It's the same one ye had last time," he told him as he took up a sack of potatoes and some carrots and put them on the table. He took a seat next to William and started peeling them. William took his dirk out of his belt and began to help him.

"Thank ye," he said as he brushed some peelings off his lap. "I was going to go see Margaret tomorrow morning before I left to go back to camp. Ye dinna think it's too dangerous do ye?"

Ewan shrugged. "I ken ye can take care of yerself. As long as ye keep low, nothing will happen to ye."

William smiled at him. "Thank ye. At least some people still know what I'm capable of."

Ewan smiled gently at him. "Yer uncle doesna mean any harm, Will. He only worries about yer safety. Mostly for yer mother's sake, I dare-say."

William nodded. "Aye, I ken. Och well. It's my own fault, though I really canna help it."

Ewan shook his head. "It was no one's fault but Edward Longshanks, curse him." He turned and spat on the floor. "I hope someday ye are able to meet him face-to-face, Will. And when ye do, ye'll have to tell him what we're all thinking about him."

William smiled slightly at this and turned to look at Ewan. "I hope I do too, Ewan. And I will tell him every bit of what we're thinking. Though first, I hope to meet face-to-face with Jack Moore."

Ewan nodded understandingly. "Aye, I ken. I hope ye get the chance to do the same favor as he did yer father, Will."

William nodded grimly. "So do I, Ewan. So do I."

That night after dinner, William bade his uncle and Ewan goodnight and went up to his room where he sighed in the relative comfort and slipped out of his boots and plaid and crawled into the soft bed. He moaned happily as his always stiff and sore body relaxed and he dropped off to sleep almost instantly, in the knowledge that there was no danger there.

Chapter Twenty-Seven

The Wrong Move

The next morning, William woke reluctantly, not eager to get out of the comfortable bed, but he could smell Ewan's fresh bannocks cooking in the kitchen below and soon the growling of his stomach forced him to get up and start the day. He laid his plaid out on the floor and pleated it then he lay on it and belted it around his waist and stood up, tucking it up in his belt. He grabbed his sword and cloak and went down to the kitchen where Ewan smiled up at him just as he was cooking the last of the bannocks on the griddle.

"Yer uncle said this would wake ye up," he said. "I know as much anyway. It always seems to be the only wake up call in the camp. Forget the pipes, I say, when bannocks and porridge can work such wonders." William laughed along with him as he sat down at the table and piled several bannocks onto a plate and covered them with butter and jam. "Aye, I say the same thing, Ewan. I'll be off right after breakfast. Is my uncle up yet?"

Ewan nodded. "Aye, he's taken his breakfast to the common room."

William stood, taking his breakfast up as well. "Thank ye, Ewan. I'll see ye again before I leave."

He left the kitchen and went to the common room where he found his uncle sitting eating at his desk in the corner as he looked over several things. Ronald Crawford looked up as William came in and smiled at him.

"Good morning, William. I trust ye slept well."

William grinned. "Ha, after sleeping at the foot of a tree for months, that bed near killed me," he said good naturedly as he took a seat by the fire and started eating.

Ronald smiled at him. "I suppose it might have that effect."

When William had finished his breakfast, he stood to take his leave. "I should be going, Uncle. I ken that Margaret will probably wish me to stay for lunch and I need to be back to the camp by tonight otherwise they may start to worry. Thank ye for keeping me the night."

Ronald stood to say farewell to his nephew. "It was nothing, William. Have a good trip, and say hello to Margaret for me, will you?"

William nodded. "I will do that. Good bye." He went back to the kitchen and dropped his plate off with Ewan.

He belted his sword on and positioned his cloak over it so that it was concealed. Ewan gave the cloak a few tugs to make sure it would stay where it was supposed to be.

"See ye tomorrow, William," he said. "I'll be at the camp in the morning with some more provisions."

William smiled and nodded. "Thank ye, Ewan, see ye then."

He left the kitchen and stepped out into the yard. He waved to several of his uncle's maids who were taking the washing down to the river and they waved back with giggles as he passed. William made his way casually into the town keeping up the appearance of a rouge or traveller as he looked around from street to street, always on the lookout for English soldiers. He made his way to the place where he knew Margaret's house lay. On the way there, he had to pass through a busy part of the town where a lot of the tinkers and traders had set up their booths. He caught sight of one of his uncle's gillies walking off with a net of fish he had just sold half of to a vendor. He raised a hand slightly to William as he passed and William nodded in return. He walked on casually when he heard something behind him that made him turn.

"You, Scot, who are yew taking those fish to?"

William narrowed his eyes as he saw several English soldiers crowding around the young gillie. He stopped in his tracks, watching what would transpire. He knew it wouldn't be good.

"I'm taking them to my master, the sheriff," the gillie said shakily, trying to push past them, but making no headway.

"Oh, really?" the man who had spoken before said. "Ye would do better to take them to our General Moore. Let me take them off yer hands for yew." he made a grab for the net but the gillie stepped back quickly, only to find himself pressed against another Englishman.

"Where are yew going so fast, lad?" he asked, reaching out for the boy. "I think I'll be taking those off you now."

"I'm sorry s-sir, I canna let ye do that!" the lad stuttered and tried to pull away. The other soldier grabbed him by the hair so that he dropped the net with a gasp, then slapped the boy hard across the face.

"We'll be going now," he said to the lad as he threw him to the ground and picked up the net.

Time to step in, William thought to himself and stepped forward with sure strides, his hand inside his cloak on the hilt of his short sword.

The Englishmen looked up as he came over to the group. "What right do ye have to be taking those fish off that lad?" William asked dangerously.

The man who had first addressed the gillie, sneered at him. "It's no concern of yours, no matter our reason," he said. "Be gone with ye, or I'll be sure to make yew sorry as well. No one messes with the king's soldiers."

"Well, no one should mess with the gillie of Sheriff Ronald Crawford of Ayr, either," William retorted. "He's the real authority here, nae matter what ye might think."

"Why yew!" the Englishman said angrily as he

raised a staff and struck William with it. The Scotsman reeled back from the blow but recovered himself before another could fall and grabbed the man by the collar, shoving him hard so that he lost his footing and fell to the street, cracking his head against the cobbles. William snatched the dropped net of fish and thrust it into the startled lad's hands.

"Run!" he commanded him and the lad needed no second bidding, taking to his heels like a frightened deer.

"Hey!" said another Englishman and drew his sword, brandishing it at William. The young Scotsman already had his sword out of its sheath and was holding it in front of him as the man struck out at him. His hood fell from his head and he cast the cloak aside so it would not hamper his movement. Then he engaged the Englishman and traded blows with him before he knocked his sword aside and smashed his helmet in causing the man to fall onto the road in a senseless heap.

It seemed that someone had raised the alarm for before William knew it, there were English soldiers coming from every direction. He cursed himself for being so foolish as he looked from left to right as quickly as he could, trying to see a way out of his mess. He leapt back before an Englishman could gut him and dashed off in the opposite direction and down an alley where no Englishmen were coming from.

"Come back here, whelp!" one of them shouted after him and he heard the sound of mailed boots pounding down the cobbled streets. William didn't stop until he found a brick wall that he set his back against, awaiting the English soldiers. They were right on his tail and he was fighting again almost before he could get his breath. He had still escaped injury, but when he saw the numbers that stood against him, he knew he couldn't hold out forever.

Aye, William, ye fool, what have ye gotten yerself into! he shouted to himself as he fought off the attacking Englishmen.

"Bring him down, lads! He's weakening!" one shouted as William fought vainly to keep up his guard against too many odds.

"Ye'll never take me alive!" he shouted back at them defiantly.

"That's all right, lad, we weren't planning on it," one sneered at him and struck out at the young Scotsman with a spear. The point gouged William in the side and he clapped a hand to the wound, gaining another to the left arm. He ground his teeth and fought even harder, knowing his life depended on it. He thought of nothing but the fight at hand, though he couldn't help sparing a small thought for his poor mother and how sad she would be when she found she had lost another son.

An Englishman who was closest to him, struck out at him extra hard as he realized the Scotsman was weakening. William caught the blow but it broke off the blade of his sword. He gave an angry grunt and threw the hilt at the man, hitting him in the face with it, causing him to reel back as the other soldiers rushed forward and began to beat William with their sword blades and spear poles until he was brought down onto the stone street, enveloped by the Englishmen and too exhausted to try to struggle anymore. One of the men pressed a sword point to his heaving chest and leaned over him with an evil sneer.

"Say good-bye to this cruel world, whelp," he said in mock pity.

William closed his eyes, waiting for the stabbing pain. But it never came. He heard someone pushing through the throng of Englishmen, cursing and threatening them, and then he felt the sword pushed aside and opened his eyes again to find himself staring up into the ugly face of Jack Moore.

"You fools!" Moore cried, shoving the man who had been about to kill William hard so that he fell into the other men. "Do you know who this is?! Idiots! This is William Wallace! You don't know how lucky you are not to have killed him!" Jack looked down at William with an evil sneer. William glared back up at him, still breathing heavily.

"Jack Moore," he said. "So we meet again. Just as I told ye we would."

Moore smiled down at him pityingly. "No, Wallace. This is not the time when we will fight." His smile changed to one of contempt. "I have my orders from the Earl Percy. I have to uphold them. Though I wish nothing more than to kill you now. Slowly, mind. But perhaps Percy will order something more then a hanging. I suppose you know the punishment for treason in England?" He laughed and the others joined in.

William made one last attempt to struggle into a sitting position, ready to fight Jack Moore hand-to-hand if he had to. But the English commander kicked him hard in the chest and shoved him back down onto his back. "Chain him," Moore commanded his men and they stepped forward, wrapping chains around his torso, pinning his arms to his sides and then wrapping them around his legs so that he couldn't move at all. They put a shackle around his neck as well and Moore tugged it cruelly as they heaved him upright.

"Get him over my horse," Moore said. "We're going strait to the tolbooth."

William snorted in anger as he was slung over the back of Moore's horse. The Scotsman was powerless against so many chains and he just stayed still, knowing there was no way he could get away now. He only hoped he might get a chance to escape before Earl Percy arrived.

***

William was not put immediately into a cell when he got to the tolbooth in Ayr, a dour place that looked as if it had seen many a prisoner who had not left the place alive. He was taken to the guardroom where Moore had him tied up with a rope hung over the rafters and his hands above his head. Moore circled him with obvious relish as he knotted the end of the leather whip he held in his hand.

"You have no idea how refreshing it is to have you right here in my grasp," Moore said with a small sneer at William.

The young Scotsman glared at him. "I'm sure it is, Jack. But before long ye'll regret it. I can assure ye that."

"You're in no position to assure anything," Moore laughed at him. "Let alone tell me what *I'll* regret!" He stopped pacing to look William in the eye. "You really are a bold one, William. I like that in an enemy. I am so used to being surrounded by fools and weaklings. It's nice to know the person I'm fighting with, though only a lad, actually has some boldness. Though, like most, it might just be all talk and no action. Pain can make even the boldest men quiver." He cast his eyes to Simpson who stood in the corner, his head bowed like any obedient servant, though William detected a perpetual shiver in the man's body.

"I can tell ye right now, Moore," William said. "That there is nothing ye would dare do to me that would break me. Ye know as well as I that if ye kill me, then Percy would kill *ye* in my stead."

Moore sneered at him. "You are only too right," he growled. "But that will not stop me from having a little fun with you. I may never get the chance again."

William shrugged as well as he could with his hands above his head. "Do what ye wish to me, Moore. It willna bother me either way. But know that Wallace's are hard to break."

"Oh, I know that far too well," Moore said, tracing the scar on his cheek. "This was all your father could give me though when we fought."

"I think you're lying," William spat at him coldly. "My father could have torn ye to ribbons." He winced as

Moore lashed the whip across his bare shoulder blades. He kept his mouth shut and stayed silent as Moore had at him with the whip even though the pain was considerable and he could feel the hot blood dripping down his back. Finally Moore stopped and coiled his whip again, coming back around to look William in the face.

"I can see that you are indeed right," he observed. "You are far harder to break then any other man I have ever dealt with. You Scots are indeed bold. But if you think you can win this war, then you are fools as well. You could never hope to fight against all the power of England."

William smiled slightly at him. "We'll see about that," he said as Moore motioned for him to be cut loose. William rubbed life back into his hands and picked up his shirt from the ground, slipping it back on carefully over his raw back. Moore watched his discomfort with relish as he motioned to his men to follow him.

"Hold him tight and follow me. We'll take him to his cell." Moore led them off into the dark corridors of the tolbooth. William was shoved along by the two beefy guards who each held one of his arms. They dragged him over to the cell that Moore opened for him where he would stay until Earl Percy's return. A fire flamed in his veins again and he made one last attempt to escape as they struggled to get him inside. Moore jammed a mailed fist into his stomach though and William crumpled to the ground, gasping for breath.

"That's enough of that!" Moore cried as the two guards grasped William's clothes and flung him bodily into the cell, slamming the door behind him. The breath was knocked out of William a second time as he landed on the cold stone floor and he levered himself up on one arm, turning to glare at Moore who was staring through the barred window in the heavy wooden door.

"Rest up, William Wallace," he said with a sneer. "You'll get plenty of time to consider all that you have done. I'm sending a letter off to Percy right away. It will still be a while yet before he gets back here to see to your trial." And with that, he was gone before William could retort. He hauled himself to his hands and knees and crawled to the door, standing up and grasping the bars, pressing his face to them to see out into the tolbooth, watching Moore and the guards retreat down the corridor. He sighed and winced. He was sore from his beating and exhausted from the fight. He turned from the door and went over to the pile of dirty straw in one corner of the cell and curled up, taking off his plaid to wrap himself in. He huddled under the tartan and winced, not wanting to admit that his hurts really did pain him. He couldn't help but think of his friends and family. What would they think when they realized he would not come back? He sighed tiredly and closed his eyes. Exhaustion finally won out over everything else and he fell into a fitful sleep.

Chapter Twenty-Eight

A Commander Lost

That night in William's camp, his companions waited anxiously for his return. It wasn't until Ewan came to the camp alone the next morning, though, that they figured something really had gone wrong. John went to meet him and relieved him of some of his baggage.

"Hello, Ewan," he said. "Is Will with ye?"

Ewan shook his head, a curious look on his face. "No, he's no', should he be?"

John shrugged. "I dinna ken, ye tell me."

Ewan put the things by the campfire. "Ye mean he's no' back yet?"

John shook his head. "Nae."

"Well, where is he?"

"I was hoping ye could tell me." John sighed heavily and sat down on the log, resting his head in his hands.

"John?" Marion came up and when she saw Ewan alone, she sat next to John heavily. "He's no' wi' ye," she whispered.

Ewan shook his head and sat next to her. "Nae, but I'm sure there's a good explanation. William can take care of himself and I'm sure he'll be back before long. He might have just gotten caught up in something and is late in coming back."

Stephen and Kerlie came up and the Irishman shook his head. "Ewan, nothing would have detained William *this* long. It's mid-morning already and he was supposed to be back before sunset last night."

"William may be many things," Kerlie added. "But I've never known him to be late like this."

Ewan was forced to agree. "Aye, I ken."

John sighed again, looking up at his companions. "Look, I know it's never a good idea to jump to conclusions, but I think William's in trouble. What do ye think?"

Stephen nodded. "Aye, I think he is."

Ewan stood up again. "Look, I'm going back to Ronald Crawford's house to see what he has to say about this. There's nothing that goes on in the town without him knowing about it. John, Kerlie, Stephen, why dinna ye come with me?"

The three lads nodded readily and began getting ready to go. John called to Keith. "Keith, ye have command, Marion, ye too, help keep these lads in line."

Marion shook her head. "Nae, I'm coming with ye. I'm not hearing anything second hand."

John shrugged. "All right, come on then. Let's get going."

They left the camp and made their way to Crawford's house where they went in the kitchen door as Ewan opened it for him. Once they got in, Ewan motioned them to follow him and called out for William's uncle. "Mr Crawford?"

"I'm in the study, Ewan," came the tight reply.

Ewan had a bad feeling as he led his companions into the study. They found Ronald Crawford standing by the fireplace, one hand resting on the mantle as he stared into the fire.

"Mr. Crawford?" Ewan began as the other man turned around.

"Ewan, please tell me what I say isn't true," he said, his voice tight and his eyes stormy. "Please tell me this is all a huge misunderstanding."

"Sir?" Ewan asked hesitantly.

"Why, Ewan, did I have Jack Moore come here this morning and tell me that William has been captured and is now languishing in the tolbooth?"

Marion grabbed Stephen's arm to steady herself. "What?!" she cried.

John sat down in the nearest chair and buried his face in his hands. "That's it then. What happens now?"

"Nothing happens until Percy gets back from

London," Crawford said angrily. "After that, William will be tried and most likely executed."

"We canna let that happen!" Marion cried. "We have to do something!"

"That's what I'm trying to do," Crawford said, motioning to a half written letter on his desk. "I am writing to Percy myself, though I doubt it will get to him before he leaves London. I feel the complete fool in this situation. I am the sheriff of Ayr, and yet there is nothing I can say that will change their mind about him. Curse the English and their blasted tyranny!" He slammed his fist against the mantle.

"Then there's nothing we can do?" John asked in disbelief. "We canna help him?"

Crawford shrugged helplessly. "I don't know, John. I don't. I can't think clearly enough at the moment to come up with anything."

"Can we at least visit him?" Kerlie asked.

"I should at least be able to do that," Crawford said. "Though, I fear that if they see you then they will arrest you as well."

John nodded and motioned to Marion. "Let her go wi' ye at least, Mr. Crawford," he said. "No one will arrest her."

"Please," Marion said. "Let me go."

Crawford hesitated a moment, then he nodded. "All right. Come Ewan. The rest of you lie low here. We'll be back before too long."

"Marion," John said before she left. She turned to

look at him expectantly. "Tell William..." he swallowed hard. "Tell him that..."

Marion shook her head at him. "Nae, John, I'm not telling him any of that. Hush ye. We'll see him again. I have nae doubt that we will all do everything we can and more to get him out of there."

John nodded slowly. "Aye, ye're right."

Marion forced a small smile and then turned and followed Crawford and Ewan out of the house.

They walked through the town until they got to the tolbooth. Crawford went up to the door and knocked on it. A small window opened and a man peeked out. His greasy hair fell around his face as he grinned at Crawford.

"Ah, sheriff, wot be yew wanting here?" he asked.

"I came to see my nephew," Crawford said sternly. "Let me in to see him."

"Sorry, I can't do that," the man said. "He's not to have any visitors at all."

"Confound it, man, I'm not only the sheriff of this blasted town, I'm his flesh and blood, *let me in to see him!*"

The man shook his head and laughed. "Do ye think that Jack Moore cares one way or another *who* you are? Nay, sorry, sheriff, no one is allowed to see him." He grinned. "But yore more than welcome to come to his execution!"

Crawford grabbed Ewan as he made to reach out to the man with a growl, looking as if he wished to strangle him. Marion glared at the man and shook her fist at him. "You can tell Jack Moore that he'll rue the day he ever met

William Wallace," she told him coolly.

The man looked at her in amusement. "Oh, I'll be sure to tell him, lassie. I'll be sure to tell him that!" They could still hear him laughing after he closed the little window.

"Curse the man!" Ewan growled as Crawford led him away. "We canna leave William to that!"

Marion shook her head, tears in her eyes. "No, we canna. Mr. Crawford," she turned to William's uncle. "Please, is there anything ye can do?"

Crawford sighed helplessly. "I will try to do whatever I can. But I make no promises."

Ewan put his arm around her shoulders. "It's going to be all right, Marion. We'll think of something," he told her.

Marion looked up at him, wiping the tears from her eyes. "I know, Ewan," she said. But she couldn't help but wonder what they could do. There was nothing that she dreaded more at the moment than going back and having to tell the others what had happened to William. She shuddered at the thought. *Oh William what will we do?* she wondered helplessly as they went back to Ronald Crawford's house.

***

William had spent most of the night pacing around his cell, looking at every possible way to get out and finding nothing. He sighed as he pounded a fist against the stone wall. He leaned forward to rest his forehead against the cold, damp stone and thought feverishly of what he could possibly do to get out. He thought of his uncle and comrades desperately, wondering what they were thinking at the moment and even more desperately hoping they would not do anything stupid. He would never forgive himself if they ended up getting killed or locked up as well for his own stupidity. He heard someone walking down the corridor then and turned as his door was unlocked.

Moore stepped in with the jailor who set a tray of food down by the straw. The jailor left the cell and left Moore standing in the door, his arms crossed over his chest as he gave William a sneer that crinkled the scar in the corner of his eye.

"How do you find your accommodations," he asked William.

The young Scotsman glared back at him, taking up a stance of defiance. "Oh, quite fine, actually. I absolutely love the view. There's nothing I find more refreshing than stone and filthy hay."

Moore smirked, looking more as if he was cringing. "You're very cheery for one in your position."

"I try to make the best in any situation," William told him cooly. "Even when I am standing three feet from my mortal enemy without even a sword in my hand. Though I daresay I wouldna even need that to kill ye. I'd settle for strangling ye with my bare hands."

If he was hoping to scare Moore he didn't succeed. The man tutted at him. "Ah, I doubt you could manage that. Because I *do* have a sword, *and* a knife into the bargain and I would be able to do away with you very fast. But I wouldn't, of course. No sense depriving the gallows of your sorry carcass." He motioned to the food the jailor had brought. "Best eat up. You don't want to loose your strength."

"I'll not eat anything ye give me," William told him defiantly.

Moore raised an eyebrow. "Won't you? I would if I were you. If you don't eat, we'll shove it down your throat and that won't be pleasant, I can assure you." He turned to leave.

William glared after him, reaching for the tray to throw at his back, but the door was already closed and he looked down at the food they had brought. The only thing it contained was a few salted herrings which he looked at distastefully. He picked up the tankard and took a gulp. He quickly spat out the water in it. At least he thought it was water. It was so scummy he wasn't sure. He sighed and sat down heavily in the hay. His stomach growled despite the fact that the food wasn't very inviting. He realized that he had eaten nothing since yesterday morning and that only made him feel hungrier. He held out for only a little bit longer before he ate the meager rations they had given him. He cringed as he drank the water then shoved the tray and tankard over to the door. He then lay down, rubbing his stomach that was still growling whether in protest of the meager meal or the condition of it he wasn't sure. He sighed heavily. Aye, something had to be done. He was sure of that, though he still didn't know what.

Chapter Twenty-Nine

Desperation

"What are we going to do? There must be a way to get him out of there!"

Marion, Ewan and Crawford had just gotten back from the tolbooth and brought the bad news to the others. John looked at them all in desperation. He banged his fist against the desk, causing the inkwell to jump. "I will no' leave William to this! He came and rescued me from a horrible fate, I would love nothing more then to repay the favor. I *should* repay the favor!"

"We all would," Stephen said grimly. He ran a hand through his tangled hair. "We would all give our lives for William like he would for us."

Marion turned to glare at him. "Don't ye be thinking

along those lines, Stephen Ireland!" she told him sternly. "And ye either, John! You are not going to give yerself up for him, even though we all *would*. No one is going to die if we can at all help it. There has to be a way out of this where everyone will come out alive."

Ewan looked to Crawford who was sitting at his desk scribbling a new letter. "Who are ye writing now?" he asked.

"My brother, Richard," Crawford said. "I think he should know what's going on."

"Will ye write William's mother?" Ewan asked hesitantly.

Crawford was silent a few minutes as he finished the letter and sealed it. "Not yet. Not until I know there's absolutely no way we can help him. There's no reason to give her extra anxiety if it's not needed."

Kerlie sighed. "I suppose we'll have to go back and tell the others," he said grimly.

Stephen nodded ruefully. "Aye. I don't look forward to it, to be sure."

Marion shook her head. "None of us do, but we have to tell them. Why dinna we go back to the camp and get it over with. We'll probably be back and forth here the next couple days, Mr. Crawford," she said.

The man nodded. "Aye, I understand. I'll make sure I find out all the new information and tell you. Ewan get these letters off for me would you?"

The red-haired man nodded as he took the letters from Crawford and left with the others as they made their way back to the woods.

Before they parted with Ewan, he turned to them with a sad look. "This is indeed a sad day for Scotland," he said to them quietly. "I hope she does not loose her truest son."

There were tears in all the other's eyes as they looked at Ewan. John shook his head. "Aye, let it no' be so," he murmured.

Ewan held up his hand to them as he turned around. Marion took John's hand and started them off to the woods. They were all silent on their trip back and they walked slowly. When they got back to the camp, the lads could tell from their looks alone that the news would not be good. Keith stood to meet them, a grim expression on his face.

"What happened?" he asked.

"William's been captured," Kerlie said as John sat down and buried his face in his hands.

Keith sat down hard amid the gasps and cries of derision from the others. He shook his head in disbelief. "I-I was hoping it wouldn't be that, though...I dare-say it was what we were all thinking."

Stephen nodded. "Aye." He looked around at them all. "Well, does anyone have any ideas?"

They all looked up blandly at the Irishman, surprised at his bluntness. Donald held up his hand.

"We break him out!" he said bravely. "We'll fight the whole English garrison if we have to!"

"Aye!" Jacob cried out, grabbing a sword and

swinging it around his head. "I'm ready!"

"It's no good thinking of things that canna be done," John told them, raising his head to look at the group. "We have to think of something else. I just dinna ken what. Please, help me. I dinna ken what to do."

They all looked at each other, searching their comrades eyes for some ray of hope, but none was to be found. None of them knew what to do. They could only imagine what would happen if they didn't think of something.

***

When Richard Crawford got the letter telling of how William had been captured, he set off immediately for his brother's house in Ayr. When he got there, he jumped off his horse and hastily made for the door, as the groom ran out to care for the tired beast.

He knocked on the door impatiently and when Ewan came to open it, he pushed inside. "Where's Ronald?" he asked.

"Right here," Ronald Crawford said, coming to see who was at the door. There was relief on his face as he saw his brother. "Thank goodness it's you, Richard, and not that monster of a general, Moore."

Richard didn't look relieved at all as they walked into the common room. He took the letter from his tunic and waved it in his brother's face. "I do hope this isn't a jest, Ronald, because if it is then it's in the poorest taste I have ever seen!"

"No jest, Richard, on my honor," Ronald said

grimly. "Though I wish to goodness it was."

Richard sighed heavily and sat in the nearest chair, pulling a bonnet from his head. "So how did it happen?"

Ronald sat down opposite him. "From what I've heard, it was because Moore's men were making sport of one of my gillie lads. William saw them and tried to get them to stop, but when they wouldn't, it came to blows and they overpowered him and, well, you know the rest."

Richard sighed as he closed his eyes and ran a hand through his mussed hair. "All too well. Och, William," he moaned. "Why ye of all people?!"

Ronald was silent. Richard looked up at him angrily. "Ye should have prevented this, Ronald. Ye are the sheriff, ye have the power."

Ronald stood up angrily. "I have no power anymore! Not since the English Earl Percy has come to occupy our city! This was completely out of my power, though I can assure you, I have up to this point done everything I could!"

"Except get him out," Richard said stiffly. "If you won't then I will."

"Are you daft, man?!" Ronald cried. "It will only make things worse! Jack Moore wouldn't hesitate to put you on the gallows beside William!"

"Maybe he'll put me there in his stead," Richard said steadfastly. "That lad means the world to me. He has nae father anymore. He's all alone in the world. Our sister's heath is failing and I dare-say she won't last much longer. We can't hasten her to the grave by letting her second son die without at least trying to do something to save him."

"Do you think I don't know that, Richard?!" Ronald snapped. "Why, do you not think that I wouldn't..." He stopped, running a hand over his face as he sighed. "No, you're right. Something has to be done."

Richard sighed as well and looked over to his brother with a hopeless light in his eyes. "Can I go to see him?" Ronald shook his head. "No. It's not permitted. Trust me, I've tried. Moore is a hard man and he knows what he's doing."

"Can I at least send him a note?"

Ronald shrugged. "You can try. But let me take it. I don't want them to know there's more then one family member in the town."

"Who is this Jack Moore person anyway?" Richard asked as he settled down at the desk to pen a letter to his nephew.

Ronald snorted. "Person? Hardly. He's a monster; a demon for want of a better word. There's nothing good come out of him being here. I used to be the justice here, but ever since he came with Percy, I have no power. Percy dotes on him like a child and Moore follows him like a dog. He has his own version of 'justice' that pretty much means that anyone who gets in his way pays in some way or another. His idea of punishment is rather more...creative then it should be. I'm sure you can only imagine."

"Aye, I can," Richard said grimly. "What does he have against William?"

"They met the day after he got here," Ronald said

with a sigh. "And it wasn't a social meeting, if you follow me. Also, I believe that he killed William's father."

Richard looked up with surprise. "Does William know?"

Ronald nodded. "Aye, he took Alan's sword off Moore when they first met."

Richard stayed silent for a few minutes. "I suppose we can't expect Moore to make the same mistake twice?"

"He didn't when he caught William, did he?" Ronald said in annoyance. "William swore to kill him and I believe he still will. There's not much that will stop a Wallace when he has his mind set to it."

Richard smiled at this. "Nae, there's not. I hope he gets his chance. Och, Ronald, we have to get him out of there. Why can't you just suggest a duel between them? I imagine Moore would like to get a crack at William himself."

Ronald shook his head. "No, it wouldn't work. Percy has ordered him to keep William alive until he gets back from London. Moore wouldn't go against his orders even if it meant personal gain. No, it would never work."

Richard sighed as he began writing again. "Well, hopefully, we can at least get this letter to him. Make sure he doesn't give up hope."

"I highly doubt William would ever do that," Ronald said, hoping he was right.

***

William was surprised when he received a letter the next morning with his meager breakfast. He picked it up cautiously, wondering if it was from Percy when he saw his uncle's seal on it. Moore looked at him expectantly as the young Scotsman looked up at his captor.

"You are quite a lucky prisoner to be receiving messages," Moore said with a slight sneer. "Though I thought it might make you happy. I can't have you depressed and dying on me. That would look bad on my record."

"Heaven forbid I put a black mark on it," William told him sarcastically as Moore left the cell. William immediately ripped open the letter and held it close to the window in the door so he would have enough light to see it by. He was surprised to see that it was in his uncle Richard's hand writing and wondered if his uncle Ronald had told him of his condition.

The letter read as this:

Dear William,

I am saddened by the news that you have been captured by the English. Your uncle Ronald and I are doing everything we can think of to try and get you out. Please, whatever you do, do not loose hope! You have many friends and none of them will let you die without a fight. Besides your position, how are you? Are you in good health, or are you sickening? Ronald doesn't know how long it will be before Earl Percy gets back from London. Hopefully not before we think of something. Ronald tried to send a letter to him asking for your pardon, though he has not gotten a reply and he doesn't really expect to. I hope you have not lost hope, William. Remember what I told you. The day that makes a

man a slave takes away half his worth. Don't let them break you.
When the darkest moments arise, they most often bring forth the
sunniest skies in the end. I hope to see you again soon if fate
allow, and leave you with the words I spoke to you before:
Freedom is the best of things. Don't ever let yourself be a slave.
Love, your uncle Richard

William folded the letter and tucked it carefully into a fold
of his plaid. Tears welled in his eyes and he didn't bother
to wipe them away.

"Dinna worry, Uncle," he whispered to the shadows.
"I willna let them break me. Not as long as I live, nor
after."

***

Later when they came to bring him supper, William asked
Jack Moore if he could send a letter back.

"Do I look like a messenger?" Moore growled
angrily. "No out-going correspondence. Parchment and
ink are far to expensive to be wasted on prisoners
condemned to the gallows."

"What will ye say, Jack, if Percy comes back and
decides to pardon me?" William shot back at him.

Moore gave him a half sneer. "He won't, surely.
Though even if he did, I would still kill you myself." He
then left, slamming the door behind him.

William lay down on his straw, leaving the food on
the tray. He wasn't hungry, though he always seemed to
be before. He stared up at the ceiling of his cell. He
wouldn't loose hope yet. No, but nothing was going to

stop   his   heart   from   feeling   sore.

Chapter Thirty

Languishing

Over the next couple weeks, William's companions racked their brains in vain for every possible escape plan they could think of. Ronald and Richard Crawford tried all they could to persuade the English authorities to release the young Scotsman though to no avail. Everyone was exhausted, no one was sleeping much or eating and they all walked around with hollow eyes and dark faces as if they were half dead. They lost more hope as the days dragged by.

William, despite all his hopes, felt himself growing weaker by the day. The rations they kept him on were not sufficient to a strong young lad like him, and being cooped up in a cell with foul air didn't help either, especially since he was used to fresh air and life outdoors. Most of the time now, he just lay in the straw, staring up at the top of his cell or dozing fitfully. His stomach hurt from hunger and he felt as if someone was running a dagger through him. He was dismayed to find that he could now see his ribs under his shirt. He had always prized himself with a well built body.

He also began to get sick. The herring were not sufficient enough to stave off malnutrition and the water they gave him was almost always bad. He discovered that after a while, he couldn't sit up without his head spinning so much that he almost retched.

It only grew worse when Moore started to notice his ailing condition. One day, he crouched down beside him, figuring he couldn't pose too much of a treat in his position and spoke to him in a mock pitying voice.

"Poor William, feeling the effects of the life in prison. Remember to eat up. Percy will be back before too long; in another week at the most."

"I *am* eating, ye great fool," William told him. Even his insults lacked strength. "It's the condition of the food that's causing me to sicken. Not to mention yer ugly face staring at me day and night."

Moore laughed at this and patted William none to gently on the shoulder. "You're too kind, surely, William. Rest up, get better."

William reached up and struck out at Moore, catching him a hit across the face. Moore reeled back in surprise. The Scotsman still had more strength then he had thought at first. He clapped a hand to his right eye and glared down at his captive. He thudded his foot into William's side before he left the cell, too angry to say anything. William rubbed his ribs with a wince and reached for the food that had been left him. He may as well eat it. It wouldn't do him any worse, nor any better. After he had finished he fell off into a light sleep. He hadn't rested well for days. He closed his eyes, but it was a long time before sleep came. There wasn't a dream for him to escape into either. Just fevered visions that sped before his eyes too quickly to make any sense of. He languished in the cell in the dark hours of the night, nothing more to do than await his fate.

***

Jack Moore left the tolbooth to ride over to Crawford's house. He was in the most happy mood, a cocky leer on his face as he knocked on the door, politely as you please.

It was Ewan who opened the door to him and he couldn't help the look of contempt on his face as he saw who it was. "Yes?" was all he could muster to force out without a curse.

"Where's Crawford?" Moore asked. "Hop to it."

"What do you want here now, Moore?" Ronald said, coming into the entryway.

Moore took off his helmet and made a mocking bow to the sheriff. "I simply came to tell you that I have received a letter from Percy that says he'll be back within the next week. I just thought you may like to know. Also, William is not in the best of health at the moment. I believe it's best that Percy is coming back so soon. He may not last the week as it is."

Ewan stepped forward, unable to control himself. "I think *ye're* the lucky one that Earl Percy is coming back so soon. William has vowed to kill ye and he *will,* no matter what ye do to him."

Ronald pulled the Scotsman back before Moore could strike him. The Englishman was furious. "I've told you before, Crawford, that servant needs a lesson in respect to his superiors! I don't understand why you still have him under your roof. If any of my servants ever spoke to me like that, they would be flogged!"

"I'll deal with my men the way I see fit," Ronald told him sternly one hand still on Ewan's arm. "Now be gone, Moore. I've told you before, you have no right on my property."

Moore turned, putting his helmet back on his head. "Good bye, then, Crawford. But I'll be back to tell you when the execution will be."

Crawford slammed the door on him and the others, who had been in the study, came out.

John looked hopelessly at William's uncle. "There's still nothing to be done?" he asked.

Ronald paced back and fourth, a hand on his chin. "Let me think," he pleaded.

They were all silent as he thought, though William's companions were all still fuming madly. Finally Ronald shook his head with a sigh.

"Well, I have one last idea. It may work. If William

has taken ill, we may be able to get Margaret in to see him."

Marion's face brightened immediately. "Yes, Mr. Crawford, do ye think she could help him? Maybe even get him out?"

"It might work," Ronald told her. "We can only hope at the moment. Ewan, why don't you take them all over to her house and talk over the plan with her. Stay there for the next couple days. But don't take too long. If Moore is right, and he probably is, then Percy could be here any day. We have to wait long enough so they won't expect anything, but not so long that it's too late to do anything for William at all."

Richard nodded, warming up to the idea. "I like it, Ronald. It may just work." he turned to the others. "I want to see William come back with you."

Kerlie nodded. "So do I," he said. "Let's hope it works."

They left soon after, in higher spirits then they had been for days. They only hoped their plan would work out.

***

William began to feel even sicker. He could only lay in the straw now, too weak to move and too sick to eat. Moore had made sure to inform him that Percy would be there before long and that his suffering would soon be over. He didn't thank him for this, nor was he mad. He had lost all feelings he might have had before. Even his anger against Moore was as dim as the cell he was stuck in. The night he had gotten the news about Percy, he began musing on his friends and family and how he would probably never see them again. He thought fondly of John and Kerlie with their undying loyalty and Stephen with his, odd, enigmatic smile and his fondness to talk about fairies. He thought about his two uncles who he loved fondly and knew they were just as anxious as his friends would be. He saddened as he thought of his mother. He didn't want to know what she would think when she found out about his fate. He only hoped his uncles would break it to her gently and little John too. William could only hope he would grow up to be like their father. Then he thought of Marion. He really didn't have anything against the lass, in fact, he had really begun to like her a lot. He might not have minded marrying her one day. For a lass, she was rather likable, even though he had never known anyone else to compare her to...

Darkness was clouding his mind and he found he couldn't resist it any longer; didn't really want to. He closed his eyes once more and succumbed to it.

.   ***

Jack Moore was busy preparing for Percy's return. The earl was due back the next day. He had his men building a scaffold out in the town square. He smiled as he watched them, though it was a bit bitter. He wished he would have gotten the chance to fight William Wallace hand-to-hand. But then, he would still get to act as executioner. He rubbed his goatee, pleased with that thought, then went to retire for the night.

Chapter Thirty-One

Freedom is the Best of Things

It was the morning of the day that Percy was due back. The jailor went to William's cell to bring him his usual rations. Moore was busy that morning, seeing to the last minute things that needed to be done so he did not accompany him. The jailor unlocked the door and entered the cell, bending to place the food beside William.

"Get up ye lazy savage, I brought yer food," he grunted, nudging William slightly with his foot. "Earl Percy will want to see ye at yer best when he comes."

When William didn't stir, he knelt beside him and grabbed a handful of his hair, raising his head that had been resting in the crook of his arm. The young Scotsman still didn't respond.

A cold fear clutched the jailer's belly. He didn't see any life left in the young man. He stood shakily, sweat beading on his brow despite the coldness of the dungeon. He knew what he had to do, though he dreaded it. Finally, he worked up enough courage to go see Jack Moore. He knew he wouldn't see the sunset that day.

***

He was quite correct in his assumption.

As soon as Jack Moore found out that William was dead, he was so calm, the jailor didn't know what to think at first.

"He's dead you say?" Moore asked him, his usually growly voice only a rasp. His face not portraying his feelings.

"Y-yes, sir," the man said, totally confused. He had expected Moore to fly into a horrible rage, this was the last thing he had expected and somehow it scared him far more.

"I see," Moore said slowly, looking over the quacking man with relish. "Well, there's only one thing to do now."

"S-sir?" the man asked, trembling.

Jack reached out and put a hand on the man's shoulder, squeezing him tight. "Someone has to pay, my friend," he said with a small smile.

The man wept in fear as Moore snapped his fingers to his men and they came to accost the jailor. Moore motioned them to follow him.

"Well, we didn't make that scaffold for nothing, did we men?" he inquired with a slight smirk as they walked off to the town square with the new victim in tow.

***

Margaret walked through the town with Ewan at her side, carrying her basket of things she was bringing to the tolbooth. Marion had pleaded to come with her, but Ewan had argued against it, saying that if it came to trouble, it would be better for himself to be there instead of only two women. Marion had finally agreed to stay, though unhappily, but she felt better for the fact that John, Kerlie and Stephen were staying as well.

Margaret and Ewan heard the screams before they got to the tolbooth. They both stopped and listened for a few minutes, trying to figure out what it was.

"What is that horrible noise?" Margaret asked.

"It's not our William, that's all I know," Ewan said and swallowed hard. "I bet it's Jack Moore trying out that new scaffold on someone who has displeased him. Sounds like it's coming from the center of town. Come on. If he's busy, our mission will only be easier."

They kept on their way to the tolbooth and reached it as the screams continued. Margaret rapped on the door and a young guard opened it, looking at them with curiosity.

"Yes?" he asked.

"I'm here to see to William Wallace," Margaret told him with a small motherly smile. "I heard he was ailing. I'm a healer, you see. I came to care for him."

"Then you haven't heard yet?" the young man asked.

"Heard what?" Ewan asked.

"William Wallace is dead," the guard told them with a shrug. "They think he died in the night. Moore wasn't happy about that at all. I daren't think what he's doing to the poor wretch of a jailor right now." He winced as the screams loudened. "I fear it's far worse than what they had planned for Wallace."

Ewan and Margaret looked at each other in disbelief. This had not been on their list of worries. Finally Margaret gathered her wits enough to speak again.

"Wh-where is he?" she asked, trying to keep the tears from her eyes. "Can we have his body at least?"

The young man nodded. "I don't see why not. Moore has no interest in the dead. Come," he motioned them to follow him. "They put him behind the building to bury him later. I'm sure the men would be grateful if you took him off our hands." He led them behind the tolbooth and Margaret gasped as she saw William's body crumpled on top of a heap of trash from the jail. Ewan saw him as well and anger clouded his face. The Englishman left them to go back to his post and Ewan stepped slowly forward to see to his friend. He reached down and took William's pitiful form into his arms, tears streaming down his cheeks.

"I'll kill them all for this, I swear I will!" he said angrily under his breath as Margaret brushed some filthy hay from William's hair.

"Hush, Ewan. Now is not the time," she told him

gently. "Let's get him back to my house and clean him up a bit."

Ewan somehow managed to swallow his anger and followed Margaret back to her house. He didn't even notice the screams that still continued relentlessly from the town square. He could only think of the grief in his heart at having let his comrade, his leader, down like this. He looked down at William's cold pale face and his heart broke.

***

John and the others were waiting impatiently for Margaret and Ewan to get back from the tolbooth, both dreading and anticipating their return.

"How much longer do ye think it will be?" Kerlie wondered out loud.

Stephen shrugged but didn't say anything. They were sitting in the kitchen. Margaret had left them food on the table, but none of them felt like eating. They sat around, staring off into space, waiting for news of their friend.

Finally, they heard the door open and they all got to their feet and hurried out of the kitchen.

"Bring him into my bedroom," Margaret said.

Marion was the first to reach them. She gasped when she saw William lying limp in Ewan's arms. She ran to him and grabbed his cold hand in hers, her tears falling onto his still face.

"Ewan," she said, looking up at him. "He's not..."

Ewan didn't say anything, but they all could see

what he dared not to speak. The lads all moaned in despair. Stephen took Marion into his arms and she cried onto his shoulder.

They took William into Margaret's room where she had turned down the bed and was bustling around busily. "Lay him down, Ewan," she commanded, and the Scotsman laid William gently out on the bed. The others watched curiously as she bent over William and put her ear to his chest.

"He's dead, what are ye doing?" John asked bitterly.

"Hush, John," she commanded and everyone was silent. She listened for a long time, her eyes closed, then she pulled her head away, a small smile on her lips. "Just as I thought," she said in a relieved voice.

"What do ye mean?" Kerlie asked anxiously.

"Margaret?" Ewan inquired.

"There's still life left in him," the old lady said. "Not much, but I think I'll be able to bring him back."

Marion gasped, her tears changing to those of joy. "Oh, Margaret, do ye really mean it?"

The old lady nodded as she filled a bowl of water from a pitcher. "Aye, of course I do, now, lads, get this fire going, we need to keep him warm, I'm going to clean him up a bit."

John wiped tears from his eyes and went to help the others stoke up the fire. Margaret turned to Marion and Ewan. "Go make him some broth, we canna waste any time in getting him fed." Marion nodded and followed Ewan into the kitchen, glad of something to do. Margaret washed the grime off William and by the time she had finished, his eyes started to flicker, though he didn't waken. Margaret smiled and pulled several warm blankets over him and tucked them around his shoulders. She stroked his forehead gently as the lads looked anxiously on. She turned around to face them, giving them a reassuring smile.

"Don't worry, lads, he'll be fine soon enough."

Marion and Ewan came back in with a bowl of broth. "Here, Margaret," the lass said, handing it to her.

"Thank you. Now, Marion if you could hold his head while I feed him?"

Marion sat on the bed and propped William's head up on her lap as Margaret fed him the broth. It took a while to get it into him, but when she had, she sighed and stood up, pulling his blankets up more snugly. She turned to Stephen.

"You and Ewan need to go tell William's uncles what is going on," she told him. "Tell them we'll move William over to his house tonight. I think it might be better and probably quieter over there. Now that everyone thinks he's dead, he will be safe."

The Irishman nodded and he and Ewan left the house to go and bring the good news to the others. Margaret looked to the others and gave them a smile.

"Well, is anyone hungry?"

They all sat down to a meal in the kitchen this time, finally able to eat again since they knew William would be all right.

Stephen and Ewan came back late in the afternoon and told them that Ronald and Richard Crawford were waiting impatiently to see William again. They had also ridden to the camp on the way back and told the lads the news, much to their joy.

"I do hope they don't try to swarm the house," Stephen said as he grabbed a roll off the table and stuffed some cheese into it. "That would give us away."

"I'm sure we can keep them in line," Margaret told him. "Now what you lads can do is make a stretcher so we can carry William to his uncle's house tonight."

That night Margaret and Marion brushed William's hair out and dressed him in clean clothes as if readying him for burial. Then, after dark, they loaded him onto the stretcher, his sword placed in his hands, and carried him off through the town as if they were on a funeral procession and made their way to Ronald Crawford's house. Margaret had to keep the two uncles from fretting over William like mother hens as soon as they brought him in the door. Marion and her companions had a hard time keeping from laughing at the rather comical scene.

"Leave him be at least until we get him into a bed," Margaret scolded them as they crowded around the stretcher.

"Are you sure he's not dead?" Richard asked her skeptically, looking William over doubtfully.

"It's all for precaution. It wouldn't do for them to think he is anything else but dead." She shooed them off and motioned to Ewan and John who were carrying

William to bring him upstairs and to his bedroom. They lifted him off the stretcher and John propped his sword up in the corner of the room. When they got him snugly under the covers again, Richard Crawford sat on the side of the bed and took one of William's hands in his. He looked worriedly into his face.

"Are you sure he'll be all right, Margaret?" he asked.

"Hush ye," she told him sternly. "His companions trust his care to me, why dinna ye, Richard Crawford? He may look bad now, but he's a strong young lad and he'll get better before ye know it. He's too determined to die on us now."

Richard sighed as he stood up again and Margaret put a hand on William's forehead, a frown creasing her brow slightly. "He has a fever coming on, I believe. Nothing I wasn't expecting. Marion, hand me my bag please."

She mixed some of her herbs into a bit of brandy and poured it into William's mouth. He coughed slightly on the fiery liquid but settled down again. He wasn't as pale as he had been before, but it was only because of the flush of the fever. Margaret sighed as she put the tankard aside. "It's going to be a long night, I'm thinking."

William's fever only worsened as the night wore on despite Margaret's medicine. They all took turns watching over him. John took his turn first, sitting by his companion's bedside and cooling his face and neck with a wet cloth. He sighed sadly as he watched William jerk and moan slightly in his fevered dreams. He took his burning hand and squeezed it comfortingly, even though he knew he probably didn't notice it.

After a few hours, Marion crept into the room to relieve him. He looked up tiredly, his eyes dark underneath. She gave him a slight smile. "How is he?" she asked.

"Not any better," John told her as he stood to give her his seat. "Though I dinna think he's any worse either. We can probably give him some more of Margaret's medicine."

Marion nodded and administered the physic while John raised William's head. He put a hand on Marion's shoulder before he left. "See ye later, Marion," he said.

"Sleep, John," she told him, even though she knew him better than to figure he would actually take her advice no matter how tired he was. She sat by the bed and reached out, stroking the damp hair from William's forehead.

"Please get better, William," she whispered. "I...We all need ye."

But William, of course, didn't answer, neither was she sure he had heard her. She sighed as she settled back to take her turn in watching him. Margaret was right. It was going to be a long night.

***

The long night turned into a long three days. William's fever gave Margaret and everyone else a very hard time and refused to break. Everyone was anxious for him to wake, though he still seemed too weak to consider it, even though he seemed to be fighting the fever with every ounce of his being.

In his fevered state, William was never really sure if he was awake or if he was dreaming. Sometimes he heard snatches of conversation though he couldn't make any sense of it, and sometimes he thought he saw his friends or his uncles hovering over him, though he could never be sure he hadn't just dreamed them up as well. Mostly, he dreamed of Jack Moore and his unspeakable horrors, and these dreams made him moan and toss and wish to wake up though he couldn't.

On the night of the third day, Marion was taking her turn by his bedside. He had calmed considerably by then and she hoped it meant an end to his fever. As it was, he didn't seem as hot to her anymore when she put a hand to his brow and this took a bit of a weight off her heart.

She was dozing off a bit; she hadn't slept more than a few snatches since they had gotten William back and she was thoroughly exhausted. His moan snapped her back to attention and she took his hand in hers, pressing it gently to comfort him. He was stirring a bit and his eyes flickered. She held her breath as his eyes half opened and roved around the room until they landed on her face. He looked at her questioningly, then whispered, "Marion?"

She nodded, a smile coming to her lips and tears in her eyes. "Yes, William. I'm here," she told him.

He smiled slightly back. "Good," he murmured and closed his eyes again.

Marion let out a sigh of relief and allowed herself to

finally fall asleep, laying her head on the bed beside William's shoulder. .

Chapter Thirty-Two

Invalid

William was not incredibly happy to say the least with being stuck in bed, but he didn't have the strength to get up for any length of time and he couldn't do it without help. This made him bad-tempered and his sickness became more of a hassle to his friends than to him.

One day he was sitting up in bed arguing with Margaret about letting him go outside.

"Please, just for an hour or so," he pleaded. "The fresh air will make me feel better, I've been stuck in a dungeon for a month."

"And what if ye're seen?" she asked him, putting her hands on her hips. "Ye're suppose to be dead, William

Wallace, and I believe it best if we keep up those pretenses for as long as possible."

William sighed in exasperation. "I canna just sit here and eat food all day! It will just make me fat! Exercise will make me braw again."

"Have ye seen yerself, Will? Ye need to get some more fat on yer bones. Muscle will come later. We have to feed ye up and nourish ye or ye'll just get sick again and I doubt that would please ye very much either."

"Fine then, I'll stay inside," William growled, slouching back down into the bed. "But I'm tired of being in here, can I no' at least go down and sit by the fire in the common room or Uncle Ronald's study?"

Margaret sighed. "I suppose a change of scene wouldn't do you any harm. I'll go get the lads to help ye down."

In a few minutes, John, Stephen and Kerlie burst into the room, grinning. "Your faithful servants, General, sir!" Kerlie cried cheekily.

"Delightful," William said sarcastically as Stephen and John each grabbed one of his arms and helped him from the bed while Kerlie settled a cloak over his shoulders. "Woops," he sighed as his legs gave out a bit and he leaned more heavily on his friends.

"That's all right, Will, ye'll feel better soon," John told him reassuringly as he and Stephen steadied him.

"And we'll get ye outside sometime too when Margaret doesn't see," the Irishman said and winked.

William couldn't help a smile as they hauled him

down the stairs and into Ronald's study where they fussed around with his blanket, spreading it in his lap and gave him a stool to prop his feet up on. Kerlie bowed mockingly.

"Will that be all?" he asked.

William swatted at him half-heartedly. "Wheesht, ye daftie. I dinna need half o' this. And please make sure Margaret doesna bring me any more food. I'm stuffed."

The lads saluted him with mock soberness. "Don't worry, General Wallace, we'll make sure ye dinna have to see another bannock if ye dinna wish it," John said.

At just that moment, Margaret and Marion came into the room with a tray of food and drink and they set the things down on a small table beside William's chair.

"Eat up, Will," Marion told him with a smile and then she and Margaret left.

William glared at their backs, then when they were gone, he waved to the food. "Well?"

The other three lads leapt on it eagerly and it was gone before too long. Richard Crawford came in and snatched up the last bannock on the tray before Stephen could grab it, and spread it with honey.

"Well, at least they're feeding ye well, William," he said with a twinkle in his eye. He was completely glad to have his nephew restored to him. "Though I tend to agree with ye, you *will* get fat if Margaret keeps this up. We all will for that matter." He bit into the bannock and wiped honey from his chin.

William rested his head against the back of the chair

with a sigh. "Aye, see if ye can tell Ewan to make me some real food. Something like stew, not any of this peely wally pastry stuff."

Richard winked at him. "I'll do that for ye, Will. And don't worry, I'm sure you'll have some eager helpers ready to be rid of the rest of it."

They all laughed at this. Everyone felt better now. So much better.

***

At least all of William's companions felt better. While he was recovering, Henry Percy returned from his trip in London, only to find that the criminal who's capture he had been awaiting with the utmost anticipation had died under the care of his jailor. Or, rather, under the care of his *former* jailor, since the jailor who had made the mistake would never get the chance to make another one. Moore was chastened a bit as well, though Percy didn't blame him for the loss of William Wallace.

"It is regrettable to be sure," he said after Moore had told him the news. "But I can't say the outcome is unsatisfactory. I was going to kill him anyway. We just didn't have to bloody our hands to do it."

Moore nodded though inwardly he was seething. He had wanted the young Scotsman's blood for so long that he had gone into something of a rage when he had found out that he was dead. The jailor wasn't the only one to pay for the incident, though no one else had been so unfortunate as to loose their life over it as he had. Moore had been even angrier when he had found out that the guard had let the old woman take Wallace's body away. The least he would have liked to have done was hang it on display as a warning to those who might get the same foolish ideas as the young hot-headed Scotsman, but no, now it was too late. His body was probably buried now. No use in thinking of it anymore.

But he did think of it. It seethed in him like a disease. He had never been one to let something or someone go when he had been wronged or humiliated by them. He never felt peace until he had killed them by his own hand. He had never been deprived that before and this was driving him mad. He didn't listen to what Percy was saying now as he talked about his trip to London. He had already forgotten the Scottish whelp. But not Moore. No. He wouldn't forget William Wallace for a long time yet.

If only I had you in my grasp now, he thought menacingly to himself, a soundless growl forming on his lips. *You'd be so sorry that you would plead to go back to the grave!*

***

William also thought of Moore during his recovery. He couldn't help it. There was never a day that went by that he didn't think about his father. And whenever he thought of his father, it was only reasonable to think of his killer. He tried not to dwell on it too much, but he secretly knew that his main reason for wanting to recover so fast was so that he could get strong enough to fight again. It wasn't just selfish of him, though, he knew that by getting rid of Jack Moore, he would be doing the whole vicinity good and probably in the long run, the whole of Scotland too. He sighed one day as he was sitting in the kitchen, helping Ewan peel potatoes for supper.

"What's wrong, William?" the Scotsman asked his companion.

"Nothing really, Ewan," William said as he dug an eye out of one of the potatoes. "It's just that I am simply tired of being here. I'm feeling much better now. But Margaret willna let me do anything but rest and eat."

Ewan chuckled at him a bit. "Aye, she's like that isna she? Oh well, soon enough we'll steal ye back to yer camp and then ye can just be William Wallace, the patriot leader of Scotland and no' William Wallace the invalid."

William grinned at him. "Hopefully that will be sooner than later, Ewan. But ye forgot the part that I'm a ghost now."

"Aye, that's right," Ewan grinned back. "The *ghostly* patriot leader of Scotland. I suppose that gives ye the upper hand."

"It certainly gives me the advantage," William mused. "It's too bad Moore doesn't seem to be so superstitious. He doesna seem to believe in all Stephen's fairy stories."

"Aye, but his men are more than a little superstitious," Ewan told him with a wink. "Ye could give them a right fright if ye wished."

William nodded. "Aye, I could. I'll have to think of my plan of action. I dinna want to make this a huge battle. I just want to fight Jack Moore hand-to-hand in a fair fight."

Ewan snorted as he took up a knife to start cubing the vegetables. "A fair fight with Jack Moore? Ye should ken by now he doesna fight fair."

"I ken that, Ewan," William said solemnly. "But *I* do. And nae matter what *he* does, I willna break my honor for his sake."

Ewan nodded. "You're a just person, William. Nothing bad will happen to ye if ye always keep yer honor."

"Let's hope not anyway," William said with a rueful smile. "I already got put into jail for doing what I thought was right. But that's the life of an outlaw, I suppose."

Ewan smiled at him. "Aye, it is."

William smiled slightly to himself as he continued to work. He would never regret what had happened. Why regret something you can't change? He sighed slightly. Now there was only one thing more he needed to do. And that was avenge his father and do away with Jack Moore.

Chapter Thirty-Three

Back to the Beginning

William, at long last, was recovered to Margaret's liking and was, for the first time in several months, making his way back into the forest to live with his companions again. He was so happy to be back that he proposed a party and the others backed him up heartily and decided to dedicate it to his successful recovery.

That night, they danced around the campfires while all the lads who could play an instrument, skirled, beat, twiddled and strummed to the best of their ability. Stephen entertained them all with ballads about Robin Hood and comically changed them to fit William and his lads.

William laughed as the Irishman finished one to much applause. He grinned at his audience and sat down next to William grabbing a tankard John handed him and took a swig thirstily.

"So, William, I bet ye're glad to be back," the Irishman winked at him.

William sighed happily. "*More* then glad, Stephen!" he said. "Ye have nae idea how hard it is to be laid up."

"Nor would he ever," John said from his seat on the other side of William. "I have doubt that Stephen can ever get wounded. He is one of the Fair Folk."

"Aye, ye're right," Stephen told him with a grin and a wink. He stood up. "And that reminds me of another ballad I should sing ye all to remind ye that the Fair Folk are not the types to be messed with!" He was off again and singing another ballad before anyone could stop him.

"Och, well at least he has a passable voice," Kerlie said with a mischievous grin as he came up. "But when are we going tae dance again? It's my turn with Marion."

"Who said?" Keith asked angrily, coming up behind him. "It's *my* turn with Marion! Ye had the last three dances!"

"I didna!" Kerlie told him sternly. "That was Donald dancing with her last!"

"Well, I didna get one yet!" Keith complained.

"Nor did I!" John said, cutting in. "Besides, I'm over both of ye in rank. Second in command, ye ken."

"Well, if it's a matter of rank..." Keith stuttered, getting angry.

"Then I as *general* get the next dance," William said, standing up and giving them all a smug grin.

"Since when do ye care anyway, Will?" Keith

snorted.

"Well, it doesna matter now anyway," John said with a roll of his eyes. "Stephen already stole her."

They all looked over to where the dancers were clapping and spinning around in a circle and Marion was cutting a reel with Stephen. They were both laughing happily and the other lads looked on in annoyance.

"Well, I never thought I'd see the day when Will Scarlet stole Maid Marion," Kerlie said blandly.

"Has Stephen christened himself Will Scarlet?" William asked him, not being able to help a smile.

Kerlie shrugged. "Well, if ye're Robin, and John is most likely Little John, then I suppose so?"

"Then who are ye?" John asked him.

"Friar Tuck," Keith said with a grin.

"*Right*," Kerlie said and stuck his tongue out at the younger lad and swatted him in the head. "Well, then I'm all for a new ballad. One where Maid Marion runs off with *Friar Tuck!*" And with that he marched off and they could soon hear the dancers laughing as he cut in to dance with Marion and Stephen came back huffily to the campfire. William and John looked up at him mischievously.

"Hello Scarlet, lost Maid Marion?" John said cheekily. "She *is* Robin's ye ken."

Stephen made a face at him. "Well, what are ye going to do about it, *Little John?* Perhaps Robin will give ye back to the evil Sheriff of Nottingham or should I say Ayr?"

William shook his head, laughing slightly. "The

sheriff of Ayr is my *uncle* remember. Nae, but I like the connection of Moore and the sheriff. And our real king is gone too. Though no' on a crusade like King Richard."

John nodded solemnly. "Aye, unfortunately. And it's also unfortunate that Edward Longshanks is nae fool like Prince John."

Stephen waved at him hurriedly. "Let's not start talking serious again, lads. Remember, this is a night of celebration. Do ye remember what that is?"

John shoved him as he stood up. "Of course, ye daftie. And I agree. Come on, Will, let's go see what that commotion is."

The starting of a riot seemed to be happening over in the group of dancers. Angry voices arose and William immediately stepped between Keith, Kerlie and Donald who were all arguing with a more then annoyed Marion. Keith and Kerlie were both clutching one of Marion's hands and Donald was trying to shove them off so he could take her hand instead. William shoved them apart as John and Stephen wrested Marion from their grasp and she sighed in gratification.

"What's going on here?" William asked the three, with an angry look in his eye. "What's the meaning of this foolishness?"

The three looked sheepishly at him. Marion stepped up to him and pointed to them. "They wanted me to dance with them. They're being fools. Like wee lads."

Ewan, who had come up to see what was going on, smiled slightly. "Lads are like that, love," he told her.

"Well, how are we going to settle this?" William asked the three who were blushing by now.

"Well, it's obvious isn't it?" Stephen asked, grinning at them. "Just like any gentlemen would settle it. An archery contest!"

They all looked at him blankly for a few minutes then Kerlie smiled and William did as well. He nodded. "Aye, I like the idea. What do ye say lads? Who wants a chance to shoot for a fair lady's hand?"

Most of the lads raised their hands and shouted out their agreement. Marion had to laugh as William bowed formally to her.

"But of course we willna do it without your consent, fair lady?"

Marion smiled and nodded. "A fair contest of archery is something I will allow, I believe, good sir," she said. "Let it commence."

All the lads, including William, John and Ewan lined up in front of the targets and the lads who were not participating came to stand around with torches to light the place up more. Stephen, who was acting judge, passed out bows and arrows to all the contestants.

"All right, lads, this is how it's going to work. We have about twenty lads here, so the best ten out of them will move on to the next round, and the five out of that and the two out of that and then the last two will go head to head and we will decide a winner."

They all nodded. Stephen turned to Marion and smiled at her. "Would ye do the honors, my lady?"

Marion smiled back at him and held her hand up to the archers. "Gentlemen. Bows at the ready. On the count of three. One...two...three...Fire!"

The arrows whizzed into the targets and Stephen walked down the line and disqualified the lads who were not close to the mark. Donald was knocked out in the first round and he protested loudly. William and his friends had all stayed in though, and Stephen issued the next round. Of the ten that shot, William, John, Ewan, Kerlie and Keith were still in the competition. They all eyed each other with sly grins, as Stephen called out the next ready.

"All right, lads, this will decide our final two. Bows ready?"

"Aye," the lads told him.

"Then, fire at will."

The shots were close but after much decision from both Stephen and Marion, they decided that William and Ewan had the truest hits. Keith and Kerlie groaned loudly and made faces at their successors as they left the shooting area.

"Use one target this time, William first," Stephen told them with a grin as he stood behind them to watch the final match. "Are ye ready?"

"Ready," William told him as he held his bow taught, preparing to fire.

"Fire at will," Stephen told him.

William took his time sighting and held his breath as he shot. The arrow landed dead center in the target. The lads 'oohed' at this and William couldn't help a grin.

"Bad luck, Ewan," John said.

The red-haired Scotsman simply smiled and took his time sighting the arrow as he still kept his position. Finally, after almost a minute, he shot and there was a gasp from the lads. Stephen ran to look at the hit and turned around with a grin to the others. "Well, it looks like we found a new Robin Hood!" he said. "How did ye learn to spit arrows, Ewan?"

The Scotsman grinned a bit bashfully. "Well, I used to practice when I was a lad. I guess it paid off."

"Paid off?" William grinned as he clapped Ewan on the shoulder. "Nae, I think it's just that I'm destined to loose every shooting competition I enter. But ye won it fair. Go and claim Fair Lady's hand."

Ewan handed John his bow and went over to Marion where he knelt and took her hand, kissing it lightly. "My lady."

"Sir Ewan," she said, stifling a giggle. "It seems ye have won the honor of a dance." Ewan stood and they went off to the dance again as the lads picked up their instruments. Stephen grinned as he stood at William's side, his arms folded across his chest. He saw how William was looking after them and turned to him with a mischievous wink.

"Dare I sing a ballad about Robin Hood and Maid Marion?" he asked.

"Ye dare what ye want," William told him with a crooked smile. "Will Scarlet."

Stephen grinned at him again and skipped off,

singing a song about the two lovers. William shook his head as John came up with an armful of bows. He turned to his friend who was looking at him slyly.

"What?" William asked him, his smile disappearing.

"Nothing," John told him with a wink. "I'm sure ye ken anyway." He looked over at Marion meaningfully and William gave a half exasperated sigh, half laugh as John went off to put the bows away. He watched the dancers from afar for a few more minutes. He could hear some of the lads laughing at Stephen as he sang the verses of his song expressively with shameless gestures in the directions of William and Marion. William sighed again and then made his way to the dancers. Ewan had just finished his dance with Marion and she gave him a kiss on the cheek before he left her.

"Is there room for a dance from a second place archer?"

Marion turned around to see William smiling at her. She grinned and curtseyed. "Of course," she told him and he took her hand and they whirled around.

"So ye *can* hit a target dead center," she told him with a teasing light in her eye.

William turned his nose up at her. "I didna come here to be insulted," he told her.

She pressed a hand to his lips. "Hush. I didna insult ye. I'm just teasing ye. Ye take offense too easy, Will."

"Perhaps I do," he told her, unable to stop the smile spreading over his lips. He took a quick look around at the other lads who seemed contented at the moment. He tossed his head to the right. "Do ye want to go somewhere quiet for a few minutes?" he asked her. "I want to talk to ye."

Marion nodded with a smile. "Of course." She took his hand and trotted after him as he led her out of the light of the campfires and into the shadows of the woods. There was a full moon that night though, so they could still see each other in the silvery light. Marion smiled at him as he sat her down on the roots of a large tree and turned to face her.

"Is it no' lovely tonight?" Marion asked him as she looked around.

He nodded at her. "Aye, that it is. Marion," he reached out and took her hand. "I realize that I never thanked ye."

"For what, William?" she asked.

"For saving my life when that man was going to kill me," he told her. "If ye werena such a good archer, then I'd probably be dead right now."

Marion shrugged modestly. "It wasna only me. Stephen shot the other man. I could only fire one arrow. Mine may have hit first, but if Stephen hadna killed the other man, then ye would be dead right now, no matter what I did."

He smiled at her. "Ye're too modest." Marion smiled slightly at him. Her face was beautiful in the moonlight. "But ye've done more for me than that. Ye keep the lads together here, Marion. Without ye, I think we'd all be dead."

"Now ye're talking foolish," she scolded him gently.

"Perhaps," William told her with a laugh. "But I canna deny that I'm glad to have ye here. No matter what I said at first. I...well...I've become just as fond of ye as the other lads have. And I would be sad if ye were to leave."

Marion squeezed his hand tightly. "Dinna worry, I'm no' planning on leaving any time soon. I wouldna dare leave ye when ye need me to help ye fight Jack Moore and the English."

William smiled fondly at her. "Jack Moore is certainly a problem. It will be his time soon. Very soon."

Marion caught the look in his eyes and looked at him solemnly. "William, are ye planning something?"

He nodded. "Aye. I'm always planning. But this I will enact tonight I think."

Marion stood up and looked down at him. "William! Ye canna go fight him right now! Ye just got back!"

William stood up to assure her. "Hush, Marion. I'm no' fighting him. I'm simply going to send him a message."

"What if ye dinna come back?" Marion asked him, grabbing his hand. "Like last time? William...I canna..."

He reached out and took her face between his hands. "Marion. Ye willna loose me again. I promise. I'll be back."

She shook her head, pulling away from him. "No! I canna let ye do it all alone. Let me come with ye!"

"No," he told her gently. "No, this is something that I need to do alone. If I dinna, then it could go wrong. But if I do, then there will be nae harm done."

Marion blinked unshed tears from her eyes.

"William...I..."

He wiped one of her tears away with his thumb. "Marion. Let me tell ye something else. When I was laying in the tolbooth, I realized that ye were more than a friend to me."

"What are ye saying?" she asked.

"I'm saying, Marion," he told her, putting his arms around her waist and drawing her close. "That I love ye."

"Will," she started, but he hushed her, pressing his forehead against hers.

"Dinna say anything yet," he told her and leaned forward a fraction more and kissed her. She was so surprised that she didn't realize she had wrapped her arms around his neck until he stopped kissing her. They looked at each other a few minutes, surprised, then William smiled and turned his face, closing his eyes.

"Ye can slap me now, if ye want," he told her. "I'm sorry."

"Sorry?" Marion asked him softly and he turned back to see a smile spread across her lips. She grabbed his face between her hands and kissed him again, much to his surprise. When she pulled away, he grinned at her.

"Well, lassie, I take back that apology then!" he told her and she laughed. He took her arms and pulled them from around his neck. "But I really must go before the night is gone," he told her.

She reluctantly let go of him. "If ye must, Will. Be safe."

He nodded to her and bowed gallantly. "I will be. I'll

be back before dawn. I promise it this time!" He turned to leave the shadows. "Keep the lads in line. If they ask, just tell them the truth and tell them also that if they come charging around Ayr, then it will be dangerous for us all, but if they stay here quiet and have breakfast ready for me when I get back, then everything will go rather nicely!"

She giggled and waved to him, unable to feel scared for his safety this time. They were in love, who could hurt them? "All right, Will, I'll tell them. See ye at breakfast!"

He waved back to her and went to his sleeping place while she rejoined the party. He grabbed his cloak and put it on, hooding his head and taking up his bow and arrows. He then went to saddle his horse and mounted up. Before he could leave though, John caught him in the stable.

"Where are ye going?" he asked.

William smiled down at him from the saddle. "I'm going to pick a fight," he said simply and spurred his horse into motion as John stood behind him with his mouth gaping, watching William trot off through the dark forest.

Chapter Thirty-four

Wraith

Jack Moore hadn't really slept since the incident with William. It had been almost a month now. The longest month Moore had ever experienced. He spent all his nights since then tossing and turning in bed, sleepless. And when he did sleep, he had dreams of William Wallace coming back from the grave and killing him as he slept. He hated these dreams. They were foolish and they made him feel weak. The worst part about them was that they actually scared him. He chastened himself relentlessly about the fact that they did, but it was only the truth. He couldn't help it. Whenever he was caught up in one, which was almost always when he finally drifted off to sleep, he felt as if he was clutched in death and he couldn't wake until he pulled himself upright, stifling a scream. The last thing he needed his men to know was that he was having nightmares about a lad half his age coming to kill him. Not to mention the fact that the lad was *dead!* So he didn't sleep. He wandered the halls of the house during the day, unreachable to everyone. He didn't chastise his men. In fact, he didn't do much of anything but mumble to himself with the most awful sneer anyone had ever seen on his face. It scared the men at first but after a few weeks, they seemed to get used to it and simply ignored him as he did them. He rarely ate either, only enough to stay alive. Percy tried to talk to him, but didn't get much out of him.

"My dear Jack, you have to take care of yourself. Don't let this get to you so," he said one night as they sat down to dinner. "He was only a lad."

Moore stabbed his knife into the tabletop making Percy flinch. "He was not *only* a lad," he snarled. "He beat me and crossed me too many times for me to just let him go! I needed to kill him with my own hands."

Percy sighed, watching with a cringe as Moore hauled the knife from the table, digging a hole into it in the process. "My good man, if you have the need to kill someone, go and see if you can find the rest of his men at least. Perhaps it will give you reason again, and it would be very good for the rest of us too, not to mention my dining table. I have a feeling that they are planning something. After all, the fall of their leader will most likely provoke them to action."

Moore looked silently at his reflection in his knife blade. A slow smile found it's way to his lips. "Hm, not a really bad idea I suppose. I'll start tomorrow." He grabbed his tankard and drained it, then stood, sheathing his blade back in his belt.

"And get some sleep, Jack," Percy told him as he left the room. "You don't want them to have the advantage on you."

Moore nodded and went straight to his room where he dressed in his nightshirt and lay down on the bed, closing his eyes and trying to sleep. He thought that Percy's suggestion might have cleared his mind enough to let him sleep. He finally drifted off, but once again, his dreams took the form of the ghost of Wallace coming back for revenge.

***

It really is rather fun being a wraith, William thought with a grin as he rode his horse as quietly as he could through the dark, deserted streets of Ayr. He came to the house Percy had commandeered for himself and his officers and saw a guard sleeping on the doorstep. He dismounted silently and drew a dagger from his belt. William bent over and pressed it to the sleeping man's throat. The guard started awake and reached for his sword hilt, but William placed a foot firmly on his wrist.

"Ah-ah," he scolded with a smile. "None of that. I willna hurt ye. Just tell me which window is Jack Moore's?"

The man gulped against the blade. "Th-the third one

on the right of the h-house, I think, sir."

William nodded and reached under his cloak and brought out a flask of ale. "Thank ye. Now take this for yer trouble."

The man grabbed the flask greedily and took a sip instantly. William turned and got back on his horse. He trotted it to the right side of the house. This side was more open and looked out to a wide street. *Perfect,* William thought to himself as he took his bow and an arrow from the back of his horse.

***

Jack Moore heard the clop of horse's hooves on the cobblestones outside his room. In his dreams, he imagined Wallace riding up on a horse, ready for revenge. He tossed and moaned in his sleep, trying to find something to defend himself with. Then he heard the hoof beats stop and he sat bolt upright with a gasp, sweat soaking his hair and nightshirt. His chest heaved with heavy breathing and he jerked his head from side to side, looking around the shadows of the room to see if anyone was there. When he saw he had just dreamed it all, he relaxed a bit and wiped the sweat off his face.

Thunk!

He nearly jumped out of the bed, grabbing a dagger from under his pillow, when the arrow whizzed through his open window and lodged itself in the wall right above his head. He looked out the window quickly and saw a cloaked and hooded rider sitting on a horse with a bow held in front of him as if he had just shot. Moore gathered his wits and snarled out at the rider.

"Who are you?!" he demanded, his voice sickeningly weak. He cleared his throat.

"Tell me now!"

The rider didn't say anything. He fixed another arrow to his bow and shot the second one right next to the first. Moore looked up at it and saw that a message was attached to it. He grabbed the paper and hurriedly looked over the lines. The writing was all too familiar to him.

Didn't I tell you not to rest easy, Jack? I still have a score to settle. It would be very inconvenient for me to have died so soon. Before I could finish you off.

Wallace! Moore hissed and looked out the window quickly. There was no one there. He leapt from the bed and ran to the window, leaning out as far as he could to see down the street. But William wasn't there. He had gone. Or vanished. Moore felt an unbidden shiver go down his spine. But it was not one of fear. It was one of anticipation. A horrible leer spread over his face as he crushed the letter and let it fall to the floor. He knew one thing for certain. Spirits couldn't write letters.

***

"*What* were you thinking?"

William had just gotten back to camp in the early dawn light and John had come to greet him with that comment. He glared at his friend, as William dismounted from his horse, throwing his arms in the air in indignation.

"Seriously, Will? Going strait into the hands of your enemy? *What were ye thinking?!*"

William shook his head at John as he took the hood from his head. "Och, John, have a little faith in me. Ye ken I had the upper hand there. Moore was really frightened. And I could have shot him if things had gotten really bad. Though it wouldn't have happened. Besides. I know that now, Moore will let nothing get in his way of a hand-to-hand combat with me. He wants it as much as I. We both want a chance to prove ourselves to the other."

"But, Will, Jack Moore doesna hold to honor, he'll cheat and he'll kill ye!" John cried. "Ye must know that!"

William smiled slightly at his friend and put a hand on his shoulder. "Johnny, have a wee bit of faith in me. Ye know I can fight. I can take care of myself, and as for Jack Moore and his pranks. I think we can all keep an eye on that."

Marion ran up, seeing he was back and threw her arms around him. "Oh Will, ye're all right!" she cried.

"Aye, as I said," William told her with a fond smile, wrapping an arm around her waist. "And I'm famished. Where's that breakfast I ordered?"

Marion led him to the campfire and sat him down, as Stephen and Kerlie pressed food and drink upon him.

"So what happened?" Kerlie asked as he handed William a bowl of porridge.

"Aye, what *did* happen?" John asked. "Ye may as well tell."

"As I said, John," William told him between bites. "I

went to pick a fight. Jack Moore now knows that I'm still alive and ready to fight him. He's no' going to stop at anything now until he succeeds in finding me."

"And how is he going to do that?" Stephen asked with a laugh. "He knows he can't find our camp. He's failed too many times."

William grinned back. "Aye, isna that the truth? But I have nae intention of *letting* him find the camp. I am going to go to him. I have a feeling he'll wait for me to do just that."

"But how can ye be sure?" Kerlie asked him.

"I canna be," William said. "But one way or another, I'll meet with him. And we'll fight. And he'll die."

"What is yer plan then, Will?" John asked him.

"I'm going to leave after I have a few minutes of rest and I'm going to go to town, present myself to Moore, and we're going to fight it out."

"Will, ye canna do that!" Marion gasped. "Jack Moore has the whole garrison at his back! He could snap his fingers and ye'd be captured! It's walking into a sure trap."

William took her hands in his, smiling. "I highly doubt he would do that, Marion. Jack Moore and I are destined to fight it out man to man. He will do just that."

"Then let us come with ye!" John told him.

"Aye," said Stephen. "Ye may need some help."

William smiled at them sadly. "Nae, I'm afraid not, lads. I dinna want to give Jack Moore any reason to kill me. If ye go, then I would be worrying about your lives and I would be off my guard. If I go alone, I have no one to worry about but myself. I ken ye'd do the same in my position."

The lads were silent then, respecting his decision and knowing he was right. Marion sat beside William with a sigh. "Ye willna even let me go, Will?"

"Ye least of all," he cried. "Marion, if I lost ye..."

She shook her head and took his face between her hands. "Nae, William. But If ye're going, at least take this with ye." And she leaned forward and kissed him.

The lads gaped at them in disbelief. Kerlie swallowed hard. He turned to Stephen. "Did she just...?"

The Irishman nodded, a grin on his lips. "Aye. She did."

William stood up, pressing Marion's hands in his. "Thank ye, lass. Now, I'm going to rest a bit before I go. I didna sleep at all last night. Stephen, wake me in about half an hour." He left to go to his sleeping place as his comrades looked after him, having mixed feelings about the proceedings.

"He seems rather happy," Kerlie commented, breaking the silence.

Stephen nodded. "Aye, he does. I think William is simply glad that after today all our problems with Jack Moore will be over."

"Ye dinna seem to even consider the fact that William could die today," Marion said, her lip quivering.

Stephen put his arm around her shoulders, giving her a reassuring smile. "As William said, Marion, have faith in him. There is nothing that can stand in your way when you are avenging a family member."

"I'm guessing ye speak from experience," John said softly.

Stephen nodded slowly a sad smile on his face. He squeezed Marion before he let her go. "As I said, don't worry. William can take care of himself. However..." and he met the eyes of the other three. "I for one do not think he should do this alone."

The others nodded their agreement. "Aye," John said. "I was thinking the same thing."

"We all were," Kerlie told him with a grin. "We canna leave William to it alone. But we'll wait. I think what we should do is send someone to go tell William's uncles and see what they think about the situation. Then we can go to Will's rescue if that's what needs to be done."

"But we shouldna let him see us," John warned. "He'd know. And he's right. If he knew we were there we would only cause a distraction. But we *should* be there if he needs us."

Marion nodded. "Yes, we should be. I dinna want him to die alone. We have to make sure he gets through this. I'll go to Mr. Crawford's as soon as William leaves."

John nodded. "All right. We'll follow ye as soon as possible. Too bad Ewan already left."

"Aye, but that's all right, we'll get it to work," Stephen grinned. He drew his sword and placed it between them. They all grasped the hilt together. "Together we fight, divided we fall," he said to them.

"Aye!" they all cried back at him.

William slumbered restlessly. His adrenaline was pumping through his veins and he couldn't keep quiet very long. He dreamed of his fight with Jack Moore. Whether it would be ill fated or well, he didn't know. Stephen woke him before it could be decided. The Irishman bent to place a hand on William's shoulder and the Scotsman jerked awake, grasping a dagger he had slept with clutched in his hand. Stephen grinned at him.

"Time to wake up," he said.

William sighed and smiled back, sheathing his dagger back under his pillow. He stood and took his father's sword up in its baldric and slung it over his back. "Thank ye, Stephen. Now I really must be going." He put his cloak on, positioning it over his sword and pulling the hood over his head. "I'll see ye later. I dinna ken when, but I will be back. I promise."

"Ye better be," Stephen told him firmly. He looked over to where Marion was standing with John and Kerlie by the campfire. "Ye'll be sorely missed if ye don't come back."

William smiled sadly. "I ken," he said. He went over to them and clasped John and Kerlie by the hands.

"Lads," he nodded to them and they nodded back. He turned to Marion and took her hand, kneeling in front of her. "My lady." Marion couldn't help a slight smile. "Sir William."

He grinned as he looked up at her. "I fight for your honor as well as mine," he told her. "And if I get out of this alive, would ye marry me?"

"Oh, William," she said, tears in her eyes. "Dinna promise me anything yet. What if something happens to you?"

He stood up and looked her in the eyes. "Marion. Nothing is going to happen to me. I promise. And I also promise that I will marry you. Now I must go. Moore will get restless." He kissed her quickly and gave his comrades pats to the shoulders and then he left to go to the stables. He saddled a horse and mounted up. He raised a hand to his lads. "See ye later!" he called to them, then set his heels to his horse's sides and was off before they could say anything.

"He left before I could tell him I loved him," Marion said quietly.

Stephen smiled at her. "I know, but you'll get a chance later. Now it's time you be going too. Take my horse."

Chapter Thirty-five

Disaster

Marion rode swiftly to Ronald Crawford's house. She jumped off as soon as she got there and tied her horse up in front of the barn. She jogged up to the door and knocked on it quickly, impatiently waiting for someone to answer it.

The door opened after a few seconds, revealing Ewan. He smiled when he saw Marion and opened the door up more. "Marion. What are ye doing here?"

"Ewan, is Mr. Crawford here?" she asked him.

He shook his head as he closed the door behind her. "Nae, both Ronald and Richard are out in the town. Why? Did something happen?"

"William's gone to fight Moore," Marion told him worriedly. "I wanted to tell his uncles about it."

"He's gone to fight Moore?" Ewan asked, suddenly alert. "Where?"

"Well, ye know he went to send him a message last night, and this morning when he got back, he decided that he was going to go out and meet him for their last fight."

Ewan shook his head silently. "Och, William. Jack Moore isna going to play fair."

"Dinna worry, we'll be there. Just as soon as I tell Ronald and Richard what's going on, I'll ride back to the camp and John, Stephen and Kerlie are going to go and find William. That way if he needs help, we'll be there."

Ewan nodded. "I hope it's enough."

Marion leaned close to him and spoke as if confidentially. "Ewan, to tell ye the utmost truth. From the stories I've heard, I highly doubt that any of Jack Moore's men would get in the way of someone who wanted to kill him. Do ye follow me?"

Ewan started to smile. "Aye, I think I do. Why dinna ye come into the study and have something to eat or drink? I'm sure Mr. Crawford willna be gone long."

Marion went into the study and sat down by the crackling fire, taking off her cloak and settling down to wait, though nervously. She couldn't get the thought out of her head of William walking into a trap and getting captured again, this time being at Jack Moore's disposal. She shuddered at the thought and pushed it from her mind as Ewan brought her a tray of refreshments. She smiled at him and poured herself a tankard of cider.

"Thank ye, Ewan," she told him. "But ye should

know me better than to think that I will be able to eat at a time like this."

"I know," Ewan to her with a small smile. "But I ken what Mr. Crawford would say when he saw I hadna given ye anything."

Marion giggled slightly at this as she took a sip from her tankard. "Och, Ewan, at least I have ye to keep me company. I would go mad otherwise. Guess what? William asked me to marry him!"

Ewan grined at her and clasped her hands in his. "Then my congratulations!" he told her.

She looked down at the floor. "Yes. Let's only hope he lasts the day."

"Losing hope in William willna help him," Ewan told her firmly. "I ken ye canna help but worry about him. But ye need to keep heart. If ye dinna then something will be bound to happen."

She smiled up at him again. "Yes, ye're right. I'll try not to worry anymore."

There was a sudden knock at the door and Ewan stood swiftly, a frown on his face. Marion stood as well.

"Is that Mr. Crawford?" she asked doubtfully.

Ewan shook his head. "Nae. He wouldna knock."

"Maybe it's William," Marion suggested hopefully.

"Stay here, Marion," Ewan told her, starting to the door. "We'll find out soon enough."

He left the study and went to the front door. He took a deep breath before he reached out to open the door. When he did, he stopped in his tracks.

"Well, well, well, what have we here?"

***

William had left his horse in his uncle's barn before he left for the town of Ayr and now he walked through the town that seemed suddenly deserted of the English soldiers that usually plagued the place. He didn't think much of it though. His mind was only filled with thoughts of Jack Moore and his demise. He didn't think anything of it at all until he got to the house where Moore was staying and saw that it was mostly deserted. He looked into the barracks not far away and saw they too were deserted. A bad feeling started up in the pit of his stomach. Was he wrong? Had Jack Moore gone out to find *him?* He decided to take one last chance and went to the tolbooth and spied around for a few minutes seeing if Jack Moore might be there, but there was no sign of life there either except the normal guards. He turned around and headed back through the town, planning on going to ask his uncle if he knew what was going on and get his horse again to ride back to the camp in case Moore had somehow found out how to get there.

He was just passing through the place where all the vendors were setting up their stalls when he pretty much ran right into his uncle Richard. The man steadied his nephew by grabbing his shoulders and looked him in the face with surprise.

"William, what on earth are you doing here, lad?" he asked in shock.

Ronald who was walking beside his brother, glared

at William sternly. "Come, William, what's the meaning of this?"

"Uncle, where is Jack Moore?" William asked quickly, not in the mood for explanations.

"Jack Moore?" Ronald asked. "William what are you up to?"

"Where is he, Uncle?!" William cried.

Ronald and Richard both seemed shocked at his outburst. They looked at each other then turned back to their nephew with the desperation in his eyes. Ronald shook his head.

"William, I truthfully don't know. He left with what looked to be his whole army early this morning. I have no idea where he's going."

"His *whole army?!*" William cried in exasperation. "I have to go. NOW!"

"William!" Richard called after him. "William, what are you doing?!"

"I canna talk now!" William shouted over his shoulder to them. "I have to get back to the camp! I'll tell ye later!" Then he rounded a corner and was out of sight.

"I have a really bad feeling about this," Ronald said with a sigh.

Richard shook his head. "I have a feeling the end of all of this is coming soon." He turned to his brother and put a hand on his shoulder. "Don't worry, Ronald. I have a feeling Jack Moore will get the worse of it. William is a Wallace."

"So was Alan," Ronald said grimly.

"But William is fighting *for* his father," Richard told him. "He won't loose."

"I hope you're right, Richard." Ronald looked up at the sky with a sigh.

***

Ewan stood in the doorway for a fraction of a second, just looking into the ugly, evil face of Jack Moore before he took the door into both of his hands and slammed it on him with a grunt of desperation. Unfortunately, Moore had already stuck his mailed boot into the doorway and pushed into the house before Ewan could stop him. The Scotsman looked around for anything he could use as a weapon and grabbed a candle sconce from the wall. He brandished it in Moore's face.

"Stay back!" he growled. "*Stay BACK!*"

"How brave of you," Moore sneered at him and swatted the candles out of Ewan's hand. He reached out and grabbed the Scotsman by the front of his tunic, bringing him forward and pressing his snarling face into Ewan's. "But bravery is oftentimes overrated, thrall. You've crossed me one too many times before. Now it's time you learn to respect your betters." He hauled Ewan into the study where Marion had grabbed the fire-poker and was starting out of the room. Moore motioned to his men almost lazily. "Take that away from her. She may hurt herself."

Marion brandished her weapon at the men who came to accost her. She swung it at one of them and stabbed him in the leg with it. He howled in pain and dropped down. But as Marion had struck out at him, three other men had gotten behind her and now they grabbed her tightly and held her between them so she couldn't get away.

"You coward!" she spat at Moore. "Why don't you try fighting alone? If William Wallace was here right now, he would challenge you to a duel and it would be the death of you, ye can be sure of that."

"So bold for a lass," Moore told her with a sneer as he handed Ewan to more guards who held him tightly. Moore stepped toward Marion and took her face between his thumb and forefinger. "And Wallace and I will be fighting soon enough. Just as soon as I find out *where he is*." He looked at her meaningfully and cocked an eyebrow.

Marion growled at him. "I'll not tell ye anything, ye pig!"

He smiled at her. "Oh don't worry, my dear. You won't have to say anything." He turned to Ewan. "He'll do all the talking." He walked over to Ewan who was held by three guards. He struggled to get away.

"If ye're thinking of getting information out of me, Jack, ye're going to be out of luck."

Moore swung his fist at Ewan's face and gave him a hard hit to the jaw with his gauntleted knuckles. Ewan sagged against the guards, but managed to pull his face up to look at his tormenter. "Ye hit like a lass, Jack," he said with a grin.

Moore punched him in the stomach and Ewan doubled over with a gasp, falling to his knees. Moore kicked him several times in the side as he lay on the ground, trying to gain his breath back. Moore sneered at his victim as he looked down at him, enjoying his helplessness.

"I've wanted to do that for a long time," he told him. "This is how servants should be treated when they misbehave. They should be punished. Not encouraged so that they will only do wrong again."

Ewan rolled up to avoid Moore's blows. He looked up at him defiantly. "I'm no' yer man, Jack Moore. I can say what I bloody well want to ye."

"That's it!" Moore growled. He snapped his fingers to his men. "Tie him up and stretch him over the desk. I'll flog it out of him." The guards hauled Ewan to his feet again and ripped his tunic off. They tied his hands in front of him and dragged him over to the writing desk and shoved him onto it face first, holding him down. Jack Moore took a whip from his belt and advanced on the Scotsman.

"Stop!" Marion pleaded. "Dinna hurt him!"

Moore struck out at her with the whip and it lashed across her cheek. She pulled back slightly at the stinging pain and felt blood run down her face.

"I would be quiet if I were you," Moore told her dangerously and bent to look into Ewan's face that was pressed against the desk top. He gave him a small smile.

"So you're one of William Wallace's men. I should have known. I also should have known that his uncle was in on it too. Oh well. When I get back, I'll have him tried for treason to the crown."

"*If* ye get back ye mean," Ewan spat at him.

"You seem so sure that I either won't get there, or, if I do, I won't come back," said Jack Moore, an amused smile playing across his face. "Do you really think that young whelp, William Wallace, can kill me? You must not. Otherwise, you'd have no reason to resist me, when I asked you to take me there. So? Where is he. Will you take me there?"

Ewan shook his head. "Nae, I willna."

"All right then," Moore said. "You'll regret that decision, I think." He stood up again and nodded to the guards who held Ewan. "Hold him tight," he told them and started the flogging.

Ewan squeezed his eyes shut, keeping his exclamations of pain to himself. Moore's whip cut across his back like fire. Marion winced in sympathy at every blow that fell. Ewan never said one thing as he was being flogged. When Moore finally stopped, he bent over again to talk to Ewan. The Scotsman had tears of pain in his eyes but he stared at the man defiantly.

"So, my friend?" Moore asked him. "Have you changed your mind?"

Ewan shook his head. "Nae, I havena. I would never give William up."

Moore gave a small regrettable sigh. "I'm sorry to hear that." He straitened up again and started flogging Ewan once more. Simpson who was standing in a corner, looked down at his feet, wincing with every crack of the whip.

Finally, Marion could take it no more. She head-butted one of the men and jabbed her elbow into the other's stomach. They let go of her for only a split second as they shouted in surprise and she ran forward, leaping at Jack Moore. She grabbed his upraised arm and stopped his whip midair.

"Stop hurting him! Stop it right now!" she shouted at him.

"Marion, no!" Ewan told her. "Stay out of it!"

Jack Moore reached out and grabbed Marion by the throat, dropping his whip. "The bold lass has more spirit then I thought at first," he said with a sneer. "I think I have a new idea. Perhaps a different type of leverage will loosen your tongue, Scotsman."

"Don't ye touch her!" Ewan cried at him.

"Ewan still willna tell ye," Marion told him bravely. "I'll tell him not to."

"We'll see what he has to say," Moore told her menacingly. He drew a dagger from his belt and spun Marion around so that his arm was around her neck and the dagger pressed to her chest. "I will kill her, Ewan," he told the Scotsman. "I will if you don't tell me where William Wallace is staying."

"Ye wouldna!" Ewan said. The guards had let go of him and he had slid off the desk, kneeling on the floor. "Even a man as evil as ye couldna kill a lass in cold blood."

"Couldn't I?" Moore asked in a taunting voice, pressing the dagger harder.

Ewan shook his head. "Nae, how could ye?"

"You don't believe me?" Moore sneered. He flicked his dagger to one side and Marion gasped as he sliced her on the arm. He turned to smile wickedly at Ewan. "As you can see, I *can* and I *will.*" He brought the dagger back to press against Marion's chest, right above her heart. "So you best decide soon. Otherwise her death will be on your head."

"No, Ewan," Marion pleaded with a gulp but Moore tightened his hold on her neck.

"You stay out of this, girl," he growled at her and turned back to look at Ewan. "What do you say, Ewan? Shall I spill her blood on this floor? Leave her body for Ronald to find when he gets back? We'll see what the sheriff has to say about that. I imagine that William has taken a liking to this lass since he's kept her around. What do you think he would rather have, Ewan? His lady love or his discretion?"

Ewan was silent. He knew what he had to do, but he didn't want to admit it.

"Well, Ewan, time is running out," Moore taunted him. "For everyone. Make your choice."

Ewan stood up stiffly, a deep scowl on his face. He glared hard at Jack Moore with his sneering face, knowing that he was going to get his way of things. Ewan nodded once. "All right, Moore. I'll take ye there."

"Excellent!" Moore exclaimed and shoved Marion away from him. She fell into Ewan's arms and looked up at him.

"Ewan, how could ye?" she asked him, tears in her eyes.

"Marion, I couldna let him kill ye! William would die of grief. It's nae different. They'll get to fight and only Jack Moore will die. Now let's get this over with."

"Yes, let's," Moore told him with a grin. He threw Ewan's tunic to him. "Best get dressed then."

Ewan pulled the tunic back on gingerly and Marion took his hand worriedly. "Are ye going to be all right?"

Ewan nodded. "Aye, I think so." He put his arm over her shoulders. "I'm so sorry this had to happen."

She shook her head. "Nae, it's no' yer fault. Let's just get going. The sooner William kills Jack Moore the better. I only hope he's back when we get there. Otherwise the inquisition might go on."

Ewan sighed. "I didna think of that. Let's just hope William realizes what happened and goes straight back to the camp."

"Tie them both," Moore commanded and soon Ewan and Marion were both trussed with their arms pinned to their sides. Moore looked around as he was leaving the room. "Where's that dog, Simpson?" he shouted. "Bring him here."

Simpson was shoved toward him through the milling men. "Ah, there you are," Moore said when he saw them. "March beside me. I want you to see everything. And take special care as to the landscape. This is the way that you failed to find for me."

Simpson nodded, looking down at the ground. "Yes,

my liege."

Moore turned to Ewan with a smirk. "That is how servants should act, for future reference. Though I don't see much in your future if I win the fight. Which I will."

"Simpson isnae a servant, he's a broken man," Ewan spat at him. "And that's something I'll never be! Besides, you'll never win the fight. William will kill ye."

"We'll see about that," Moore told him. "Something will have to happen to you all after I kill William Wallace. I can't just leave you to roam the woods causing problems for the crown. I suppose the rope's end will be the fate of any who fought under him."

Ewan glared after him, but Marion shook her head. "No use exciting him further," she whispered to him. "May as well give him what he wants. He's too spontaneous."

"I think I'll take that advice, Marion," Ewan whispered back.

They marched off into the forest, dread filling them at the thought of what was ahead.

Chapter Thirty-Six

Reconciliation

Ewan and Marion led Moore through the woods, knowing that if they made one wrong turn or took too long, Moore would start threatening again and nothing good would come of it. Moore was grinning the whole time, awaiting his meeting with William Wallace with the utmost anticipation.

"What will we do if he's not there?" Marion asked Ewan as they stumbled through the woods, pulled by the men.

"We'll stall for time," Ewan told her. "Dinna worry, we'll think of something."

John, Kerlie, Stephen and the other lads were completely unaware of the danger when it marched into their camp. They all made a quick grab at weapons that were always close to hand and rose to fight, but it was already too late. Jack Moore's men had surrounded them. Moore strode up to John and unsheathed his sword, pressing it under the young Scotsman's chin, raising his face.

"Ah, it's you," he said with a wicked grin. "As you can see you're outnumbered. Fighting now would only result in defeat and death. Also," he motioned to the guards to bring Marion and Ewan forward. "We have captives who are friends of yours. I'll kill them if you don't surrender in the next three minutes."

John looked hopelessly around at the others. Stephen caught his eye and nodded. John turned back to Moore and laid his sword on the ground. "All right, we surrender."

Moore sneered at him. "Wonderful!" He snapped his fingers and his men came and accosted the three leaders, holding them tightly. Simpson gasped as they went to grab Stephen.

"That's the evil fairy!" he told them. "Don't touch him! He'll kill you with a look alone!"

Moore backhanded Simpson and he fell to the ground with a whimper, holding his hands over his face. The three men who had been about to grab Stephen had quickly backed away and turned around three times before they spat on the ground. Moore shook his head at them with disgust.

"Yew fools!" he growled. He went forward and

grabbed Stephen by the wrist, drawing his knife. He slashed it across the Irishman's arm viscously. Stephen winced silently as blood dripped into the loam at his feet. "See? He bleeds just like everyone else!" he told the men and shoved the Irishman into the custody of the guards. "Put them with the others and keep an eye on the rest. I don't want anyone getting away." He looked around the clearing with a critical eye. "Rather cozy place you have here," he said with a lopsided grin. "But where's your leader, Wallace?"

"He's not here," John told him firmly.

Moore turned around to look at him and the others. "Oh really? Where is he?"

"Out," John told him, looking at him defiantly.

Moore advanced on him, his dagger poised. "Are you so sure of that? Perhaps he's hiding somewhere here?"

"William Wallace doesna *hide!*" Kerlie told him angrily. "He wants to kill ye. He went to find ye!"

"Oh, he did, did he?" Moore seemed to consider this for a minute then he lashed out with the knife and slashed Kerlie down the left side of his face. The lad shrunk back with a cringe. Moore chuckled slightly as he wiped the blood from his knife. "Oh, there is such loyalty in your band, it almost sickens me!" he motioned to his men surrounding the clearing. "These wretched dogs know nothing of loyalty. They follow me out of respect."

"We *respect* William Wallace," Stephen told him. "Ye're men follow ye out of *fear.*"

Moore grinned at him. "You're probably right,

Irishman. But please, if you value the lives of your friends as well as your brave young leader, tell me where he is."

"It *is* true," Stephen told him with a glare. "He's away. He went looking for ye."

"And leave you all here just for me to find?" Moore laughed. "Hm. Perhaps William is not as smart as we all thought."

"Ye bloody murderer!" Ewan spat at him. "Ye never would have found this place if ye hadna forced us to show ye!"

Moore shrugged. "You're probably right. Though, I still think William is closer than you say. Perhaps when he sees his friends in danger, he will come to me." He eyed all the captives in front of him and smiled. He reached out and grabbed John by the throat, shoving him up against a tree. "You know what I'm capable of. What do you say? Shall I shoot another arrow into you to pull out? Or shall I do it to one of your companions?"

John grasped Moore's wrists, trying to loosen his grip on his throat. "Do what ye want to me. Dinna hurt the others. William will come in his own time. As soon as he realizes what has happened, he'll be here. Not before, no matter what ye do! Ach!" He gagged as Moore squeezed him tighter, his oily smile spreading across his face.

"Stop it, Moore!" Ewan demanded. "Dinna bother them!"

Moore turned to him and shoved John to the ground where he gasped for breath and clutched at his bruised throat.

"Ewan," Marion warned, putting her hands on his arm

Moore shoved her away from the Scotsman. She fell in front of Stephen who immediately knelt to untie her arms. Ewan looked Moore in the eye. He was still smiling. Ewan glared back at him.

"Ye think ye're so tough, Jack, threatening people who have nae defense. I call that cowardice!"

"Ah, Ewan, would you give your life for these young whelps?" Moore asked him. "You seem the kind of fool. I won't disappoint you then." Before anyone could stop him, Moore drove his dagger into Ewan's middle. The Scotsman doubled up with a gasp, looking up at the Englishman with deadly eyes. Moore smiled at him thinly as he pulled his dagger out of him. Ewan fell to his knees, clutching at his wound.

"Ewan!" Marion screamed and rushed to his side, throwing her arms around him as he fell and cradling him against her. She looked up at Moore with such hatred he almost took a step back. "You *MONSTER!*" she screamed at him.

He smiled down at her. "Yes, I am a monster. Perhaps now that you know I am not playing games, you will tell me the truth about William?" He turned to the others. The three lads gazed at him with all the hatred they could muster. Moore held his bloody dagger up for them to see, his horrible grin spreading over his scarred face. "Who's next?"

He strode toward them, looking at all three. Finally,

he reached out and grabbed John by the front of his shirt and spun him around so that he grabbed him by the hair and pulled his head back, his dagger pressed to his throat. "I won't kill you so fast," Moore sneered at John, then turned to the Scotsman's comrades. "Tell me now where William Wallace is, or I start cutting him apart bit by bit. I think I'll start with his tongue."

"Jack..." Stephen said warningly.

"Where is William Wallace?!" the Englishman screamed at them.

"Right here, Moore."

Jack spun around to see William riding into the camp. He leapt off the horse and threw his cloak to the ground, striding forward. He reached behind him and grabbed the hilt of his sword, pulling it free of its sheath. "Let him go, Moore. This is between ye and me!"

Moore smiled, cocking his head to one side as he shoved John away and sheathed the dagger in his belt again. "Ah, William, here you are. We were just waiting for you. Finally come to fight me, have you?"

"Shut up, Jack," William growled as he fell into a fighting stance. "No more smart comments. We fight to the death. Just ye and me."

Moore unsheathed his sword as well. "Of course, William. My men won't interfere. To the death it is. Though, on my part, I can't promise it being a quick one."

William spread his arms and bowed slightly to his opponent. "Quite all right, Jack. The longer ye take to kill me, the longer I have to finish ye off. Ye *will* be the one to die today. Ye realize that ye dinna have a chance."

"It's never good to go to a fight so sure, William," Moore told him with a cock of one eyebrow. "The boastful ones always loose."

"I'm not being boastful," William told him firmly. "Take it into consideration that ye killed my kin. I will avenge my father and my brother." He held up his father's sword in a salute. "They will rest in peace today. That is one thing I *can* assure ye of, Jack Moore."

Moore smiled at him. "Oh, William. Don't make me feel sorry for you. It is rather a pitiable position you have thrust upon you. Don't take it to heart."

William smiled back at him. "Dinna worry, Jack. I willna." He brandished his sword. "But I didna come for a battle of words. I came for blood and steal."

"I couldn't have said it better," Moore told him and crouched down as well.

They circled each other, locking eyes, anticipating the other's movements, hands twitching on sword hilts. William fainted forward and Moore jumped back in defense and that started the fighting. William lunged full force at him and they clashed their swords so hard that sparks flew. William spun around to catch the second blow and Moore took a low swing, hoping to wound William in the legs but the young Scotsman jumped over the flashing blade and swung high at Moore, causing him to duck. They clashed blades again. Moore was surprised at how strong the lad was. He was a far cry from the wasted young man he had held captive in the tolbooth. He was strong once again, and fierce. He had everything in the world to loose, but yet he fought as if he had nothing. No cares whether he lived or died. Moore found himself satisfied. This would be a challenge. He smiled to himself.

"Why are ye smiling?" William asked him as he parried a blow and struck out again, causing Moore to side step.

"No reason, really," Moore told him as he swung at William's head. "Just surprised at how strong you are. For one who has been dead recently."

"*Nearly* dead, Jack," William corrected him with a smirk. "Wallace's dinna die easy."

"No, they are infernally hard to kill," Moore told him with a scoff. "Your father and brother certainly held on to the last. I finally was able to kill your father with his own sword though. Ah, I see you didn't know that part of the story."

William angrily struck out at him with a growl, hoping for a hit but finding only cold steel under his blade. He disengaged and staggered back a few paces, taking a few seconds to breathe. "This blade, Moore, will soon enough taste *your* blood and then it will be cleansed."

Moore laughed at him, taking a breather as well. "We'll see what will transpire. This battle is not half over." He leapt forward and struck out at William, driving the Scotsman back up against a tree. Their swords stayed locked and Moore pressed forward on the blades. William grunted and strained to break the contact, thinking of the best way to do it without leaving a way for Moore to decapitate him. Moore inched the swords closer and closer to William, forcing the Scotsman's own sword against his shoulder. William gritted his teeth as the blade dug into him and he felt the blood seep down his arm. Moore laughed at him.

"Looks like I got first blood after all," he told William. "And it's on your own sword!"

William said nothing, he was inching a foot forward and it was pressed against the inside of Moore's leg. Almost at the same time the Englishman realized what he was doing, William had already made his move. He kicked out hard and knocked Moore's foot from under him, making him fall to one hand. William leapt free of the confines of the tree, pressing a hand to his wound with a wince. Moore leapt up off the ground and brandished his sword again. Anger clearly flashed over his face.

"Why you!" he growled and charged forward, his sword raised above his head. He gave a mighty downward strike and William dodged it, bringing his sword up to cut Moore in the side, only to find that he was wearing chain mail under his tunic and his blade glanced off it without any harm done. Moore laughed at him.

"Aye, we have this thing called armor in the English army," he sneered. "I see you don't wear it in Scotland!"

"That's because Scots arena afraid of blood and pain," William told him defiantly, crouching again.

"That's good because there's going to be a lot of it before we're done here today," Moore told him and struck out at him again. "Most of it yours."

William blocked the blow he thrust at him and sidestepped, though not in time to avoid Moore's seeking blade. It dug into his side and he gasped, clasping a hand to the wound, blood seeping through his fingers.

"Still able to go on, William?" Moore asked him tauntingly. "Or do you wish to rest up and fight again some other time?" William growled and ran at him, swinging his sword around his head in a glittering arch. Moore caught the blow but it slid off his sword blade and dug into the unprotected part between his neck and shoulder where his chain mail didn't cover. Moore gasped and pulled away, clapping a hand to the wound.

"So ye *can* feel pain," William observed blandly. "I was beginning to wonder. I ken ye can feel fear. I saw it in yer face when I visited ye last night."

"That wasn't fear, and pain is nothing!" Jack Moore growled at him with a twist of his lip, spit flying from his mouth as he shouted. "Never insult me! I'll gut you for it!"

Moore struck out and William leapt back, the tip of Moore's sword cutting him across the midriff. He winced, but kept up his guard, knowing that if he failed now, Moore would certainly get the upper hand and he would be dead. He needed to push the pain from his mind. He looked over to his friends who were all watching him with bated breath. He saw Marion with Ewan laying in her lap and new anger flared up inside him. *What happened to Ewan?!* he cried silently as he turned back to face Moore with new hatred in his eyes. The Englishman smiled at him.

"Ah, yes, William, it's true. I have killed your trusty friend. He needed to be taught a lesson, and he got his education."

William growled at him and leapt forward to engage him again. Moore fended him off easily this time, having seen the blow coming. He laughed at his opponent and stopped his sword before it could land a blow. "Ah, William, you're weakening," he said simply, a bright light in his eyes. "You've been wounded too many times, you're loosing too much blood. You have no chance now."

"I still have a chance," William told him, breathing heavily. "Remember, I'm fighting to avenge those I loved. Ye can never contend with that!"

"One of us needs to die, William," Moore said almost kindly. "And, at the moment it doesn't look like it's going to be me." He struck out again, rushing forward. William was shoved back and Moore took the few seconds breathing space to reach down and grab a handful of loam and damp dirt. When William straitened back up, he threw it at his face. The Scotsman instinctively ducked as the dirt flew into his eyes. Moore quickly turned his sword around and swung the hilt at the side of William's head.

William fell to his knees, dazed by the blow. Moore kicked the sword from his loosened hand and thumped a boot into his wounded side. He reached down and grabbed William by the front of his shirt, looking down into his bleary eyes, tearing from the dirt.

"The tide has been turned, William," he sneered and brought up his mailed fist, punching William in the jaw.

William fell to the ground and rolled over, levering himself up to fight but Moore thumped a boot into his stomach and William gasped for air, doubling up on the ground. Moore brandished his sword as he stood over William. "You're loosing." He slashed the sword across William's shoulders. The Scotsman cried out in pain as Moore leaned over him, grabbing him by the hair and hauling him to his feet. William struggled to get away from him but Moore grabbed him by the throat and slammed him up against a tree, knocking the breath out of him a second time.

"Hush now," he said with a leer. "It's no use fighting anymore. I've won."

William grasped his hands and tried to pull them from his neck. "No, Moore," he choked out. "Ye havena won until I'm *dead*!"

"That will be soon enough," Moore told him.

William kicked out at him and his foot connected with Moore's shin. The Englishman cursed and let go of William's neck shoving him into the tree so hard that he was knocked cold and slumped to the ground.

"I'll flay you alive before I kill you!" Moore spat at him and drew his knife from his belt.

Marion had been watching the fighting, holding her breath, crying out whenever William had taken a blow. Now when she saw Moore with his wicked knife and William lying prone at his feet, she knew she had to do something. She lowered Ewan gently to the forest floor and grabbed a sword from one of the guards who had been watching the fighting intently, rushing forward before he could say anything.

Just as Moore raised his knife and was about ready to bend over William, Marion lunged in front of him and struck out at the dagger, sending it flying off to stick in the ground a few yards away. Moore leapt back with surprise, bringing his sword up in front of him again.

"You leave him alone!" Marion cried at him, brandishing her sword.

"Ah, the bold lassie," he sneered at her. "What do you think you can really do to me?"

"Many things," Marion told him with a small smile.

"Of course," he smiled back and struck out at her half heartedly, expecting to bring her down. Marion parried the blow and gave him another. Moore ducked with surprise.

"This is a fun game, lass, but it can't go on forever, I have a price to collect in blood." He struck out at her and when she blocked the blow, he maneuvered his sword so that he gashed her in the arm. Marion gasped slightly, but glared up at Moore and struck out at him once more.

William came awake again, wondering blearily why he wasn't dead, then he saw Marion facing off with Moore. He started up with a jump. *Marion!* He looked around and saw his sword lying several yards away and started crawling over in its direction.

"How?" Moore wondered out loud as Marion spun around and struck out at him again, her blade singing against his.

"I learned from an Irishman!" she told him and

parried another blow he aimed at her before he locked his sword against hers and tried to press her down.

Marion knew she couldn't keep up the block forever, she was too much lighter than Moore and soon he would press her back.

Stephen saw this too. He drew a dagger from his boot and caught her eye. Marion saw what he was trying to get across and she gave him a nod. She let go of the sword with one hand and Stephen threw the dagger. She caught it deftly and stabbed it into Moore's thigh.

The Englishman howled in pain and staggered back, pulling the dagger from him. He looked up at Marion again and growled at her.

"You'll pay for that!" he shouted, raising his sword to strike her down.

Marion raised her sword, preparing for the blow, but suddenly, she was knocked sideways and fell to the ground. She looked up, throwing her hair back from her eyes and saw William standing in her place, his sword blocking Moore's at the last minute.

"I thought we agreed this was our fight, Moore," he growled as Marion stood and quickly got out of the fighters' way. William glared at his enemy, breathing hard from the exertion but still on his feet. Moore shook his head at him.

"You are harder to kill than I thought," he said. "But as I've said, I've killed Wallaces before. They aren't invincible."

"Maybe not," William said as he parried another

blow, the sword feeling like a dead weight in his hands now, where it had once felt so light. "But they're determined. And they do *not* forget!"

Moore gave him his oily grin. "Neither do I, William." He swung his sword around his head and brought it down forcefully, William caught it, but the force brought him to his knees. He gasped in pain from his wounds and struggled to push the sword aside. He finally found a last reserve of strength and shoved it into the ground, rolling over once and coming up again. He gave a battle yell and charged forward, making to stab at Moore, but the Englishman was ready for him. He brought his sword up quickly, pressing the blade to William's throat, stopping him in his tracks with his sword buried in the ground between Jack Moore's feet. William looked up at him, panting heavily, his whole body shuddering from exhaustion. Moore smiled at him kindly.

"You fought well, William. I may make your passing easy for that. If you admit you're finished, that is."

"I would admit it, Jack," William gasped out, glancing down to where his sword was planted. "*If* I was. I think ye need to think again." With a mighty grunt, he swung his sword up and dug it into the back of Moore's left leg. Jack Moore fell onto his back with a grunt, loosing his sword in the process. William wasted no time in stabbing him in the chest. Moore gasped in disbelief, as the sword drove through tunic and chain mail alike. He looked up into William's face. The young Scotsman was flushed from the fight and his eyes flashed in vengeance. "That was for my father!" he spat at him and pulled the sword free as Moore groaned. William knelt over him and pressed his blade to the Englishman's throat. "And this is for Malcolm since ye have nae heart to bleed!" He killed Jack Moore with one motion of his sword and the Englishman gave one last sigh and died.

William stayed kneeling there for a few seconds, breathing hard, sweat falling from his face. Finally he pulled himself upright with the help of his sword and staggered over to where his friends were standing, watching him.

He turned to the Englishmen first. "Your leader is dead," he told them. "What will you do? I think fighting us would only result in all your deaths."

Simpson who seemed to have changed a bit when he saw Moore die, stepped forward and bowed in respect to William Wallace. "I know it would be the wish of Jack Moore for us to kill you all. But I for one am willing to let this go." He looked around at the other men and they nodded their agreement. Simpson smiled to William. "We have no quarrels today. You were brave and should be rewarded for it." he saluted him. "I will also be so bold as to say we owe you a debt of gratitude."

William smiled back at him and gave him a salute in return. "Then it has been paid. Thank you, Captain."

Simpson smiled wider and called all the men to withdraw. They trooped out of the clearing and went on their way back to the town of Ayr. William watched them for a few seconds before he went to Marion and knelt beside her, taking her face between his bloody hands.

"My dear Marion," he whispered. "Where did ye learn to use a sword?"

She smiled at him a bit sheepishly. "Stephen taught me, William," she told him and took his hands in hers, looking at him worriedly.

"Then I'm very glad ye didna listen to me," he told her with a laugh.

"William ye're wounded badly," she said.

He pushed her hands away as she started to untie his sark to see to him. "Leave it," he said and turned to Ewan laying nearby, struggling to keep his pain at bay. William smiled at him sadly.

"Och, Ewan," he said, taking the man's proffered hand. "I'm sorry." Ewan shook his head. "Dinna be. I was the fool." He winced and clutched William's hand tightly. The young Scotsman looked down at him worriedly.

"We'll get ye back to my uncle's house," he told him. "Margaret will take care of ye."

"She'll take care of *both* of ye," John told him, coming to his friend's side and helping him stand upright. He looked him over with a sigh. "Ye took some hard blows, Will."

William grinned. "Perhaps I did, but it will take more than a few scratches to bring me down." The lads smiled warily at him as they watched him sway on his feet. Marion stood to take him by the arm. "Now, if ye dinna mind, lads. I think I'm going to pass out," he said and fell forward into their waiting arms.

They lowered him to the ground and John turned to Marion. "Let's get them to Crawford's. Then one of us can go for Margaret. We'll soon have them sorted out for the better."

Marion knelt and kissed William gently on the forehead. "Yes, he's had a hard day." For some reason this made them all laugh. They were so happy to be rid of their enemy that they were simply relived.

Keith came up and saluted them. "What should we do with Moore?" he asked.

"Leave him to rot," John told him with relish. "We have to move anyway. Ye're in charge until we get back."

Keith saluted again and the others got their wounded onto stretchers and set off for Ronald Crawford's house. Feeling like they were stepping into a new life. A better one.

Chapter Thirty-Seven

All Things Come to an End

"William? It's all right, William, ye can wake up now."

William opened his eyes, trying to take stock of where he was. He saw blurry figures standing over him. He blinked several times to clear his vision and finally realized that it was all his friends, John, Stephen, Kerlie and Marion. His uncles and Margaret were also there, standing a little back from the bed. He tried a smile at them. "Hello," he said softly.

Marion smiled back at him and sat on the bed, taking his hand gently in hers. "How do ye feel?"

William thought a moment. "All right, I think," he told her. "How long was I out?"

"All night," John told him with a grin. "Ye had a

nice long sleep, but Margaret took care of yer wounds soon enough to prevent fever. Ye'll need to rest up for a while though, I'm sorry to say."

William groaned in protest. "Och, ye could at least give me some good news, Johnny lad," he laughed slightly and winced, his hand traveling to his side where he found that his whole body from shoulders to waist was covered in bandages. "Och, well, it's a small price to pay for my victory."

"That it is," Richard Crawford told him with a smile at his nephew. "You fought well, I heard. And now Ayr is rid of its worst pest."

William nodded. "Aye, that it is. But I couldna have done it without all of ye." He looked up at all his friends and smiled.

Marion stroked his forehead gently, smoothing his hair back. "I'm simply glad it worked out for the best. I had so many bad moments when ye were fighting. I thought for a moment that Jack Moore would rip ye to pieces."

"He would have. But he didna," William told her with a fond smile. "Thanks to ye."

Marion looked down with a slight blush. "I was really not that brave, William. When Moore came to capture Ewan and I, I was truthfully terrified."

William sat up slightly then, looking around. "Ewan? Where is he, is he all right?"

The others looked at each other sadly. Margaret stepped forward. "William, Ewan is very bad off. There's not much I can do for him."

"Let me see him," William pleaded, levering himself up more, ignoring the pain that sung through him.

"Ye'll hurt yourself, Will," Marion told him sternly, trying to push him back down.

"Please let me see him," William said again and Margaret sighed.

"All right, William. I think it might be for the best anyway. Do help him though, lads, so he doesn't hurt himself."

John and Kerlie each pulled one of William's arms over their shoulders and took him gently around the waist and led him slowly out of the room. He leaned heavily on them, his legs wobbly, though he did his best to walk for himself. They went across the hall and opened the door to another room. William saw Ewan laying in the bed, tossing restlessly. John pulled a chair over to the bed and they deposited William onto it.

"We'll leave ye," John told him and he and Kerlie left the room, closing the door behind them.

William turned to Ewan. The man opened his eyes and looked up at his friend. He reached out to take William's proffered hand, smiling weakly.

"Ah, William, I'm glad to see ye awake," he said, his voice hoarse. "Though bandaged up right well, I see."

William smiled at him and looked down at himself. "Aye, I am, and the wounds smart right awful, but Jack Moore is dead, man. That's certainly cause for celebration."

Ewan nodded. "Aye, that it is. A great cause for

celebration. Too bad I willna get to join in."

"Ye'll get better, Ewan," William told him. "Ye will."

The redheaded man shook his head. "Nae, William. No' this time. I fear I'm done."

William sighed. "Och, Ewan, I'm sorry. I'm so sorry."

"Why should ye be sorry?" Ewan asked him. "Ye killed my murderer."

"But he wouldna have stabbed ye if I had been there earlier," William told him. "I was the fool. I should have known what he would do."

"Nae, Will," Ewan told him, squeezing his hand in comfort. "Dinna ever think it was yer fault. I canna rest easy if I know ye're blaming yerself for my death."

William looked back up at him, his eyes shining with unshed tears. "Ewan, ye're a man I would have wished to go the whole way with me. Ye're the truest man I think I've ever met."

"There are more true brave hearts to be found, Will," Ewan told him. "Ye're one of them. And yer friends waiting out there for ye are as well. I have a feeling that ye will never be lacking in friends. And if it ever be so, I daresay it will only mean that every lad out there is dead. They would never betray ye, William."

William smiled at him. "I believe they willna, Ewan. I am very fortunate in my friends. I'm glad to have been able to count you one too, Ewan. I'll...I'll carry a stone for you."

Ewan smiled and reached out his other hand to

sandwich William's hand between his palms. "William, promise me one thing. Never give up on Scotland. She needs ye. Just like everyone out there does."

William nodded. "I never would have considered it. My father fought for Scotland until his death. I would do the same. I would die for Scotland."

"I hope that day doesna come," Ewan told him with a sad smile. "For if it did, Scotland would loose her truest son. I dare-say she would never find another."

"I wouldna say that," William told him with a smile. "I'm sure there are probably other sons of Scotland waiting to be born."

"None as loved as ye," Ewan told him, then he coughed and he gasped, breathing hard for a few seconds before he looked back up at William. The young Scotsman clutched his hand tightly, seeing the pain on his friend's face.

"Ewan," he whispered, shaking his head, not knowing what else to say.

"William," Ewan said, his voice hardly a whisper. "William, I was very lucky to know ye. Take good care of Marion. She loves ye."

"I ken that," William smiled sadly at him.

"And remember, William," Ewan continued, smiling at him. "Freedom is the best of things. Never be a slave." His eyelids slid shut and he took several more shallow breaths then died. William clutched his hand still, tears streaming down his face as he looked at the still form of his friend.

"Dinna worry, Ewan," he whispered. "I'll never be a slave." Then he laid his head down on the bed, his forehead resting on Ewan's hand and wept for his friend.

Marion opened the door quietly and slipped across the room to kneel by the bed at William's side. She put her arm around him gently, careful not to hurt him and pressed her face to the side of his neck.

"I'm so sorry, William," she whispered to him. "I'm so sorry." She kissed him and wiped the tears from his cheeks.

"He died for what he believed in," William told her, looking up slightly. "There...there was no dishonor in it." He rested his head on her shoulder with a sigh and she held him gently as his tears dampened her dress.

"No, Will, there wasna. He preferred it. It was a hero's death."

William nodded. "Aye. That it was."

They stayed there sitting by the bedside of their passed friend, thinking on his legacy and how it would go on.

***

"We'll build him a cairn, like a true hero," William told them as they all stood over Ewan's grave the next morning outside Ronald Crawford's house.

The others nodded. "Aye," Stephen said. "Come on lads, let's all add a tribute to him."

They looked around the property to find stones and brought them back to lay in a pile on Ewan's grave. They all looked down at their handiwork with sad smiles.

William crouched carefully and laid down a bunch of heather on the stones.

"We willna forget," he told his companions. "Not Ewan, nor the rest who give their lives for Scotland's freedom. Whether it be our comrades, ourselves, or those we never knew. They shall be remembered. That's the way it should be. And that's the way it will be."

They all nodded and John bent over to help William back onto his feet. "Aye, it will. Now ye should get back to bed, Will. Ye still need to rest."

The young Scotsman turned back to the house, leaning on John's shoulder without another word. John helped him back up the stairs and William sat down on the bedside.

"Thank ye, John," he said.

"Are ye all right, Will?" the other lad asked worriedly.

William nodded. "Aye, I am." He gave a small smile.

Marion slipped into the room. "I'll take care of him, John. Make sure he takes his medicine and all that."

John nodded to her with a small smile. "I'll leave that to ye then," he said and left the room, closing the door behind him.

"If ye're going to torture me, get it over with," William told her with mock dignity. "I'm too weak to resist."

Marion giggled slightly at him. "I was just teasing about the medicine, Will. Dinna worry, the only thing Margaret wants ye to have is sleep and rest."

William pushed himself up and took Marion around the waist. "No' quite yet, Marion. No' until I make sure of something." He grinned at her. "Are ye still willing to marry me?"

"Of course, Will!" she told him. "Why shouldna I?"

"Och, I dinna ken," William shrugged. "I thought ye might no' want to marry a wounded, supposedly dead outlaw."

Marion reached up to take his face between her hands, smiling up at him. "Och, and who ever said I wouldna? I love ye, William Wallace. I doubt anyone else could suffice."

William gave her a small sideways roguish smile. "No' even Stephen Ireland?"

She laughed and slapped him gently on the cheek. "Nae! I want *ye*, Will!"

"Well, all right, then, if ye insist," he shrugged and leaned over to kiss her. When he pulled back he looked at Marion kindly. "I'd love to continue this conversation, Marion, but I think that I'm going to fall over."

"You poor thing," she crooned with a laugh and helped him into the bed pulling the covers over him. She leaned over him and kissed his forehead. "Have a good rest, Will. I'll be back with something to eat when ye wake."

"That sounds nice," he murmured, breathing easily, his eyes already closed. Marion turned quietly and tiptoed out of the room, smiling. She was glad everything felt all right. She took a last look at William's sleeping figure.

"What is in store for ye William Wallace?" she whispered out loud, though she couldn't conceive the answer.

Chapter Thirty-Eight

A New Beginning

Two months later

William breathed deeply as he looked around their new camp. They had spent all the last week moving all their old stuff to the new location. It was even deeper in the woods and would probably never be found by anyone, not even the deer and other wild animals that lived there. His wounds had healed eventually, and as soon as Margaret had let him go, he was off back to the camp to help the others move it. They left Jack Moore's body to rot in the place it fell. He had not had any trouble with the English in the time since his fight. He knew the "peace" wouldn't last forever, but it was enough to get him back on his feet and get his lads into safety again.

When Captain Simpson had gone back to Henry Percy after their meeting with William Wallace, he simply said that Jack Moore had gotten lost in the woods and when he still hadn't appeared several days later, Percy feared the worst and didn't bother to send out a search party, much to the pleasure of the men of his command. They were all much happier without the tyrant rule of Jack Moore and got on about their business with much more efficiency since they no longer had to fear for their lives if they made the smallest mistake.

Richard Crawford had gone back to his estates after William recovered, with many an encouraging word to his nephew, and Ronald was very proud of the lad as well, in his own way. He began to raise money for William's army and kept them supplied with the things they couldn't hunt for.

The Scottish resistance was still gaining more fighters by the day, news of the deeds of William Wallace, the young patriot, traveling all over the reaches of Scotland by word of mouth and bringing in more men and lads from all over.

One day, William stood gazing out at his handiwork, thinking of their future as he often did. He suddenly felt someone approach from behind and slip their hand into his. He turned and smiled down at Marion as she stood by his side, looking out at their camp.

"Quite impressive, General Wallace," she told him with a grin.

"Yes it is," he told her, putting his arm around her waist and drawing her closer to him. "I think we're almost ready to take on the English army."

"I do as well, Will," John said, coming up with Stephen and Kerlie, a grin on his face. "We're getting bloody board sitting here doing nothing!"

William grinned back at him. "Well, Johnny, we should get to training again then. Everyone has gotten fat and lazy while I was recovering. Am I the only one who keeps up discipline in this place?"

Stephen grinned. "Nae, ye know I can be very persuasive when I have a mind to it." He winked and Kerlie took several comical steps away from him.

"Scary, insane Irishman," he muttered and ducked with a grin as Stephen threw a punch at him.

"Now, now, children," John told them with a grin. "I think a bit of food is in order."

"We just ate," William told them indignantly. "Ye can go and take yer starving body over to the practice fields, John Graham! We have lots of new recruits to train. We dinna want to send them to battle with no experience!"

"Nae, heaven forbid, we'd all leave them in the dust when we charged," Kerlie said with a cheeky smile.

William threw his arms up in mock exasperation. "Ye're impossible, the lot of ye!" he cried. "How am I going to take this army into battle against the English?"

"Quite well, I should think," Marion told him, smiling. "Remember, we're all in it together." She put her hands on his shoulders and looked up at him, fluttering her eyelashes. "Some of us more then others."

He laughed and gave her a kiss before he turned back to the lads, grinning at them. "She's right lads, we're all in this together. Ye do ken that? Nae turning back."

They nodded with grins. "Aye, we ken that, Will," John told him, sobering slightly. "There's nothing ye can do to stop us now. We've signed on for life, I'm afraid."

"Aye!" Kerlie cried, unsheathing his sword. "We'll fight to the end with ye, Will! Ye can be sure of that!"

Stephen grinned and winked. "And one part of Ireland will always be in the fight as well."

"Can ye ever keep yer noses out of anything?" Kerlie teased him, ducking another punch.

William grinned at them, drawing his own sword. "To all ye sons of Scotland," he told them. "I just want to tell ye that there is no better love than that of freedom. Life is nothing without liberty. We're here to make sure Scotland can enjoy that right they were given. We fight until our hearts cease to beat. We fight for our generation and all those to come, so that our sons and grandsons and all our bloodline down through the years can be free. We will never give up, nor give in, no matter the cost. Our one goal is Scotland. A free Scotland." He looked into the loyal faces that surrounded him, he stuck his sword in the ground and they all clasped the hilt together. William met each of their eyes in turn. "For Scotland. For Freedom. Alba gu brath."

"*ALBA GU BRATH!!!!!*" they all shouted together.

William sheathed his sword again, a smile on his

face. He breathed a deep sigh. A new life was on the horizon. The beginning of something wonderful. He would embrace it with every ounce of his being. Of this he was certain.

Roch the win i the clear day's dawin
Blaws the clouds heilster-gowdie owre the bay
But thair's mair nor a roch win blawin
Thro the Great Glen o the warl the day
It's a thocht that wad gar our rottans
Aa thae rogues that gang gallus fresh an gay
Tak the road an seek ither loanins
Wi thair ill-ploys tae sport an play

Nae mair will our bonnie callants
Merch tae war whan our braggarts crousely craw
Nor wee weans frae pitheid an clachan
Murn the ships sailin doun the Broomielaw
Broken faimilies in launs we've hairriet
Will curse 'Scotlan the Brave' nae mair, nae mair
Black an white ane-til-ither mairriet
Mak the vile barracks o thair maisters bare

Sae come aa ye at hame wi freedom
Never heed whit the houdies croak for Doom
In yer hous aa the bairns o Aidam
Will fin breid, barley-bree an paintit room
Whan MacLean meets wi's friens in Springburn
Aa thae roses an geeans will turn tae blume
An a black laud frae yont Nyanga
Dings the fell gallows o the burghers doun.

-"Freedom Come All Ye" Hamish Henderson

From that time on, William Wallace dedicated his life to Scotland's fight for freedom. He fought many skirmishes, chased the English from all the leading towns in Scotland and eventually met Edward's proud army at the River Fourth at Stirling and sent him homeward to think again. He took his army into England, looting all the English towns, then back up to Scotland with the English on his tail to fight at Falkirk where the Scots saw great losses. He went across the sea to France to plead Scotland's cause and more men to help.

Wallace was betrayed by a man named John Menteith and was taken down to London to experience a cruel murder at the will of Edward Longshanks, but even though he died before freedom came back to his country, his legacy spurred on the fight, inspiring Robert the Bruce to carry it on until it brought the Scots to the fields of Bannockburn where they charged the English once again and won their freedom.

Author's Note

So, as I said in the beginning of the book, I took a lot of liberties in writing this. Let me explain some to you now, so you will not get the wrong idea about the history in general.

First off, William did attend a school or collage in Dundee that his uncle sent him too. There was a bit of confusion about his uncles while I was researching and I still am not quite sure weather Richard and Ronald were the same person or not or if one was a Wallace and not a Crawford. There was something different in all the accounts I read, but since I needed two characters, I decided to put them both in. If this is not accurate, I apologize. I do know that the Dundee uncle was neither of them. One of the uncles did tell William that "Freedom is the best of things". This is a well known fact.

Also, William's brother Malcolm did not die with his father, though I believe Blind Harry said he did and since I was mostly following his story line with this book I stuck to his tradition. Malcolm was actually seen along with John in later history and they both were executed in London after Wallace was himself.

And yes, the kilts. Kilts were really only worn in the Highlands at this time, but who wants to read a Scottish book without kilts?

What I did in this book was take stories from Wallace's early life and put them all together. In actuality, if any of these stories happened at all--which I think a good number of them did--they probably would have been over the span of several years and not the few months I have in this book. The story about Selby is very well known and is most likely true. He tried to take William's dagger and mocked him for wearing such fine clothes; being an Englishman, Selby did not think William worthy to dress in them. The story where William was fishing and the Englishmen came up to him is true as well, though Jack Moore was not a part of this!

Jack Moore, was my own creation. I wanted William to have a personal villain, so I made one up. Perhaps I kind of named him after someone? Well, whoever it was is anyone's guess ;-)

The circumstances of William's capture are all almost exactly the way I had them recorded. He saw his uncle's gillie being mistreated by the occupying

Englishmen and wanted to do something about it. He was backed against the wall, his sword broke and he was taken captive, again, not by Jack Moore personally. Lord Percy had wanted him kept until he got back to London and William was thought to be dead, thus getting a free way out of the tolbooth. His childhood nurse came to claim his body and as she was cleaning him for burial, she saw his eyes flicker and realized there was still life in him. I do not know what her name was, so I just called her Margaret.

On the subject of William's friends, Stephen and Kerlie are anyone's guess. They were characters from, once again, Blind Harry's epic, and have been used in various other works as well. Wallace did have several recorded Irishmen fighting for him though, so Stephen may very well have been one of them. Kerlie is sometimes knows as John Kerr, the Kerrs being a known Scottish family. Blind Harry called him Kerlie. John Graham was a known supporter of Wallace. They actually met up later, but I thought it would be nice to put John in this book. Wallace probably would have known John from a young age, weather or not John joined on with Will at this time, I can't tell you. You can read Nigel Tranter's novel *The Wallace* and see what he says about the whole thing with John.

As for Marion Braidfoot, it is most unlikely that she would have been allowed to stay out in the woods with a bunch of lads without someone getting really mad. However, I wanted her to be in the story, so I kind of explain away a lot of things like where her father is and how he would feel about that. Her father was Lord

Braidfoot and did have two places, one in Lanark and a manor outside. Marion and Wallace did not actually meet like this either, they met while Wallace was in town one day with some companions and when he went to the kirk, he saw Marion there and it was reported love at first sight. Not the way I portrayed! They did marry however, and depending on the account, had a daughter who later married into the Shaw family. I did mention that James Heselrig was the sheriff of Lanark. That is not an important piece to this novel at all, but in Wallace's later history, he was to play a major role.

Also, the Robin Hood thing might be a bit stretched at this time. The actual ballads started showing up around the mid thirteen hundreds. But it seems you must mention Robin Hood when you are talking about outlaws, so I had Stephen sing a few. Though the ballads were probably not about the Errol Flynn-like Robin Hood we think of today. The early ballads were about a man more like Wallace, a sort of desperate outlaw, and his companions hiding out in the woods.

When William tells Ewan that he will "carry a stone for him" he is quoting an old Gaelic saying, *cuiridh mi clach 'ad charn*, meaning that he will not forget. I do not know how far this actually goes back, but I love this saying and I wanted to put it into something. It comes from when the Scots created cairns to commemorate a person or an event. They would make a pile of stones and anyone passing on the road, even if they did not know what the cairn was for, would put a stone down on the cairn. There are still cairns in Scotland today and if you ever see one, put a stone on it for whoever it was for.

I truly hope you enjoyed this novel, for it was close to my heart. William Wallace is a man who must never be forgotten. Let us all carry a stone for him, shall we?

-Slainte, Hazel

Made in the USA
San Bernardino, CA
21 June 2020